Topaz Treasure by Valerie Comer
Lyssa Quinn volunteers at the Rainbow's End geocaching hunt hoping she can point folks to the true treasure found in Jesus. She's not expecting her former prof to be there, too. Kirk Kennedy's treasure hunt takes him down a path he hadn't intended when he is captivated by Lyssa's intriguing sparkle. Can he convince Lyssa that there is more than one kind of treasure? Can Lyssa remind him of the greatest prize of all?

Beneath the Surface by Annalisa Daughety
Madison Wallace isn't the most outdoorsy girl in the world, so spending two months traipsing around the Ozarks isn't her idea of fun. Especially when her sister backs out at the last minute. Grant Simmons loves the outdoors, but when his grandfather's health takes a turn for the worse, Grant is without a partner. When these polar opposites find themselves teamed up, will they find common ground and a love worth treasuring?

Love's Prize by Cara C. Putman
Reagan Graham has never been one to tempt fate. But after four years of making numbers match as an accountant, she's ready for a break. Colton Ryan is spending the summer before law school trying to relax. His plan doesn't include falling in love. But the more time he spends with Reagan, the more he can't remember why. Will Reagan and Colton risk their safe plans and their hearts to take a chance on love?

Welcome Home, Love by Nicole O'Dell
After winning her lifelong battle to get fit, Hadley Parker signs up for the annual Rainbow's End Treasure Hunt as a gift to herself. Once there, she begins to fall for the syrupy compliments of an ill-intentioned womanizer. Hunt director Noah Templeton tries to warn Hadley before things go too far. But will he manage to remind Hadley that the treasures she truly seeks are already within her. . .and right in front of her?

RAINBOW'S END

FOUR-IN-ONE COLLECTION

VALERIE COMER
ANNALISA DAUGHETY
NICOLE O'DELL
CARA C. PUTMAN

BARBOUR
PUBLISHING

Topaz Treasure © 2012 by Valerie Comer
Beneath the Surface © 2012 by Annalisa Daughety
Love's Prize © 2012 by Cara C. Putman
Welcome Home, Love © 2012 by Nicole O'Dell

Print ISBN 978-1-61626-686-8

eBook Editions:
Adobe Digital Edition (.epub) 978-1-60742-848-0
Kindle and MobiPocket Edition (.prc) 978-1-60742-849-7

Scripture taken from the HOLY BIBLE, NEW INTERNATIONAL VERSION®. NIV®. Copyright © 1973, 1978, 1984, 2011 by Biblica, Inc.™ Used by permission. All rights reserved worldwide.

This book is a work of fiction. Names, characters, places, and incidents are either products of the author's imagination or used fictitiously. Any similarity to actual people, organizations, and/or events is purely coincidental.

Cover and interior design: Kirk DouPonce, DogEared Design

Published by Barbour Publishing, Inc., P.O. Box 719, Uhrichsville, OH 44683, www.barbourbooks.com

Our mission is to publish and distribute inspirational products offering exceptional value and biblical encouragement to the masses.

 Member of the
Evangelical Christian
Publishers Association

Printed in the United States of America

TOPAZ TREASURE

by Valerie Comer

Dedication

For my dad, Aaron Friesen, who was a bold yet tactful man of God. Thank you.

For my husband, Jim, and our kids and grandkids. Thanks for believing in me. You are my anchor and my treasure.

Many thanks to my coauthors, Nicole, Cara, and Annalisa. Working with you gals has been an awesome privilege. I'd do it again in a heartbeat.

Hats off to Margaret McGaffey Fisk, Maripat Sluyter, and Nicole O'Dell. Without you, I wouldn't be here today. We all know it!

Thank You, God, for loving me and nurturing this dream within me. You are my everything.

Have I not commanded you? Be strong and courageous.
Do not be afraid; do not be discouraged, for the LORD your God
will be with you wherever you go.
JOSHUA 1:9

Chapter 1

Lyssa Quinn clutched a bright-pink folder stuffed with advertising forms against her chest and squeezed her eyes shut. *Please God. Help me be brave.* She squared her shoulders and released each cramped finger individually. She could do this.

Frigid air conditioning laced with the odor of new carpet blasted into the Missouri humidity as Lyssa shouldered open the glass door of Osage Beach's newest shop. This looked like the kind of corporate sponsor the Rainbow's End Treasure Hunt needed, with a name like Communication Location: Home of Gizmos, Gadgets, and More—gadgets that included cell phones and GPS handhelds, if the posters plastering the windows were to be believed. Along with a smaller sign that announced OPENING SOON. Well, she didn't have time to wait, not if she was to have all the advertising and sponsorship in place before the middle of June. Only a month to go.

At least the door was unlocked and the fluorescents blazed down. Stacks of cardboard boxes lined the aisles next to partially filled shelves. Somebody must be around. If she was lucky, somebody sympathetic.

But what if they weren't? Maybe she should come back

another day. Or never. How had Noah talked her into this? She glanced at the folder in her hands, covered with decals from her third-grade class. Cute stickers with chalkboards and apples. #1 TEACHER. If she could face twenty-nine kids five days a week, surely she could face one manager.

A guy in jeans strode out of the back room, his face and upper body obscured by the box in his arms. "Good morning, and welcome to Communication Location. How can I help you?"

That voice. Lyssa froze. Even muffled by cardboard, it shot her straight back to her college days. But it couldn't be. There was no reason her humanities professor would be here in Osage Beach, stocking shelves.

He slid the box across the countertop and appeared from behind it. Dark curly hair and deep blue eyes, just like Lyssa remembered. A dimple appeared as he grinned.

No way. Lyssa sucked in a ragged breath as she white-knuckled the folder. When her good friends, who just happened to be the youth pastor and her roommate, had bullied her into seeking patrons for the church outreach event, this scenario had not remotely elbowed its way into her nightmares. She pivoted and forced herself to take even steps toward the door. No bolting like a frightened deer.

"Hey, I'm sorry. I was practicing my welcome line. I didn't mean to scare you."

Scare her? Yep, shaking. Lyssa halted in her tracks. This was ridiculous. She was a grown woman of twenty-six, for heaven's sake. And just the sight of one of her professors made her flee?

But not just any college professor.

Muffled footsteps approached on the carpet. "We're not open for business yet, but I might be able to help you anyway. Is there anything in particular you're looking for? If it isn't unpacked yet, I should at least know when it's coming."

Lyssa forced herself to face him. The temptation to ask for comparisons of various GPS units rolled over her. But no, she had a reason for being here, and that wasn't it. She braced herself and looked up.

His intense blue eyes crinkled around the edges as he smiled encouragingly. And waited.

"My name is Lyssa Quinn, and I'm here on behalf of Osage Beach Community Church." She paused for a split second, but his grin didn't waver—to her shock—so she plunged on. "We're hosting our first ever geocaching event this summer, and we're looking for donations and corporate sponsors. Being as you sell global positioning systems and cell phones, both useful in geocaching, we thought you might be interested in sponsoring our event."

There. She'd gotten all the words out and publicly aligned herself with the church.

He didn't laugh, though his eyebrows angled down.

Lyssa pulled a sheet of paper from the folder and shoved it at him with trembling fingers. "If you want any further information, please call the number listed." She started to turn away. Why didn't it have the church number on it instead of her cell?

"Just a moment."

The floor gripped Lyssa's sandals like Velcro.

He glanced over the paper then met her gaze.

She tried to wrench her eyes free but couldn't. In humanities, four years ago, she'd found him mesmerizing. Even after he derided her roommate in front of the entire class.

He held out his hand.

Lyssa reached out and clutched it like a drowning woman, sweaty palm notwithstanding.

"I'm Kirk Kennedy, just in town to help my brother get his new business off the ground. Your name is Lyssa?"

She nodded and tugged her hand free. Also her gaze. The arrogant professor she'd once known didn't seem the kind to help out a sibling. Had she judged him too hastily back then? Not likely.

"Why don't you come sit down and tell me more about this event? I could use a break. I'll grab us each a cola, if you'd like."

Lyssa found her voice. "No, thanks. To the cola, I mean."

Kirk—no longer her professor—grinned and ushered her toward the door he'd come out of a few minutes before. "We've got ginger ale and root beer, too. Just name your addiction."

Her wooden legs propelled her to the back of the small shop. "I stay away from the stuff. I've seen kids in the classroom who drink soda for breakfast, lunch, and dinner, whose baby brothers and sisters get it in their bottles. So unhealthy, with all the sugar and chemicals." To say nothing of making a teacher's job more difficult.

He chuckled behind her. "Well then. Water?"

Lyssa hesitated. Probably all he had was bottled, and then she'd feel obligated to get into issues like plastic in landfills and how recycling didn't work as well as everyone had been led to believe. "I'm good, thanks."

Kirk ushered her into a brightly lit room. "Have a seat." He pulled a soda out of the bar fridge and saluted her with it. "I hope you don't mind if I indulge."

Not like her opinion would matter, and why should it? In a few minutes he'd taunt her for being on church business and send her on her way. Might as well get it over with. She laid her papers on the table and perched on the edge of a padded red seat.

He straddled the other chair and popped the tab on his

can. His chin jerked toward her pocket folder. "So, what's the purpose of this event?"

Here it came. She believed in God just as much as she believed in healthy food and drink choices. Why was it so difficult speaking up about her faith? Mentioning that the hunt was a church function shouldn't be a big deal. Dad would have managed to get in an entire sermon by now—not that she wanted to follow in his tracks. But polar opposite wasn't healthy either. Noah and Jeannie figured working this event would be a good first step to coaxing Lyssa to bravery, but they hadn't counted on Professor Kennedy.

Neither had she. Lyssa breathed a quick prayer. "Um. . . our new youth pastor wants to do a big event to get more community interaction. He's a fan of geocaching and thought it would be fun to do a summer-long treasure hunt."

Kirk took a big gulp from the can and swallowed. "Geocaching? I'm new to this business. It's really more my brother's thing." He pointed at Lyssa's folder. "Explain, please."

There he went, sounding like an authority again, just when she'd almost managed to regain confidence. "People hide small containers called caches, containing trinkets and a logbook, and then they load the GPS coordinates to the Internet."

"Lats and longs?"

She nodded. "Then other people can search for the caches and sign in when they find them."

"So the prize will go to the person who finds the most the fastest?"

"That's part of it, but in order to make the event last two months instead of two weeks, we've added other ways for participants to gain points, such as discovering certain tokens and planting more caches. There will be riddles and puzzles that need to be solved. And"—Lyssa poked her toe at the metal table leg—"they'll get additional points for coming to rallies at the church."

"I see."

Here's where that once-familiar sneer would cross his face. She peeked up at him through her lashes, but instead he looked thoughtful. "So any gadget that operates on satellite locators works for geocaching?"

No comment on the church affiliation? That was a shock, after all her recollections of sitting in his class. "Well, yes. There are dedicated satellites only for global positioning, just as there are dedicated GPS units to use them. But a lot of the newer cell phones have the capability as well."

Kirk tilted his head as he considered. "Would a 10-percent-off coupon for registered participants be helpful? Or are you looking for other kinds of sponsorship?"

Lyssa jerked her head up and stared at him. He was actually volunteering? "Um. . .that would be cool, but to be listed in our brochure, we need donations of cash or prizes. The advertising price list is on that sheet."

He glugged the rest of his soda as he glanced over the page. "A coupon might help get some folks started that wouldn't otherwise, and be great advertising for Communication Location at the same time. We'll participate. How much for the premier spot, or is that already taken?"

She struggled to her feet. "No, it's still available." Along with most of the other spaces, other than those church members had signed up for. "Th–thank you. Do you want the coupon to be valid on any units, or are there specific ones you'd prefer to include? Maybe something your supplier could discount?"

"That's a good idea. I'll ask." Kirk picked up the paper she'd handed him earlier. "Is your phone number on here? I'll get back to you with the details in the next day or two."

"I'm only available evenings and Saturdays until the school year is over, though I'll be in the church office late some afternoons." Her face burned. Sounded like she was encouraging him to call for social reasons. Attractive as he was, that was not an option, though she was certainly curious what had caused the change in him. Nah, she was probably imagining it.

He flashed her a grin. "Saturday, then? Count me in."

Kirk strode into Osage Beach Community Church, shaking his head. Whoever would have thought he'd enter a place of worship when there wasn't a wedding or a funeral? He didn't really want to think about Dale's wife's death, but it was hard since Kirk was spending the summer with his brother. The store had diverted much of Kirk's attention from deeper thoughts until Lyssa had walked in the door, but it wasn't just her pretty face reeling him in. Debbie's faith had been real. Was Lyssa's?

The woman at the church's reception desk definitely wasn't Lyssa. Maybe he'd arrived too late. Maybe she'd gotten tired of waiting for him and gone out to solicit another vendor for the inside flap of the brochure. Maybe. . .

The middle-aged woman glanced up. "Hi, can I help you?"

Kirk shifted from one foot to the other. "I'm looking for Lyssa Quinn. Is she in?"

"Down the corridor, second doorway to the left."

He turned the direction she'd indicated, nearly tripping over a sandwich board with an arrow pointing out Rainbow's End Treasure Hunt. Had the thing appeared out of thin air?

He let out a whoosh of breath. Just dropping off the ad

copy. That's all. And maybe checking to see if Lyssa wore any rings. He didn't remember any, but he'd had no clue at the time that he wouldn't be able to get her out of his mind all week. Plenty of attractive girls crossed his path, both at the college and elsewhere. But her soft brown eyes struck a chord he hadn't been able to shake.

The second door on the left stood ajar.

Kirk peered around then tapped on the open door. "Lyssa?"

She jumped when she saw him, sweeping her shoulder-length brown hair away from her shoulder with one hand. Away from a shimmery top with short flouncy sleeves. Feminine. Pretty.

Wow.

"K–Kirk."

He stepped through the opening. "Is this a good time? I wanted to show you what I've been working on."

"Um, sure. Come on in. Have a seat." She straightened a stack of papers. "Sorry for the decor. They just found a semi-vacant corner to stash me in."

Kirk was so busy soaking up the sight of her, he hadn't even noticed.

She laced her hands together on the desktop. "What have we—I mean, you—got?"

No rings on her left hand. So far so good. Kirk passed her the sketch he'd been working on. She'd so filled his mind the whole time, it was a wonder he'd managed to remember the key points of the ad. "How's this?"

Lyssa's shoulders straightened as she examined it. "Really? It looks great. I was hoping you'd come through."

Did she mean him, or the ad?

"Your brother was okay with the coupon?"

Oh. Dale.

Kirk shrugged. "I haven't had a chance to run it by him. He's up in St. Louis for the next week or two, packing up his house." His and Debbie's house. "He's been kind of. . .busy." It wouldn't be an issue, though. Dale had trotted off to church with Debbie nearly every week for years.

Lyssa raised sculpted eyebrows. "But he'll want to have input, won't he?"

"It's okay. We agreed I should start some advertising for the grand opening. The timing is super, as we wanted to kick things off the week before Father's Day."

"That sounds perfect. You wanted this on the inside flap, then?"

"Yes, please. If it's still available."

She nodded.

Kirk pulled out the Communication Location's checkbook and patted down his pocket for a pen. "If we want to make an additional donation, would you prefer a separate check?"

Lyssa's shocked eyes met his. Sparkling brown, with highlights that reminded him of the topaz lamps his mom had given him for commencement. "That might make bookkeeping easier."

He wrote out two checks and tore them from the stubs. "Well, that's business accomplished." But he had more on the brain than that. She seemed so shy. What was holding her back, when it appeared she felt the same pull he did? "Would you like to do dinner and a movie?"

She dropped the checks as though they were on fire, and her hands jerked into her lap. "I have plans."

But he hadn't even specified which night yet. She couldn't be busy all of them, unless she had a boyfriend. He had to know.

"Is there someone else?"

Her face flushed, but she didn't meet his gaze. "No one. I'm just busy." She got to her feet.

Dismissal.

What had he said wrong? He couldn't have been imagining how aware she was of him. Maybe he was just moving too fast for her. At twenty-nine, he was ready to find the right woman and settle down. Well, he could take some time. He'd be in Osage Beach all summer.

Chapter 2

Y̲ou'll never believe who's in town." Lyssa hung her
leather purse on its hook behind the townhouse's back
door and turned to the kitchen.

Her roommate glanced up from chopping asparagus at
the peninsula counter. "Hmm?"

"Kirk Kennedy." When Jeannie's brown face registered
nothing, Lyssa added, "*Professor* Kennedy. From Lincoln
University."

"Oh, really?" Jeannie slid the spears into the sizzling wok.
"Wonder what he's doing here. Not that we're so far from
Jefferson City, but still."

"Messing with my mind, that's what," muttered Lyssa under her breath.

Jeannie turned. "What?"

Never mind. "Have you seen that new business just off the
parkway? Communication Location?" Lyssa poured herself a
glass of sweet tea from the fridge.

Her roommate shook her head, black curls swinging.
"Can't say that I have."

Figured. Jeannie drove west across the Grand Glaize Bridge
to work, not north. "Professor Kennedy's brother is the owner.

It's a shop that carries cell phones, GPS units, and. . .I don't know. Games and stuff, I think."

Jeannie grated garlic into the wok with a little extra energy. "Weird. Wonder if he quit teaching. Maybe he got fired."

Lyssa hitched herself onto a stool across the peninsula and snagged a slice of red pepper from the cutting board. "Probably not. He said he's helping get things going at the store."

"How'd you run into him?"

"It's your fault. You made me volunteer to help Noah with the treasure hunt."

"Serves you right, then." Jeannie stirred the wok's contents. "God knew you needed a good challenge right from the get-go. You went in there looking for donations?"

"Yeah. There's no way I'd have gone in if I knew he'd be there. Not after what he put you through in college, class after class."

Jeannie grimaced. "He certainly kept me on my toes."

"That's not the weirdest thing. He didn't make a single snide comment about the event being church sponsored. Not one." Lyssa still couldn't figure that out. She crunched through another piece of pepper before Jeannie whisked the rest into the wok. "He made a good-sized donation on top of the prime ad."

Jeannie set the spatula on the counter and parked her hands on either side of it. She leaned across the peninsula toward Lyssa, dark eyes wide. "He *what?*"

"You heard me. He's our biggest corporate sponsor."

"Let me get this straight. Professor Kirk Kennedy, Humanities 237, Lincoln University, Jefferson City, Missouri? We're talking about the same guy here?"

Lyssa pointed at the smoke curling from the wok. "Stir supper, if you don't mind."

Jeannie whirled back to the range. "He called Christianity a residue of the Dark Ages. A crutch for feeble minds. Church was—"

"'A social club for pansies,' I believe were his exact words." Lyssa remembered all too clearly.

"Yeah." Jeannie poured a shot of lemon juice into the wok and turned the element down. "He had no respect."

"You'd never guess it was the same guy, but there's no doubt." He was just as hot as he'd ever been, for starters.

"I don't understand, Lys. He knew it was for a church event?"

"Yep. He even came by the office to drop off two checks and the ad copy. Probably the first time in his life he stepped foot in a church. And never a word." Not about that, anyway.

Jeannie tossed two catfish fillets in cornmeal then into another fry pan. "Wow. He almost did me in, back in the day."

It wasn't "almost" for Lyssa. "I hated him for what he did to you." Hated herself for being too chicken to stand up beside Jeannie.

Hated herself for thinking he was cute anyway.

"I can't say I looked forward to humanities, but being challenged did make me understand better what I believed and why." Jeannie shot a look at Lyssa. "It was probably good for me."

No answer to that. The sweet saltiness of frying fish wafted to Lyssa's nose. "Is that your mama's recipe? Smells awesome."

"Sure is." Jeannie flipped the fish. "Almost ready."

"You're lucky I came home to eat. If you hadn't told me your brother dropped off the catfish, I might've stood you up."

"Uh huh. Like you have a life." Jeannie plated the fillets.

"I was invited out for dinner."

"Oh, yeah? By whom?" When Lyssa didn't answer, Jeannie

looked up, a scoopful of stir-fried veggies in midair.

Lyssa couldn't help smirking. "Professor Kennedy."

Asparagus and spoon clattered to the floor. "Oh, no you don't. Just because I've been encouraging you to get out of your shell doesn't mean I think dating *him* is a good idea."

"Relax." Lyssa reached for a cloth to wipe up the mess. "I said no."

Changing a few words on the coupon layout was a slim excuse to swing by the church, but Kirk couldn't help himself. She'd turned him down for dinner the other day. Had she been trying to get rid of him, or was her excuse legit? Somehow, he had to know.

School-aged kids seemed everywhere in town today, so he figured classes must be out for the summer. And that might mean Lyssa would be at the church, working on the treasure hunt. It was worth a shot.

He pulled into the parking lot in time to see her exit the building in knee-length khakis and a striped tank, pulling her luxurious thick hair through the back of a baseball cap.

"Lyssa?"

She froze then glanced his way. "Um, hi."

He waved the paper. "I guess this isn't a good time to go over the ad copy?" He tried for his most charming smile.

"I can take a quick look." She headed toward him, a picture of grace.

"Going somewhere? I don't want you to be late."

"Oh, it's okay. I was just headed up to the park to hunt down a geocache. A couple of people noted on the website that they couldn't locate it, so I wanted to double-check it hadn't gotten trashed before the treasure hunt lifts off." She slipped the paper from his fingers and looked it over.

"You're going hiking alone? Isn't it. . .dangerous or something?"

"Dangerous? Why?" She flashed him a grin.

He'd do nearly anything to see that again. "Snakes. Skunks." He waved his hand. "I don't know. You might trip on a root and sprain your ankle."

Lyssa laughed. "Anything is possible, but highly unlikely. If I waited until a friend wanted to go hiking, I'd spend far too much time sitting around the condo. So I'm just careful."

The best opening he'd found yet. "How about if I come with you?"

Her eyes widened, and then she glanced away. "Oh, I'm sure you're much too busy for that. I'll be fine."

"Why not? I'm not expecting any new freight today, and Dale won't be back until later this week. It might be the last chance to do something spontaneous before the grand opening." He gestured at his white button-up shirt and dark slacks. "I'd probably want to change first, though."

"Yeah, you would." She sized him up uncertainly.

"My apartment is on the way to the park gates. I promise not to hold you back." With those long lean legs of hers, she was probably in great shape. Hopefully all that jogging he'd been doing would make a difference.

Lyssa broke their gaze and glanced back at the paper he'd handed her.

"I could use the escape." Kirk touched her arm. "Besides, I was serious when I asked you out the other day. I'd like to get to know you better. If you're interested." He held his breath.

Her hand clenched around the paper, crumpling it slightly.

Somehow that gave him a perverse hope she wasn't as immune to his charms as she pretended. Been a while since a woman had that kind of effect on him. Like, never.

Lyssa peered at him through long lashes. "Really?"

She didn't seem to know how attractive she was. Kirk vowed to wipe the uncertainty off her face. "Really."

"Okay." Lyssa pulled a deep breath. "No point in taking two cars. You can ride with me."

The only vehicle in the parking lot besides his, a green hatchback, had seen better days. Besides, it was only chivalrous for him to do the driving. But the wary expression in her eyes cut off his protest before he started. He shrugged. "Sure, no problem."

"I'll just run back and set this on my desk for later." She pivoted and jogged for the church door.

Heart lifting, Kirk watched her go. He shoved aside the question of what his brother would have to say. Dale had been after him for years to meet a great girl. It wasn't Kirk's fault Lyssa arrived right on the heels of Dale's big loss.

Chapter 3

Why had she insisted on taking Kermit? Lyssa eyeballed Kirk's car across the parking lot of the lavish complex he called home. It was probably ten years newer than hers. Her fingers tightened on the familiar wheel. It was just a small something she could control, when she had no clue why he seemed so different than her memories of him. But until she figured out what had caused the sudden alteration, she didn't want to be stranded in the backcountry without her own wheels.

Kirk jogged out of the complex in hiking shorts and a navy Lincoln Tigers T-shirt. He tossed a small daypack onto the backseat and slid into the passenger side, brandishing a bottle of mineral water.

Lyssa sighed. No good could come of this outing. So he was cute and interested in her by a flattering amount. But in the not-so-distant past, he'd been vehemently opposed to Christianity. There wasn't any recent evidence to back that up since she'd met him at Communication Location last week, but still. She must've been nuts to accept his company. She shook her head and shifted Kermit into reverse, her hand skimming the hair above Kirk's knee. Best not to think about that, either, though her fingers tingled.

She drove north on the parkway. What to talk about? She certainly couldn't admit to how unsettled his presence made her, though he probably guessed. She'd just make him do the talking.

The silence lasted only seconds.

"Tell me about yourself, Lyssa. Have you been teaching long?"

This could be neutral ground. "Three years. A lot of it has been substitute teaching."

"Takes a while to break in?"

"Seems so. I covered a maternity leave this past term, and that's given me good experience. And confidence." At least in some areas.

"Are you from Osage Beach, then?"

Lyssa clenched Kermit's wheel. "No. My best friend grew up here, though. It seemed as good a place as any to get established, since she needed a roommate and I had nowhere else I'd rather be." She'd certainly had enough of living near her father. "How about you?" She glanced over her shoulder and merged into the exit lane for Lake of the Ozarks State Park.

He stretched his legs as much as Kermit's space would allow. "I grew up in St. Louis, but I've lived in Jefferson City for"—he paused then whistled—"more than ten years now."

Not that she'd doubted his identity, but somewhere deep inside the part of her that hoped this guy was just Professor Kennedy's doppelgänger—conveniently with the same name—died. "What do you do there?" As if she didn't know.

"I'm a humanities professor at Lincoln U." He tugged his T-shirt so she could see the tiger emblem.

This was where she should say Lincoln was her alma mater.

Lyssa stopped herself from physically shaking her head. "That sounds interesting. What's the best part of your job?" Poking fun at Christians, maybe?

"I love helping shape young people's perceptions of the world around them."

Her mind screamed at her to challenge him, to tell him she'd sat in his class and hadn't seen his attitude as a positive influence. How could this friendly, fascinating man be the same guy? Kirk didn't add up. "And here I thought you wandered around the state, opening up electronics stores."

He laughed, a nice, easy sound. "No, that's a new hobby of mine. Blame it on my brother."

"Why here?"

"My grandparents had a cottage along the lake. My brother and I used to spend summers with them, so we have a lot of good memories of the area."

More money than she'd ever had, then. No surprise, considering his condo and his car. "You and your brother must be close." She glanced over in time to see his jaw clench for a brief instant.

"He's a couple years older. Yeah, we were close."

Were?

"It's been rough lately." He paused. "His wife died six months ago."

"That's too bad. He's lucky to have a brother like you." Drat. She was too forward, by far.

Kirk shot her a sidelong glance. "It doesn't always seem that way. But families stick together, right? I mean, that's what they're for."

"You'd think so." Lyssa pulled into the parking lot at the Trail of the Four Winds. Good timing. "Ready?"

Kirk grinned as he got out. "*So* ready." He leaned against the car and stretched his hamstrings.

Lyssa turned away as she adjusted her daypack. The Kirk she'd met in Osage Beach did not jive with the college professor she'd known in Jefferson. This Kirk had muscular legs and looked great in shorts. She'd never daydreamed *that* about him back at Lincoln. Why did college feel like a lifetime ago? It seemed it had happened to different people.

She cast him a sidelong glance as he locked his fingers behind his head and stretched to his left.

Maybe it *had* happened to someone else. On both sides. But how would she ever know if she couldn't get up the courage to ask?

Lyssa shuddered and began her own stretches. That question required an openness she wasn't prepared for. She didn't want that old Kirk back, no way, no how.

"So, show me how this geocaching thing works."

His words returned Lyssa to the present. The new Kirk was here, interested in many of the same things she was, or so it seemed: the outdoors, hiking, geocaching. She pulled her GPS unit out of her pants's cargo pocket. "I know where the cache is, but I think the coordinates are still in memory." She logged into the handheld and waited for the list to refresh.

Kirk moved in behind her, peering at the unit. His T-shirt brushed her arm, and his breath warmed her cheek. The scent of his spicy cologne filled her senses.

Lyssa shifted slightly away. She couldn't let him get to her. "These are the coordinates, and here's where we are now. We follow the trail until we get close then use the hints to zero in."

He leaned closer. "Basically, we've got a couple of miles to go up the trail first."

She nodded.

"What kind of hints do you mean?" He took the GPS from her and examined it.

"In this case, it's a poem. Just scroll down."

Kirk read the verse out loud.

"Trails of the Four Winds—
North, East, South, and West.
Hike until the numbers match;
See where the view is best.
Limestone low and grasses blow;
Oaks have tumbled down.
Cedar roots bind the spot;
Flowers act as crown."

He grimaced. "Does it have to be so cryptic?"

A wave of heat shot up Lyssa's cheeks. "It's a hunt, after all." She turned away and adjusted the straps of her pack. "You don't tell people 'third rock from the left'."

"But still. Hokey poetry? The rhythm is off."

"It has to get the information in there, okay? Sorry it doesn't meet with your expectations."

"Whoa." He put his hand on her arm and turned her to face him.

Didn't mean she had to look in his eyes.

"It sounds like somebody is a tad sensitive over this. Why would that be?"

Lyssa pulled back far enough that he dropped his hand.

"Aw, Lyssa. You wrote it, didn't you?"

She motioned toward the trailhead, not meeting his gaze. "You ready to hike?"

"Tell me I'm right." Kirk fell into step beside her and elbowed her lightly.

Why couldn't he leave well enough alone? Lyssa picked up the pace. Maybe he'd get the hint, sooner or later. Not that he ever had in class, but at least now he wasn't being mean. Much.

It didn't take long for him to catch on. "I was making fun of you. I'm sorry."

Lyssa couldn't stay angry when he sounded so contrite. "It's okay." She kept a wary eye on the clouds scuttling overhead as she hiked up the rocky trail. The weatherman had forecast late-evening showers, but they should get back in plenty of time. In the meanwhile, the cooler breeze cut the heavy aroma of wild roses and swept mosquitoes away, making the hike delightful. Or was that the presence of the man behind her on the narrow path? She glanced over her shoulder at him.

Kirk was practically on her heels. "So, do you have any siblings?"

That's what she got for meeting his gaze for an instant. "Two younger brothers."

His tone remained light. "That must've kept you on your toes. Or were you Daddy's Princess and could do no wrong?"

As if. "I was more like Cinderella in the before category—all the cooking and cleaning, minus the fairy godmother." Minus the handsome prince, too.

Kirk's tone softened. "Your mom?"

Lyssa stopped in the middle of the trail and met his gaze. "She walked out when I was twelve and hasn't been heard from since. My dad had no clue how to raise kids and didn't bother figuring it out. He was focused on his own stuff." Trying to save the whole world and not caring—or noticing—he'd lost his family.

Kirk caught her hand. "I'm sorry. I can't even begin to imagine how hurtful that must have been."

She pulled away. "I'm getting over it. Check the GPS. How close are we to the cache?"

He held her gaze for a long moment, like he understood how much even that bit of honesty had cost her. He couldn't get it, of course. Not unless his family was as dysfunctional as hers. Finally he lifted the unit and examined the screen. "Not too much farther. I think."

"Let's go then." She pivoted and headed up the trail. What guy in his right mind would stick around a girl like her? And he didn't even suspect there was more to her reticence. Did he?

Chapter 4

Kirk studied Lyssa sitting across from him at On the Rise Bakery & Bistro. "I would have been happy to pick you up."

Was that guilt in her eyes? "No problem. I had some errands to run. There wasn't any point in you making two trips to my place when I had to come across the bridge anyway."

He couldn't decide if there was more to it than that. "You mentioned you have a roommate?"

Lyssa toyed with her Java Chiller, not meeting his gaze. "Yes, a friend and I rent together. She works over at city hall."

Wow, she'd actually volunteered some information. "Cool. Someone you've known a long time?"

"We were college roommates."

Now they were getting somewhere. "Where did you go to school?"

She took a long sip of her mocha.

It hadn't seemed like an awkward question to him.

Lyssa looked past him, and her face brightened. "Hi, Kelsey!"

A little girl dragged a woman over by the hand. "Ms. Quinn! I didn't think I'd get to see you all summer long. I miss you."

Lyssa hugged the child to her side. "Osage Beach isn't that

big. I told you we'd probably see each other sometimes and, look, here we are."

The woman laughed, resting her hand on the wrought-iron back of Lyssa's chair. "All Kelsey ever talks about is Ms. Quinn said this and Ms. Quinn did that. Thanks for giving her a great school year."

"It was my pleasure." Lyssa wrinkled her nose and grinned at the girl.

Kirk's heart flipped. Maybe someday she'd look at him that way. Of course kids adored her. He was rapidly getting to that point himself.

"Will you be my teacher again, Ms. Quinn? Please?" Kelsey twisted her hands together. She tilted her head and batted her eyelashes at Lyssa.

"I'd love to, but I'm not sure what will happen. Maybe I'll sub in your grade sometimes."

"The school district should give you your own class, Ms. Quinn." The mother took the girl by the hand. "You're the best teacher Kelsey's had yet."

Lyssa flushed a becoming shade of pink. "Thank you. One of these years I'll get a permanent spot."

"Come along, Kelsey." The woman cast an appraising eye over Kirk as though determining if he was worthy to be seen with the hallowed teacher.

Did he pass inspection? He met the mother's eye and nodded in acknowledgment.

The girl blew a kiss at Lyssa then skipped away, clinging to her mom's hand.

Still watching them, Lyssa raised her glass, and Kirk reached across the table to clink his against hers. "You must be a great teacher."

Lyssa focused on him, her face still bemused from the encounter. "I love the kids and try to make learning fun."

"It shows." As did the complexity that made up the woman across from him—a woman he wanted to get to know better. "You made geocaching fun, too, but I'm pretty sure I haven't learned enough to pass the final exam. When can we go again?"

He waited, practically holding his breath, while she appeared to weigh a decision.

"You'll be busy getting the store ready to open."

"That's still a couple of weeks away. Deliveries tend to be in the morning, so I can get away nearly any afternoon."

Lyssa turned her Java Chiller in circles on the wooden table top. "Well, we could go Thursday afternoon. I do have to set up another cache toward Lakeland."

"Great!" Even better than he'd hoped. "I'll bring some stuff to put in it."

"I can't believe you're going out with Professor Kennedy." Jeannie planted both hands on her hips and stared Lyssa down. "Again."

Lyssa jingled Kermit's keys and reached for the doorknob. "We're not going *out* out." Probably sounded as lame to her roommate as it did to her. "It's just a geocaching hike. You've told me before that it's silly for me to go alone, so don't complain when I have someone for company."

"Just? How many of these have you gone on now? With him, I mean."

Trust Jeannie to be keeping score. "Well, there was the one on Trail of the Four Winds."

"After which he invited you to On the Rise, and you went."

Of course she'd gone. It had seemed rude not to, and besides, she hadn't wanted the idyllic afternoon to end. Maybe. . .she eyed Jeannie. "Are you jealous?"

Jeannie dropped her chin and looked at Lyssa with widening eyes. "Get serious. Not a chance in the world. The man was a jerk in college, and I'm sure he still is. Why would I envy you?"

Because he was an attractive man who was fun to be with? Not that she could explain it to Jeannie. Not that Jeannie would buy it.

"And then there was the hike in Lakeland. Today you're going. . .where? Ha Ha Tonka State Park on the other side of Camdenton?"

"Rainbow's End Treasure Hunt covers the whole lake area." Besides, she loved wandering around the castle ruins there, and Kirk had said he hadn't been since he was a kid. She couldn't wait to see it anew through his eyes. "Kirk found some miniature shields and castles to tuck into one of the caches there."

"I hope you remember you're playing with fire, Lys. Have you talked to him about God yet? Confronted him about the things that happened at Lincoln U?"

"Not yet. It'll be fine. You'll see." If only she could convince herself.

"How come you're meeting him at the church instead of letting him pick you up here?"

"I—uh. . .I have some paperwork to drop off there anyway." Lyssa held up her pink pocket folder.

Jeannie snorted. "Nice try. You'll be going into the office tomorrow anyway. You just don't want me to meet him."

"You'd confront him."

"You bet I would. It's high time somebody did. I'm not a

college kid anymore. I'm not a captive audience to someone with the power to give me a bad grade."

"I–I'll talk to him. Sometime. It's too soon." Lyssa pulled the door open. "I need to get going."

"Lys? It's okay to talk to people about their faith. Just because your dad shoves his beliefs down the throat of anyone who's breathing doesn't mean there isn't a middle ground. You can't go dating a guy who doesn't love the Lord."

"We're not dating."

"Nice try, Lys. I'll track the guy down myself one of these days and find out what his intentions are. You be careful."

Kirk let himself into the apartment at the end of a starlit evening. He'd never met a girl as intriguing as Lyssa before. On the one hand, she obviously felt an attraction to him. On the other, something was holding her back. Something major. So she was a Christian. He knew it, and she knew he knew it, so it couldn't be that. One of these days he'd ask her about her faith. Was she strong like Debbie?

He rounded the corner into the dining room, shocked to find the chandelier on and Dale seated at the table. Paperwork lay strewn across the surface, obscuring every hint of wood.

His brother glanced up. "Finally home? Where have you been?"

"Dale! Thought you weren't coming until tomorrow." Kirk crossed to the kitchen and grabbed a cola from the fridge. He straddled a maple chair and looked expectantly at his brother. Right in front of Dale, on top and dead center, lay the receipt from Osage Beach Community Church.

Dale's eyes narrowed. "Since when are we giving money to

some religious organization?" He cocked his head. "Tell me, is she cute?"

Kirk choked, spraying soda. "Is who cute?"

"The girl who talked you into this donation." Dale tapped Lyssa's round signature on the receipt.

"It's not that way at all."

"Right. Not hearing a denial."

Sometimes Kirk hated being the younger brother. Even two years was a huge gap between them. He took another sip, stalling for time.

Dale leaned back and crossed his arms, quirking an eyebrow.

"Yeah, she's cute, but that's not why—"

Dale slammed a fist onto the table. The paperwork jumped. "Start thinking with your brain, not your body. What made you think I'd want to give money to some church thing?"

"We talked about adverti—"

"Yeah. Ever heard of newspapers and radio?"

Anger churned in Kirk's gut. "Ever heard of word of mouth? Lyssa says—"

"She has a name, does she?"

Kirk surged to his feet. "They're expecting hundreds of people to sign up for this event. What's not to like about that many people knowing Communication Location has the gadgets they need?" His fingers tightened around the can until it crackled. "What's not to like about getting in a small town's good books? This isn't St. Louis or Chicago. Things are different here."

"I doubt it. You're just a sucker for a pretty face."

Making it sound like he had a new girl every week. So untrue. He hadn't dated in several years. Kirk narrowed his gaze. "You're not hearing me. You're focused on the least important part of that ad agreement." Not the least important part of his past week, however, but his brother didn't need those details. At least not yet. "It's an inexpensive way to get our business in front of hundreds of residents and tourists alike."

"Inexpensive? You're offering who-knows-how-many people 10 percent off their purchase?"

"And three of our suppliers already agreed to give us discounted product for our grand opening. It's not coming out of our pockets."

"You're absolutely right it isn't. You can call that cute girl right now and tell her to pull the ad. I'm having nothing to do with a church event." Dale rested both hands on the table and rose, leaning toward Kirk. "We'll run our own grand opening sale, and if some of those church people want to come spend their money in our store, I'll gladly take it. But I sure as shootin' am not going to link my business name with any religion." He shoved forward, his nose almost touching Kirk's. "So deal with it."

He'd blown it. He'd suspected Dale wouldn't be thrilled, but he thought his brother would see the wisdom and economy of this venture. He'd just been following instructions. Mostly.

Kirk stood his ground and stared into his brother's cold blue eyes. When had Lyssa said the printer's deadline was? The cut-off loomed for getting her glossies printed on time for the treasure hunt kickoff. Surely Dale wouldn't require pulling the ads once the brochures had been printed. But by the look on his face, Kirk couldn't bet on it.

"Bottom line, Kirk, it's my business. I appreciate that you've invested some cash. Thank you for giving your summer to help me get things off the ground. If it were any other organization, I'd be faster than you whipping out the checkbook. But not a church. I can't do it. I just can't."

"Since when? You went to church with Debbie. I had no clues you'd changed your mind. You could've given me a heads up." Not that Kirk had been bringing up religious topics, either, but still.

"In case you hadn't noticed, God took my wife, and all the preacher could say was that it was God's will." Dale snorted. "I have no use for a God like that, and I won't support preachers deluding other poor souls." He spun away. "You're not changing my mind, Kirk. Call up that cute girl and tell her no. I'm done with God, and I'm done with church, and I'm done with everything it represents. I won't have my name attached, and that's final." He stomped down the hallway. A door slammed.

The receipt fluttered to the tile floor in Dale's wake. Kirk picked it up and stared at Lyssa's round handwriting. Had his brother left him any options? Dale's mind was cast in concrete. His business name would not be on the brochures. How could Kirk possibly have guessed?

Kirk hadn't even told him about the five hundred straight-up donation. At least he could put that in his own name instead of the business. But what to do about the ad?

What to do about Lyssa? She already didn't easily give trust. After this, she'd probably never speak to him again. And that he couldn't live with. He'd call her in the morning. No sense in both of them losing a night's sleep over it.

Chapter 5

"Here you go, Lyssa." The church receptionist rounded the corner into Lyssa's office and set an open box on her desk. "The guy from the printer just dropped these off. Don't they look great?"

Lyssa peered in and picked up the top brochure. The front of the trifold declared the Rainbow's End Treasure Hunt. She turned it around to see the church photo displayed with the address and phone number plus a list of sponsors. On the inside flap was the coupon from Communication Location; then it opened to a full-page spread with details about the hunt and how it worked. This beat making third-grade bulletin boards all to bits, though she was mighty good at those, too.

"Thanks, Melanie. These turned out just how I'd hoped."

Melanie beamed. "You've done a good job laying these out, girlie. And here you were reluctant to take on the project."

Lyssa grinned. Even going around to the various businesses hadn't been so bad once she'd discovered the managers were pleasant. Getting past Kirk had been a big boost to her confidence. The rest of the sponsors had been a snap in comparison.

Her cell phone rang.

Melanie fluttered her fingers and turned to the door. "I'll

leave you to it."

"Hello?" Lyssa propped her cell up against her ear, feeling the kink in her neck from doing it too many times. She really ought to stop by Communication Location and buy a headset. Not to see Kirk, of course.

"Lyssa?"

Oh, no, she only had to think of him and he called. Hopefully, she could keep her voice calm. "Speaking. How can I help you?" Maybe if she didn't let on she knew it was him. . .

"It's Kirk. I don't know how to say this, but something's come up."

Like he already had a wife somewhere that he'd forgotten about in his zealous pursuit? "Oh?" she asked cautiously.

"My brother got back from St. Louis yesterday, and we went over the accounts last night."

Lyssa's gut tightened. He was going to say they'd overextended, that the check would bounce. But no. It had already cleared.

"He—I never expected it to be an issue, but he wants to cancel. I mean, he used to go to church with his wife, so this is a surprise to me. . . ."

She gripped the phone. Kirk's *brother* wanted to withdraw on account of it being a church affair? When all along she thought Kirk himself was the one with issues against Christians? Not that he'd shown any sign of it in the few weeks since they'd met—or remet—but she knew his past, even if he didn't know she knew.

Complicated.

"Lyssa?"

Right, she hadn't answered him. She ran her fingers over the brochures on her desk. "It's kind of too late. Everything's back from the printer." Her mind boggled to think what it would entail to redo everything. He couldn't possibly mean it.

"Back?" His voice caught. "Already?"

"I e-mailed the files yesterday morning. They knew we needed a rush job so, yes, the printed copies are sitting on my desk this very minute." She couldn't keep the bitterness out of her voice. Not that she was really trying. "All two thousand of them."

"But—"

"Do you have any idea how much it cost to have these printed?" Yeah, he'd given a donation, but she'd already spent it on the printing bill.

"Uh—I don't know what to say. I had no idea your deadline was this close."

Puh–leeze. "The kickoff is just a week away. Ideally they should have been printed at least a month in advance." It wouldn't take much of a businessman to figure that out. But then, Kirk wasn't a businessman. He was a professor, all locked away in his ivory tower where he could poke at Christians without consequence. Maybe that's what he was still doing. Maybe he'd pretended to like her so he could make her look like a fool in front of Noah and the committee. Dad would call it justice. She squeezed back tears.

"I—uh. . .Lyssa, this wasn't my idea. I'm so sorry."

Yeah, right. "I don't know if there's anything that can be done, to be honest. The check has cleared, the money's been spent, and the brochures are printed. In fact, I was just about to leave the office and start dropping them off at key locations around town."

Kirk's voice hesitated. "Well, I'll talk to Dale again, but I think he'll still want a refund. Just for the main ad. I'll pay the business back for the donation personally."

Big of him. Lyssa hardened her heart. "You can't just give money to a nonprofit and then demand it back ten days later. I'm sorry, but that's not how things work. If you'd said no the day I came asking, I'd have gone on to the next store, and eventually I'd have found the sponsors I needed. But it's totally unfair to say *oops* when it's all done." Totally unfair to play with her heart, as well, but thankfully she'd seen his true colors had never changed before it was too late.

But it *was* too late. She'd loved every minute she'd spent in his company. She'd let down her guard and fallen for his smooth charm. Why, oh why, hadn't she listened to Jeannie? She should have followed through with her first instinct and marched straight back out Communication Location's door that day when she'd recognized him.

"Lyssa? I'm sorry."

She mumbled something and clicked to end the call. Maybe her original mistake had been accepting this volunteer position in the first place. She cradled her head in her arms on the desktop. She should have kept her faith separate from her public life, no matter what Jeannie said. Jeannie admonished her to be bold for Jesus everywhere she went. Lyssa hadn't been bold with Kirk, though. Not really. She'd pretended her responsibility was over when he knew she went to church.

How much time had she spent asking God for *His* advice? She cringed. Not enough. Not nearly enough.

Kirk clicked off his cell and sank his head into his hands in Communication Location's staff room. Stuck between a rock and a hard place. Such a fun spot to be. It didn't much matter what he did next—neither Lyssa nor Dale were likely to forgive him any time soon. How had he gotten himself into this predicament? And, more to the point, how would he get out?

He could practically hear Debbie's voice. *You could always pray.*

Easy for her to say. Well, no, it hadn't been. Not when she was dying. Still, her sweet, gentle spirit had shone through, even in those last ugly days.

His brother missed her as though half his body were gone. Amputees talked about phantom pain in missing limbs. That must be what Dale was going through. Kirk should have been more sensitive. Should have allowed his brother to call all the shots. Should have known.

But how could he have? Dale had sat by his wife's side Sunday after Sunday in their St. Louis church. There had been no way to guess Kirk would incur Dale's wrath over this advertising. Debbie's death had softened him but hardened his brother.

A rustle sounded behind Kirk. He took a deep breath and glanced up to see Dale leaning against the staff-room door, holding his coffee.

"So, did you tell her?"

Kirk nodded slowly.

"Good." Dale shoved off the doorframe.

"Wait. It's not that simple."

Dale's eyes narrowed. "It should be."

"She said the completed brochures are back from the printer. It's too late to change them."

Coffee sloshed over the edge of his brother's takeout cup.

Kirk forged on. "Look, it's not as though every sponsor has to sign some statement vowing we believe like them. It's advertising, Dale. That's all. It's a big church. We'll look good to the community."

Dale took a few shaky steps into the room and slumped into the other bright-red chair. "But. . ."

Sympathy rolled over Kirk even as he could feel the win coming on. "I'm sorry we didn't discuss the campaign in more detail before you left. It never crossed my mind that there would be any issues with this. After all, you and D—"

"I remember, okay?" His brother jerked upright. "I know why you thought. . .why you didn't think. . ."

Oh, man. Kirk leaned across the table. "I wasn't trying to rub salt in your wound."

"Everything does. Intentional or not." Dale met Kirk's gaze for an instant then stared at the cup in his hands as though unaware he turned it in circles. "It's not your fault."

"I should have guessed." No, that was ridiculous. He'd slid right back into his familiar role, taking all the blame whether it was the rightful place or not. And it usually wasn't. Not that he could retract the words now.

Dale took a long, deep slurp of his brew and set the cup on the table. "If it's too late to retract, I guess it's too late. If you were anyone else, I'd take it out of your hide, but you're my brother. I'm thankful you entrusted me with your savings, so we'll just ride it out the best we can."

Gracious of him. Kirk nodded sharply and kept his mouth zipped while his brother downed the remainder of his coffee, tossed the cup in the trash, and headed back into the store.

Chapter 6

Lyssa slammed the box of brochures on the counter in front of Melanie, wishing Kirk's fingers were in the way. She'd like to crush them, crush *him*. "What am I going to do with all these? It took a week to get in line for a print run. There's no time for a do-over." To say nothing of zero time to find new sponsors.

Melanie glanced at the windowed wall between Noah's office and the reception area.

Empty. Lucky guy had escaped before Kirk's phone call. He'd have been in for an earful from Lyssa. Maybe seen some tears. They still burned in her eyes.

"He can't just cancel like that." The receptionist's voice held indecision.

Lyssa gritted her teeth. She needed advice, a plan, maybe a Java Chiller over at the bistro. Melanie wasn't going to be any help. She only drank decaf. Black.

Lyssa's cell-phone ring pierced the air, and she glanced at the display. Kirk's number. She stuffed it back in her pocket, still ringing.

"Not going to get that?"

Lyssa shook her head and talked louder. "So, you don't have

any advice for me, then? When will Noah be back?"

Melanie turned to the "Gone Fishing" clock on the office wall. "Not until after lunch."

The cell beeped. Great, Kirk was leaving a message. How much more could he say than he already had? Still, Lyssa's hand tightened around the phone and waited for the signal he was done. She held up one finger to silence Melanie and clicked to hear his voice, turning away so her face couldn't reveal her emotions any further.

"Lyssa? Sorry I didn't catch you. I talked to Dale some more, and we're working things out. Can I pick up some of those brochures? I'll swing by the church in just a few minutes. And, um, I want to talk to you."

How dare he put her through all this if it wasn't a big deal after all? She'd been scrambling through her contact list, trying to think who might upgrade their sponsorship. She'd been panicking about getting another slot at the printer. She'd been...

And now she was supposed to just smile and say, "Whew, glad it's all good"? She didn't think so. He couldn't get here fast enough to get a piece of her mind. The nerve of him.

"Lyssa, are you okay?"

Melanie. Lyssa turned to the counter and smacked the box of brochures. "I'm fine. Forget everything I said. Mr. Hot-Shot Professor has smoothed everything over, and the show will go on."

"That's wonderful! What an answer to prayer."

"Yes." Lyssa sucked in a deep breath. "Yes, it sure is."

Perspective. The heat she'd felt a moment before started to fade. No, she couldn't face Kirk like this. Not while her anger flared. "Listen, Melanie, I need to run a few errands. Kirk said he'd be by to pick up some of these brochures. Mind if I leave them right here? He can help himself to however many he wants. Oh, and there's a poster he can have for the window, too." If his bossy brother would let him put it up.

"Yes, that's fine."

"Okay." Lyssa jingled Kermit's keys and glanced at the clock. "Not sure what time I'll be back." Only when she was sure Kirk had truly gone. That Java Chiller was sounding better and better.

Kirk sped toward Osage Beach Community Church. Lyssa must have been in a meeting or something, but she'd be waiting for him. She'd be as relieved as he was that Dale had given in. Maybe they'd go for coffee then hunt a cache later.

He turned the corner into the parking lot, but Lyssa's bright-green car wasn't there. Maybe she'd walked to the church this morning. He didn't even know if she lived close enough. So many things needed clarifying, but the summer was young. They'd have plenty of time to get to know each other before the school year threatened to separate them.

Kirk swung out of his car and strode up the church walkway then in through the glass doors. He stopped at the reception desk. "Is Lyssa in?"

The woman eyed him speculatively. "No, she stepped out for a bit. You're Professor Kennedy?"

The sunshine streaming across the foyer floor seemed duller than a moment ago. He nodded. "She's not here? But I talked to her only half an hour ago." Of course that had been by cell, so she could have been anywhere. He frowned. Hadn't she said she was at her desk?

"She was here, but she's gone now." Sympathy shone from the receptionist's eyes.

Doubts flickered through Kirk's brain. "When will she be back?" He needed to know she'd gotten his message. Maybe she was already out trying to find a new sponsor, despite her comments that it was too late.

"She wasn't sure."

It took an effort to keep his shoulders back as he nodded at the woman. "Okay. Thanks for telling me. I'll catch up with her later." Where or when, he didn't know, if she didn't answer his calls.

"She did say you could help yourself to as many of the brochures as you needed."

Kirk jerked his head up. "Brochures?"

It wasn't his imagination. The woman knew something was up. She had to. She pushed the box on the counter closer to him. "Here."

He picked up a bundle of paper. This was crazy. Lyssa had obviously gotten his message. That had only been ten minutes ago, tops. She hadn't taken his call, and then she'd left.

So much for his daydreams.

Chapter 7

Lyssa sat slumped in a chair at On the Rise Bakery & Bistro, nursing a Java Chiller containing a double shot of mocha. The richly caffeinated chocolate tantalized her nostrils and swirled around inside her mouth. How could this much caffeine calm her? But it had, with a molten lava cake as helpmeet. She pressed her finger against the few remaining crumbs then licked them off.

With the last deep-brown fleck gone, she said good-bye to Kirk Kennedy. Like the confection, he'd been a tantalizing pleasure while he lasted. Her gaze drifted to the dessert case. She could get another piece of cake, but her relationships wouldn't be mended by indulging in more calories. Though it was a temptation. A strong one.

"Hey, Lys. I thought you'd be at the church office."

Jeannie. Lyssa looked up. "Just taking a break." Not that she could hide from Kirk forever, but she'd give it a good shot.

"Gonna be here for a few? I'll join you."

Whatever. Lyssa hitched her shoulder then watched as her roommate waved down a waitress and placed her order. The waitress reached for Lyssa's plate, which was all but licked clean.

Lyssa snagged the fork off it. "I'm having some of yours," she informed Jeannie.

"That bad?" Her roommate cocked her head. "You look like you just lost your best friend. But I'm here, so that's not it. What's up?"

"You were right. I was wrong."

The waitress set a molten lava cake, mounded with vanilla bean ice cream, in front of Jeannie, along with a Java Chiller.

Lyssa pulled the plate closer and dug her fork into the cake.

"Of course I'm right." Jeannie tugged the plate back and scooped a large bite. "What did I say? What context?"

Like her roommate didn't know. "Kirk. You told me to stay clear of him, but I figured I could handle things."

"What happened?" When Lyssa didn't answer right away, Jeannie poked her hand gently with the fork. "Hey. Talk to me."

Lyssa sighed and updated her roommate. "He's just playing with my mind."

"So you're even, then."

"What?" Lyssa narrowed her eyes.

"Seriously. You've been messing with him, too. How long did you expect to go in this relationship without 'fessing up to the past? Did you think you'd tell him on your wedding day? Or maybe hold it in until you died of old age?"

"I don't know. The time just hasn't been right. I hate confrontation."

"You need to let go of the issues with your parents." Jeannie tapped the fork against the nearly empty plate.

Lyssa reared back. "Thanks, Freud. What has that got to do with anything?"

"I won't even start on how your mom's abandonment crushed you at your most vulnerable age. I cried over everything when I was twelve. Mama couldn't even ask me for a weather report without me breaking into tears."

On Lyssa's first day of junior high she'd come home to find that Mom had taken a suitcase and left a note. Lyssa had only cried the once. It hadn't brought Mom back. A girl had to be tough to survive.

"But I think you resent your dad more than your mother."

"Oh, I don't know about that. What kind of mother abandons her kids, leaving them with a man so tied up in his work he barely knows their names?"

Jeannie nodded. "Don't forget the crux of the matter." She had another bite.

Oh yeah. "His *church* work. He was so busy handing out tracts and explaining the way of salvation to people who didn't even want to hear it that he had no clue what was going on in his own home."

"A respected community leader."

What, was her roommate crazy? Jeannie'd heard the stories. "When he finally went to school events, he discovered a treasure trove, a whole new captive audience he could preach at. He turned me into a pariah. Everyone laughed at me."

Jeannie set her Java Chiller, laced with hazelnut, back on the table. "And as a result, you veer away from mentioning your faith to anyone."

"I remember far too well what that ridicule felt like." Lyssa met her roommate's eyes. "That's why Kirk—Professor Kennedy—made me so crazy in college. He treated you like an outcast, and you didn't seem to care. I couldn't take it all over again."

"I cared, but I couldn't let him stomp all over me." Jeannie studied her. "But even after your dad, even after humanities, you still believe. You're still a Christian."

Lyssa spread her hands. "There isn't anything that makes

more sense to me. Faith gives me a reason for living. I do believe."

Jeannie leaned back in the chair. "If you were still dating Professor Kennedy, I'd say that you need to tell him that, one way or another, but I guess it doesn't matter anymore, if you're done with him."

Shards of ice surrounded Lyssa's heart. Jeannie was right. It was too late.

Kirk thumbed off his cell phone when his brother came in the apartment door. Two days later, and Lyssa still wasn't picking up calls from him. He and Dale had been working flat out, preparing for Monday's grand opening. "Everything ready?"

Dale swung his briefcase onto the table. "Yep. Looks pretty good, if I do say so myself." He headed over to the fridge and pulled a can of cola out of the box.

"Yeah, it does." Right down to the Rainbow's End Treasure Hunt poster in the window. Dale had grimaced when Kirk put it up but hadn't challenged him. Kirk would've been ready to argue, so maybe it was a good thing. "Ready for food? I can fire up the grill anytime."

"Sounds good." Dale popped the tab and took a deep guzzle. "What's for dinner?"

"I've got a pasta salad in the fridge and some burgers ready to cook."

A shadow crossed Dale's face as he sat back down. "I don't know what I'm going to do when you go back to Jefferson City."

"Learn to cook?" Kirk meant the words lightly but wished he could bite them back when his brother's jaw clenched.

Dale looked down. "Yeah. I might have to."

He'd never much learned how, sliding through college on

boxed mac 'n' cheese like most guys. And then married Debbie, who'd taken good care of him for most of the intervening years. Kirk, on the other hand, had eventually tired of packaged food and takeout, and applied himself to learning the culinary arts. There'd been no woman around offering to do it for him.

He headed for the balcony door. Did Lyssa know how to cook? He bet she did. Any gal that was so adamant about not drinking soda probably cared even more about the quality of her food. Kirk could quit the cola and feel less withdrawal than not seeing her. The ache of her rejection showed no sign of lifting. Surely life would settle down a bit once the store was open and the treasure hunt rolling. He'd do everything he could to make amends.

Kirk checked the propane valve on the barbecue then ignited it.

When he turned back to the kitchen, Dale sat leaning against the table, head in his arms.

"You okay, man?"

Didn't look like it. Dale's shoulders shook as he choked out, "Why did God let Debbie die?"

Like Kirk was the God expert in this family. That had been Debbie's thing. He'd thought it was also his brother's, until a few days ago. If only Dale could have this conversation with Lyssa. She went to church. She could probably help him.

"I shouldn't have moved here. I've left everything of her behind."

Which had been the point, to give Dale a fresh start. "It'll be okay. It takes time."

"I just want her back. What did I do to make God hate me?"

Whoa. Once Kirk would have said God was just a figment of folks' imaginations. After Debbie, he wasn't so sure. And

Lyssa. "*Hate's* a mighty strong word."

"I loved her. We had so many plans. She wanted to travel, and I was too busy. She wanted to have kids years ago, and I just wasn't ready until it was too late."

"You have to let go." Kirk pulled the container of beef patties out of the fridge. "We all have regrets, but it's best not to dwell on them." At least not sink oneself into them, not that he truly understood the depths of his brother's despair. He'd only begun to woo Lyssa when the lid had snapped on his fingers. Thanks to Dale.

"You?" Dale's harsh laugh echoed around the apartment. "What have you done that you regretted?"

He didn't want to go there. Kirk gave his head a quick shake to clear it. "Trust me, there's been plenty." He strode out to the barbecue, slapped the patties on, and headed back into the kitchen.

Dale narrowed his gaze at Kirk. "You were Mom's golden boy."

"Good grief, don't drag up ancient history. Get the condiments and rolls out, please. Have you seen the long-handled spatula?"

"Third drawer."

"Thanks."

Dale followed him to the balcony. "Seriously. What did you ever do that you regretted more than a day or two?"

The burgers weren't ready to flip. Kirk studied Dale leaning against the doorjamb. Could either of them handle this discussion? He took a deep breath. "I'm not so proud of the way I've poked fun of people's beliefs."

Dale snorted. "Get real."

"I am."

"Debbie was really into that religion thing. She believed right down to her toenails."

Kirk nodded and checked the meat again. Lyssa hadn't seemed to want to talk about her faith when he'd tried to steer the conversation there. Didn't mean she wasn't as into it as Debbie had been. Did it?

"You never hassled *her*. Man, you never hassled me either, when I went to church with her."

True. Kirk hadn't been an equal-opportunity troublemaker. "I didn't want to wreck what you guys had. Besides, Debbie was for real." Maybe those students in humanities had been real, too. Who knew?

"Yeah, she was. God should've left her alone. Left us alone. At least if He cared about me, He would have. I was thinking seriously about that stuff and then *whap*!" Dale thwacked the glass door. "The end."

Kirk flipped the burgers. "Debbie wasn't bitter." The joy she'd had even in the midst of cancer had done a lot to challenge his views on Christianity. She'd had strength from within, even as her body faded.

Dale pulled away from the jamb. "She left the bitterness for me."

Kirk glanced at his brother. "I don't think it's one of those things where somebody has to take the role." He took a deep breath. "Have you tried reaching for her peace instead of rejecting it?" If Dale figured out how to do that, maybe he could help Kirk. They could both use peace with God.

Silence hung between them for a moment. "Since when are you the expert? Good thing I saved you from yourself with that church girl. Next thing I'd know, you'd be preaching on street corners like that bozo in Jefferson City."

"You saved me? Good one, Dale. You found happiness with a Christian. Why couldn't I? What gives you the right to blast my chances to smithereens?"

Dale leaned closer. "Because I own controlling shares in the business. Don't get me wrong, I'm thankful for your input. Just don't try to run things."

"That had nothing to do with it. Just because you lost Debbie doesn't mean I shouldn't fall in love." Because that's what he'd been doing. Falling for a girl with gorgeous eyes. "Not trying to hurt you, man, but don't interfere with my life." If only Lyssa would pick up his calls.

"Don't burn the burgers. I'll go set the table." Dale stormed back inside.

Chapter 8

Kirk glanced out the front window of Communication Location for the hundredth time since they'd unlocked the doors at nine o'clock. Balloons and streamers fluttered from a sandwich board on the sidewalk announcing the grand opening. Inside, dozens of customers milled around the shop, examining the merchandise and indulging in doughnuts and coffee.

His throat caught. A woman stood with her back to him, her brown hair swinging across her shoulders as she turned over a package of headphones. Could that be Lyssa? Kirk rounded the end of the counter.

"Excuse me, can you answer some questions about these GPS units?"

Kirk glanced at the group in front of him then back at the woman. He bit back a sigh. "Sure. What do you want to know?" Business before pleasure.

"Colton here wants to know why this one costs so much more than the other one," the younger man said.

The young woman with the two guys rolled her eyes and stepped back, caressing the camera hanging around her neck.

She was cute, but not like Lyssa. Kirk glanced at the woman

across the store, still with her back to him.

These guys looked like an easy upsell, especially with the coupon, and Kirk needed to prove to Dale that throwing in their lot with the church program had been a good idea. He turned to the task of explaining the merits of the two units the guys had set on the counter. A few minutes later he closed the deal on the more expensive one, and the girl raised her camera to record the moment.

"Oh, come on, Reagan. Do you have to take photos of everything?" the younger man complained, leading the way out the door.

Kirk headed across the store just as the brown-haired woman turned. He ground to a halt.

Definitely not Lyssa. But she knew their grand opening began today. She'd come, wouldn't she? Just to check things out? No guarantees, of course. Not after all those phone calls she hadn't picked up. Didn't she think she owed him some sort of explanation after the chemistry they'd shared? She'd felt it, too. Her eyes had revealed her emotions, even while she pulled away from him.

The woman approached the counter, headphones in hand, and Dale stepped in to ring her purchase through.

A fresh breeze wafted across the small community park next to the church, making the muggy June Saturday bearable. Lyssa stood under a hickory tree beside the registration table. Genius of Noah to run the launch outside. People of all ages streamed into the area they'd cordoned off, from elderly men to groups of teens to families with small kids.

And Kirk.

She tried to drag her gaze away but didn't manage before he saw her. What was he doing here? Lyssa focused on straightening bags of trail mix on the table, willing him to walk on by.

"Lyssa?"

He hadn't gone past. But—to be fair—he also hadn't followed through pulling the sponsorship. He'd talked his brother into staying the course for whatever reason. Jeannie kept telling Lyssa what a close call she'd had, that he'd let his true colors show through for just long enough to remind her of them.

His grin faltered. "I'm sorry I missed you the other day."

The other day? That had been over a week ago. Of course he'd called since, but she'd resisted the impulse to accept his calls, instead listening to his recorded voice after each one. Not that she could explain it to him. She lifted a shoulder noncommittally. "All's well that ends well."

Lyssa tried to look past him, maybe reel somebody else in with her eyes. Someone who might want questions answered about the hunt, for example. Even a kid searching for his parents would be a nice change. But no one showed any signs of interest in her as they chatted in little groups of their own, carrying collapsible lawn chairs and drifting closer to the bandstand where Noah tested his equipment.

"We had a good opening week."

Lyssa's eyes flew back to meet Kirk's. "That's nice."

He stepped closer. "I'm really sorry about what happened. My brother has had some difficulty adjusting to his wife's death. He—I can't predict how he's going to react to things these days." His blue eyes bored into hers.

"I'm sorry, too." Sorry she'd trusted him, for starters. "It was simply too late to do anything about it." Too late to do anything about her heart, too. It pounded erratically whenever Kirk was near. She'd get over it, though. She had to.

"I convinced him of that."

Lyssa managed some sort of smile. "I appreciate it. I hope the treasure hunt draws a lot of people into the store so he'll be happy with the results."

"So far, I'd say that's happening. I see quite a few people here who picked up brochures from Communication Location." He poked his chin toward a table right at the park gate. "And I'm ready to do more business this afternoon when the kickoff closes."

"That's awesome." Too bad she couldn't get any enthusiasm into her voice. "Oh, look. I think Noah's about ready to open the rally." She turned away from Kirk and pretended to focus on the bandstand, but her whole body seemed magnetically drawn to him. Good thing the table stood between them, or she might make a fool of herself.

"Welcome to Rainbow's End Treasure Hunt!" Noah's voice boomed across the sound system. "Find a place to set your chair, and let's get started."

There must have been a few hundred people milling around the small park. Even though they'd planned for this many, Lyssa hadn't believed it would happen. But maybe they hadn't planned for enough. Maybe she'd run out of registration packets. Maybe—

"Lyssa? I'm sorry this thing with my brother came between us when we'd just started to connect with each other. Can we talk over dinner, maybe tonight?"

She lurched around to face Kirk. Opened her mouth and closed it again. Anything she said now could be setting herself up for further pain. Better not to give any hope—for him or for herself.

"I don't think so. It's best to leave things the way they are." Lyssa tried to stare him down, like she didn't care, but she felt as if any second she'd dissolve in tears or throw herself into his arms. She clenched the table's plastic edge to prevent that from happening then turned her back to him. Hopefully, he couldn't see her tremble.

"You just plug the handheld into your computer with the USB connection, like this." Kirk lifted his own GPS unit and fitted the cord into it. Good thing he'd come to the rally prepared. Also a good thing the church's wi-fi stretched this far.

He glanced at Lyssa across the stream of people leaving the park. Her hands flew as she talked to someone; then she smiled brightly and passed over a brochure.

Once, briefly, Kirk had been privy to that smile. His heart sank. Not anymore, and he barely knew what he'd done wrong. This couldn't all be about Dale and the sponsorship.

Lyssa's gaze met his. Time suspended for a second or two. Then she hitched her shoulder slightly, turned away from Kirk, and reengaged the African American gal beside her.

"Then what?" the young woman in front of him asked.

Right, he was helping these two gals. They looked so much alike they must be sisters, even though one was dressed for the trail and the other for the outlet mall. "Okay, so it's plugged in. Then you need to log into the website—if you haven't created an account, you'll need one. Free and easy. Then enter our zip code, and scout through the resulting caches until you find one or several you'd like to try for." Kirk glanced at the woman in front of him. "With me so far?"

She nodded, focused on the laptop screen, but her sister hung back.

He shot a glance at Lyssa, but she was busy.

Back to his demonstration. "Now, if you have a paid membership on the website instead of a free one, you click here to transfer the information to your handheld." He waited for the download to complete then removed the unit from the cord. "If you go with the free membership, you can see all the waypoints online but will need to enter them into your unit manually. It's not that big a deal."

"Good. Madison and I want to make sure we like treasure hunting before committing more money to it."

Madison rolled her eyes and fiddled with her purse strap.

Kirk bit back a grin. The amount of the membership was peanuts compared to the unit they'd bought from him the day before. "Now, when you're out on the trail, you'll have the lats and longs of your position—you know what those are, don't you?"

The sporty sister nodded. "Latitude and longitude. Those imaginary lines they draw around globes in school. Remember, Maddie?"

Madison hitched a shoulder.

Close enough. "Right. So you have those, plus the coordinates of the cache's location. Your unit will let you know when you're getting close."

"Oh, that sounds cool." The girl grinned at him. "And then you find the treasure."

Kirk laughed. "Not quite that easy." He tilted the unit for her to see the poem Lyssa had written for the first cache he'd found. . .with a lot of help from her. "Here's an example of a clue to help you find a cache once you're out there."

She frowned. "Is that supposed to make sense?"

Kirk couldn't help shooting a look across the park, but

Lyssa wasn't watching him. "It does when you're at the correct coordinates."

"Okaaaay."

Kirk handed her a brochure. "This gives you the details of how to log on to the Rainbow's End website and what to do at each cache so it will count for the treasure hunt. Good luck to you."

"Thanks! We'll have a lot of fun with this. Won't we, Maddie?" The girl grabbed her sister's arm and hauled her away, waving the GPS unit around.

Best wishes to those two.

The crowd had thinned out by that time. Lyssa finished up with a middle-aged man while her dark-skinned friend stacked brochures into a carton. The girl said something to Lyssa, and then her gaze passed Lyssa and landed on Kirk. She froze for an instant before turning her back.

Kirk frowned. Lyssa must have said something about him to her friend to make her swivel away, but what? The staring-at-a-train-wreck look on the woman's face bothered him. He'd seen that expression before. Seen *her* before.

Where?

"You're right, it's him," Jeannie hissed under her breath.

Lyssa refused to look up. He'd caught her eye too many times today already for her comfort. "Like I would lie."

"Yeah, sorry." Jeannie popped the cardboard tabs shut on the box. "Still, I hoped you were wrong. After all, you went on a date with the guy."

More than one, if she counted the hikes. "Look, can we just get out of here? Noah's team will get the tables and chairs later.

If he'd quit staring at that brunette over there. Good grief."

Jeannie didn't spare a glance for Noah. "Professor Kennedy is packing up to leave, too. If we go now, we can't avoid him."

He wasn't very avoidable at the best of times. "Kirk."

"Kirk?"

Lyssa gave her head a shake. "He's not Professor Kennedy. Not here. Not now."

Jeannie narrowed her eyes. "You'd better remember him as the obnoxious professor who hung you out to dry this past week, not the cute romantic guy you had no business going out with, or you'll be in trouble."

Too late.

"Lys, you're sure he doesn't know who you are?"

"Not a chance."

"Uh oh," Jeannie muttered, so low Lyssa barely heard her. She glanced up.

Kirk stood mere inches from her elbow, looking from her to Jeannie and back again.

Kirk shifted the briefcase to his left hand and held out his right. "Hi, I'm Kirk Kennedy, but I've a feeling we've already met." He kept his focus on Lyssa's friend, but the awareness of Lyssa right there nearly did him in. His mind reeled from overhearing that statement of her friend's. Know Lyssa from where?

"Jeannie Dawson. Nice to meet you," the girl said crisply then turned a shoulder toward him. "Ready to go, Lys?"

Kirk dropped his hand back to his side.

Lyssa glanced from her friend to Kirk, biting her lip. She picked up a canvas bag full of trail mix packages and her ever-present pocket folder, hugging it close.

Was his smile as frozen as it felt to him? "Lyssa? Can we talk a minute?"

Jeannie wedged the box against her right hip and tucked her left arm through Lyssa's.

"Here, let me carry that." Without waiting for a response, Kirk plucked the box from Jeannie. "Where are you parked?" At least he'd bought a bit of time. Maybe time to figure out what had gone wrong and how he could make things right.

Jeannie humphed, but Lyssa pointed at the parking lot. "Far end."

Didn't look like Lyssa's friend was going to give them privacy, and if Kirk's sharpening memories of his first year of teaching were accurate, he might finally have a clue why. He fell into step beside Lyssa, only to discover Jeannie had swapped spots with her. Should he openly challenge her friend's obvious ploy? But he'd been here with Jeannie before, or somewhere similar. She hadn't backed down then.

And she wasn't going to start today. "So, Professor Kennedy from Lincoln University. What brings you to Osage Beach?"

His hunch of where he'd seen her had been correct, but that didn't mean he needed to be as hostile as she was. Besides, she had a right to ask. "Helping my brother open a business."

Jeannie stopped on the path, forcing the others to do the same. "And involved in a church rally? I wouldn't have thought it of you."

A burn rose up his neck. "Things have—"

"Churches are merely social clubs for pansies, if I remember correctly. Have you turned into a pansy, Professor?"

He stared at her, not daring to seek Lyssa's eyes. "No, I..." How could he explain what had brought him to this point?

It wasn't just Lyssa and the treasure hunt.

Jeannie yanked the box from his hands. "Thanks very much for offering to carry this, *Professor*, but we'll manage just fine from here."

"About that—"

"Have a great day." Jeannie gave him a sharp nod and pulled Lyssa's arm. They started down the path.

Kirk gaped after them, the apology sputtering on his lips. It wasn't until the women entered the parking lot that Lyssa glanced over her shoulder at him, eyes wide.

"You didn't need to do that." Lyssa jerked away from Jeannie's grasp as they approached the car. "You were downright rude to him."

Jeannie slipped the box off her hip onto Kermit's hood. "Get a grip on yourself, Lys. You know he's only using you to get his business name out to the town. You offered the cheapest advertising in Osage Beach."

"No, that's not it at all." Though the cost for frontlining in the brochure had been reasonable. Was that why Dale had relented in the end? Or had Kirk stuck up for her because he... liked her?

"Look, you always had a soft spot for Professor Kennedy, even after he strung me out in class time after time. That was fine. You were an undergrad. Just a kid. Now you're an adult—a teacher—and you need to open your eyes. A guy like him doesn't do an about-face and suddenly start being sensitive to Christians. Did you hear him deny what I said?"

Lyssa shook her head. He really hadn't. Too bad she'd never probed. Too bad she'd never dared let on she remembered him from Lincoln U. She'd preferred to keep her head stuck in the sand in the hope that if she pretended everything was all right, it would be.

"I'm just trying to save you some heartbreak, Lys." Jeannie popped the hatchback and set the carton inside. "You need to get a backbone."

Why, so she could be nasty and abrasive, too? Look at her dad. Look at Jeannie. Until now Lyssa had slid through life making the fewest possible waves, trying not to draw too much attention to herself. And what had it gotten her?

She eyed Jeannie. It had gotten her a roommate who persisted in protecting her while telling her to buck up. Jeannie couldn't have it both ways. But neither could she.

Kirk had never downplayed her church affiliation when they'd seen each other here at the lake. College didn't count. Not anymore.

Lyssa whirled around in time to see his car turning onto the street. Gone. But maybe not forever.

"Let's get going, Lys. You driving, or am I?"

Lyssa set her jaw. "I am." She rounded Kermit and opened the driver's door.

Jeannie slid in the passenger side and cocked her head at Lyssa. "Give it up, Lys. You'll thank me later."

If so, it would have to be much, *much* later.

Chapter 9

Kirk opened the door to his Jefferson City apartment. No problem for him to get back in time for Monday morning, and he needed a break from his brother, if only for a day.

This place was more like it. Sure, it lacked the view of the lake the pad in Osage Beach sported, but this was all his. The wood-paneled walls and deep colors suited him more than the airy contemporary lines of the other place. He switched on his topaz lamp and paused, staring at the glow of amber amidst the brown. Just like Lyssa's eyes. Everything reminded him of her. A vision of her curled up on his brown leather sofa, reading a hiking magazine, swam into his mind.

He needed her in his life, but what could he do about the history that separated them? Yes, he could apologize, and he would as soon as he could catch her apart from her roommate, though he owed it to both women. If only he could do those first few years of teaching over again.

Kirk opened the glass door of his walnut bookcase. Yearbooks. Second shelf from the bottom. He pulled out the one from his first year on staff and checked the student index. His finger hovered over *Quinn, Alyssa*. Must be her. The odds were slim there would be two with such close names in that time frame.

The photo of a platinum blond with big glasses stared back at him. She looked vaguely familiar, but not like the Lyssa he knew. Kirk searched for *Dawson, Jeannie*, and came up with a face that had changed little over the intervening years.

He sank into his recliner and flipped the pages between the two photos. Jeannie. She'd been a vocal one in his classes back when he had something to prove as a new professor. He'd challenged her beliefs over and over, often calling on her when he'd felt like waking the class up. When his own ego had needed a boost.

The super-blond had sat on Jeannie's right. She sank back into her chair and averted her gaze. She certainly never got into the spirit of the game, and Kirk hadn't wasted any time wondering about her.

Until now.

He studied Alyssa's photo. He could almost see the treasure hunt coordinator lurking behind those frames. Lyssa had walked into Communication Location, taken one look at him, and pivoted on her heel. Now he knew why—she'd recognized him. All the walls were back up, ten feet taller. Had Jeannie protected her back then? Was she doing it again?

He'd caused it.

Kirk sank his head into his hands. Lyssa didn't trust him. And why should she? What had it looked like to her, knowing who he was all along? No wonder she'd seemed withdrawn. She'd become confident and fun when she relaxed a little, but never really let down her guard. Never freely talked about herself or where she'd gone to school. When he'd called her about pulling the funding, he had no idea how deep her scars ran. He still didn't, not really, but at least he could begin to appreciate what this had looked like to her. Like he was toying with her.

Nothing was further from the truth.

That thought slammed into him and jerked him to his feet. He shoved the yearbook into its spot and closed the glass door. Maybe a good brisk jog would clear his head.

"Excuse me, sir. Do you believe in life after death?"

Kirk swung around and eyed the man on the sidewalk. "Pardon me?"

He'd seen this guy around Jefferson City from time to time, always managing to avoid him. The man looked to be about fifty, with a full head of graying hair. He grinned at Kirk, took a step closer, and held out a folded piece of paper. A brochure, of sorts. "If you were to die today, where would you go?"

The last time Kirk heard those words had been from his sister-in-law's deathbed. Debbie had pleaded with Dale, and Kirk felt like an interloper just listening in. Her words cut him to the core.

"Sir?"

Kirk gave his head a shake. "Um, I don't really know." Yes, he did. And it wasn't heaven.

"Accidents happen." The man waved to encompass a city bus, air whooshing from the brakes as it pulled into a nearby transit stop. "People get diseases. Not a one of us can know we won't meet our maker in the very next moment."

Before Debbie's death, before meeting Lyssa, Kirk would have brushed this man aside as a lunatic and gone on his way. He'd only have remembered the conversation long enough to share the joke with someone else. But tonight was already loaded with self-recrimination and regrets. Tonight. . .he wondered where he would go when he died.

"I'd like to introduce you to Jesus." The man pointed out a bench near the sidewalk. "Do you have a few minutes?"

Kirk studied the man's face. Something about him was vaguely familiar, but Kirk couldn't place him. One of the mature students who'd reentered the halls of learning? A relative of one of his fellow faculty members? Whoever he was, could he explain Debbie's death to Kirk? He'd know pretty quickly if the guy was just a weirdo who talked out of his hat. Not that he was wearing one.

Kirk nodded and took the few steps to the bench.

The man sat near him. "My name's Ron." He pulled a well-thumbed black leather book from his pocket. "May I tell you what God has done for you?"

Anyone who'd read his Bible enough to wear it to a nub couldn't be all that bad. Kirk relaxed a little. "Tell me."

Lyssa followed Jeannie out to Kermit after church and slid behind the wheel. She turned to her friend. "Wow. How did Pastor John know what I needed to hear most?"

Jeannie slumped into the passenger seat and massaged her temples. "He has a way with words."

This sermon had been aimed straight at Lyssa. No point in pretending to deflect the words onto someone else, hoping so-and-so heard. Today, she was the person who needed to hear, and there was no denying it.

"You know, I knew those verses from Matthew 10 existed, but I'd kind of forgotten. About God denying He knows us if we say we don't know Him, I mean." How many times had

Lyssa been guilty? Not out loud, of course. It hadn't ever really come to that, being as she'd rarely stuck her nose out far enough so folks knew she was a Christian to start with.

"Telling people where it's at has never been a big deal for me." Jeannie shot Lyssa a sidelong look. "I've never understood why it's so hard for you."

Lyssa shook her head. "I've always blamed it on my dad, but that's not totally fair either. No reason to go to the opposite extreme."

"I'm pretty sure your dad means well."

"I know he does. It's just. . .he accosts everyone around him. People laugh at him, sometimes shove him out of the way."

Jeannie nodded.

"Probably there are people he actually helps." On the heels of that sermon, Lyssa had to be fair. "It always seemed to me, growing up, that everyone ridiculed him, but I know he'd sometimes come home excited because he led someone to Jesus." She jammed the key into the ignition and started the engine. The church parking lot had nearly emptied while they talked.

"So he was just spreading the Word, hoping it would find a receptive heart here and there."

Lyssa pulled the car out into the street. "I have no trouble telling people that soda and junk food are bad for them. I don't care what they think of me for that. Why is it so different to tell them about the Lord?"

"Because it matters more. Junk food affects our current life, but faith affects eternity."

Lyssa took a deep breath. "So we need to be bold. I need to be bold."

"We all do."

As though her roommate wasn't already. "Okay." Lyssa poured resolve into her voice. "Well, I know what I need to do then."

Jeannie tipped her head and peered at Lyssa. "What's that?"

"Right after we have lunch, I'm going to drive over to Kirk's." She ignored her roommate's gasp. "I'm going to tell him who I am and find out where he stands with God."

"I don't think that's wise, Lys."

"You told me to be bold."

"But not with him. He's not a changer."

"He already has changed, at least somewhat. The evidence is that he signed up to sponsor the church treasure hunt to start with. The old Kirk wouldn't have done that."

"He tried to pull back his sponsorship."

"That was his brother's fault, and Kirk made sure it didn't happen in the end. I think God is working on him." Just the thought ran goose bumps up Lyssa's arms.

"And I think you're not being sensible. You're twisting that sermon just to go see him. It's not the gospel you care about; it's a cute guy."

"That hurts, Jeannie. Really."

Jeannie's jaw set. "It's true."

"So you're willing to stick your neck out for Jesus, but you don't believe God can change people, is that it?"

"That's not what I said."

"Sure it is." Lyssa shot her friend a look as they pulled into the driveway at the condo. "Unless it's only Kirk you think God can't change."

Jeannie wrenched the car door open. She hurled herself out and leaned back in, dark eyes blazing. "Go, do your missionary thing. It's your heart I care about. *Professor* Kennedy is going to hurt you. Again. Don't come running to me when he does." She slammed the door.

Lyssa leaned her head against the steering wheel. "Is that all it is, God? Give me boldness. I need it. But please don't let me be foolish."

Kirk glanced in the rearview mirror as he turned into the apartment complex parking lot back in Osage Beach. Ron was right behind him. He'd told the guy where the guest parking was located, so Kirk pulled into his own spot, parked the car, and jogged back out to meet his new friend.

He took a deep breath. Yeah, he'd called Dale to say he was bringing a guest by for dinner—assured him it wasn't *that girl*—but still, how would his brother handle a straight-talker like Ron? Yet Dale needed to hear Ron's message as much as Kirk had.

"Hey, man." Kirk beckoned the street preacher behind him through the apartment door. "Ron, I'd like you to meet my brother Dale. Dale, my new friend Ron."

Dale looked up from the table, which was covered with Communication Location paperwork. Guy didn't look like he'd slept last night. "Pleased to meet you, Ron." But he didn't get up to shake hands or ask any questions.

Ron rested a hand on Dale's shoulder. "Good to meet you, too, son."

Dale's shoulder dipped slightly, no doubt trying to get away from the man's touch. Maybe bringing a stranger in hadn't been such a good idea. Kirk's relationship with his brother had been too rocky recently for this kind of trust. He should've waited a while, or tried to talk to Dale again on his own.

"Kirk tells me you've opened a new business here in town." Ron moved away from Dale and pulled out a chair at the end of the table.

Kirk dared to breathe. Maybe the guy, straightforward as he was, had enough tact to handle Dale after all.

"Yes, I have."

"Anyone want a cola?" Kirk opened the fridge door. Looked like Dale had gone through the better part of a case since Kirk left yesterday. He glanced up. "Dale? Ron?"

"Sure," said Dale.

Ron shook his head. "My daughter talked me out of drinking that stuff years ago. Said I didn't need to be hepped up on chemicals and caffeine." He laughed. "To say nothing of the sugar. She said I was hyper enough."

Just like Lyssa, only she'd complained of school kids. He passed a can to Dale and popped the tab on a second one. There weren't a lot of other options in the fridge.

"A glass of water would be great. Thanks."

Kirk nodded and filled a glass from the fridge dispenser. He and Dale had joked the first week they'd been in here how cool it would be to have a cola line instead of a water line. Probably wouldn't have gone over well with Ron, not that it mattered. Could he give up soda for Lyssa? Man, he'd give up anything she asked. Missing her created a vacuum deep inside.

His mind kept sliding back to her. Tomorrow, for sure, he'd connect with her. Come clean. Make her listen at least long enough to tell her he wasn't the professor she'd once known. The issue concerning his class must play at least a part in her rejection of him. Whether she'd be convinced of his sincerity or not, he didn't know. But his heart twisted every time he thought of her, and he couldn't give up this easily.

She wasn't here. Not now. Now it was this guy, Ron, whose last name he didn't even know, who had explained the gospel in a way Kirk could grasp.

"Have you lived here in Osage Beach all your life?" Ron asked Dale.

Dale measured the older man with his gaze. "No, we grew up in St. Louis, but our grandparents had a place on the lake here."

Did Kirk dare focus on dinner and trust that neither of the men would set the other off?

"So you must have had good memories, then, to draw you back."

Whew. Ron could be more tactful than he'd appeared when he stopped Kirk on the street. Yet that boldness had been just what Kirk needed.

He turned to the fridge and pulled out a package of hot Italian sausages. The bag of salad in the crisper still looked good. The pantry held a jar of pasta sauce and a package of linguine. He'd call it dinner, and it wouldn't take long.

Soon sausage chunks sizzled in the pot, loosening their peppery aroma into the air. Man, those things were hot. Just the vapors brought tears to his eyes.

"It's Father's Day today," Ron said. "Either of you a dad?"

Kirk froze, wooden spoon poised in his hand. He closed his eyes. *Oh please, God, no.* Dale wasn't ready for this.

"No, actually I'm not." Dale's voice, which hadn't warmed up in the brief exchange thus far, now sounded positively icy. "My wife had two miscarriages before she passed away a few months ago." His chair scraped. "Excuse me, please. I need to make some calls."

Kirk turned, trying to catch Dale's eye, but his brother

marched down the hallway without a glance. His bedroom door shut firmly.

"I'm sorry. I didn't mean to rub a raw spot."

Kirk eyed his visitor. "He'll be okay." Probably wouldn't have mattered who Kirk brought home. Ron hadn't even gotten to the heaven-and-hell thing yet.

"How about you? Any children?"

Kirk narrowed his gaze. "No, sir. I've been too busy building my career for a wife and family." But he was ready for that to change. Anytime.

The sausages. Kirk pivoted to wrench the jar of pasta sauce open then dumped it over the meat. He filled a large pot with water and adjusted both burners. "How about you, Ron?" Kirk leaned against the counter.

Ron stared out the patio door. "My kids are grown up now."

"I guess that happens eventually." A thought struck Kirk. "No one invited you over for Father's Day? They must live far away."

"My boys are back east, but my daughter lives here in town."

Kirk tilted his head. Interesting. This time it seemed Ron was on the defensive. "They call you?"

Ron shook his head. "Don't know. I haven't been home."

"No cell phone, man?" Kirk laughed. "We'll have to hook you up with one. It's what we do, Dale and I. Communication Location: Gizmos, Gadgets, and More."

The man gave a self-deprecating smile. "I don't really need one, thanks anyway. I doubt I miss many calls."

"Some people don't like leaving voice mail."

Ron shook his head. "I don't have that, either."

Telephone packages still provided the chance to opt out? Who knew?

When the water boiled, Kirk emptied the package of linguine into it and gave it a stir. He turned back to Ron, who watched him with something like longing. "What happened to your family, Ron? Your kids won't call on Father's Day?"

Ron's gaze shifted back to the patio door as he shrugged. "My daughter might phone, but my wife left me. Ten, twelve years ago or so. Walked out, didn't even say good-bye to the kids."

Pity welled up. "I'm sorry to hear that. Must've been tough."

The man's jaw clenched, and he blinked a few times. Tears? "I wasn't much of a husband. I didn't know how to be a father."

The pot sputtered, and Kirk jumped to readjust it. He'd clean the mess up later. Whatever.

"You told me God's in the business of forgiving us. You convinced me." Kirk studied Ron's face. "Sounds like you're in need of forgiving yourself."

Chapter 10

Lyssa strode across the parking lot of Kirk's ultramodern apartment complex, clutching her purse strap. She was nuts, but stopping now would be handing Jeannie the win. Her roommate already expected Lyssa to come home bawling in five minutes or less.

But Lyssa owed it to Kirk—and herself—to tell him the truth, and to find out what, if anything, had changed to allow him to date a "church girl." A Christian.

Her heels clicked across the tile lobby toward the propped-open interior doors. She scanned the list of names until she found KENNEDY next to 414. Was she about to make a fool of herself? Would Kirk be willing to hear her out? *Please God, don't let it be too late*.

In minutes she stood in front of the apartment door. She took a deep breath and patted down her hair. Adjusted her skirt. And knocked.

The door flew open, and a guy charged out, nearly running straight into her. "Sorry." Then his gaze narrowed. "Who are you?"

Not Kirk. A little shorter and not quite as cute. Must be his brother. "Are you Dale Kennedy?"

He scowled. "Yes. Why?"

His obvious displeasure sucked most of the bravado from her. "I'm Lyssa Quinn. Is Kirk in? I need to talk to him."

"You're the girl from church." His gaze flicked over her. "What's gotten into him lately, anyway? First you—then I had to put up with a street preacher over lunch."

Street preacher? That didn't sound like Kirk. Lyssa tried to see past Dale, but he filled the doorway. "Hey, man," he tossed over his shoulder, still watching her. "Some girl here to see you. Says she's Lyssa Quinn."

Lyssa!

Kirk was most of the way to his feet when he heard a gasp. He spared a glance at Ron and saw the older man's face pale. "You okay?"

Ron glanced furtively around. "I—I. . ."

Much as Kirk was thankful for Ron's help, he needed to see Lyssa and find out why she was here. Get things on the right footing.

It felt like the first day of school when he was a kid. Full of possibilities. Full of panic.

"Kirk?" His brother's voice hauled him back to the moment. "Want me just to send her away?"

"No." He pulled his gaze from his guest's and took a step toward the door.

Ron grabbed the hem of his shirt as Kirk passed by. "I'm not here."

Strange thing to say. Kirk pulled away from the man's grasp and rounded the corner to the door.

Dale shifted, clearing his line of sight.

Kirk caught his breath. No khakis and a tee today, or shorts and a tank. She'd pulled her hair into some kind of knot and wore a lacy pink top with a narrow brown skirt. Heels.

She was even more gorgeous dolled up. He couldn't get enough of filling his eyes with her.

Dale shook his head and pushed away from the doorjamb, heading back to the dining room, but Kirk barely noticed.

He reached a hand toward her, but let it fall. "Lyssa?"

"Hi." She twisted the strap of her leather purse. "I—I need to talk to you. Is this a good time, or. . ."

His brother's voice rose from behind him. Whatever was going on between his guest and Dale was beyond Kirk. It really wasn't a good time.

There might never be a better time. "Come on in."

She hesitated then nodded and took a step forward.

The hint of her perfume weakened his knees. "You're beautiful." He reached for her but remembered in time that he had no right. His hand fell to his side again.

Lyssa's startled eyes—topaz—locked on his. "Th–thank you."

"I'm outta here, man." Dale's voice came from behind Kirk's shoulder. "That guy is loony, and I can't handle this. I'll be back later."

Dale nodded sharply at Lyssa and swept past them both, all but jogging for the elevator.

That guy. What was he going to do about Ron? He'd invited him for dinner to learn more about his new faith, but partly so Ron could talk to Dale. That hadn't gone over so well, and now Dale was hightailing it out of here. Maybe he could get Ron to come back another time, though the man had driven over from Jefferson City. Wasn't Lyssa more important?

Kirk drew Lyssa into the dining room, where the remains

of the meal still sat on the table. Ron was nowhere to be seen.

Lyssa pulled back. "I'm sorry. I didn't mean to interrupt."

"No, it's okay. We were pretty much done. Besides, how could you have expected we'd be eating this late?" He couldn't take his eyes off her. If he sat next to her on the sofa, he wouldn't be able to help himself. She looked in dire need of a good kissing.

He needed a good distracting. "Here, have a seat at the island, and I'll clean up while we talk."

She perched on the edge of a barstool while Kirk busied himself gathering plates.

Finally he couldn't take the silence. "You wanted to talk?" He shot her a glance but couldn't read her expression.

"There are things I haven't told you." Lyssa bit her lip. "I think you may have guessed. I was a student in your humanities class at Lincoln four years ago."

Kirk nodded slowly, cautiously. "I found your picture in the yearbook. You've changed."

"I dyed my hair platinum blond back then. Tried to fit in. Basically I tried to be unnoticed." She grimaced. "It mostly worked."

What should he tell her? That he didn't remember her from class, so kudos on succeeding in her mission? But there was more to it than she'd said yet.

"It was hard to pull off around Jeannie, though. She always had opinions and wasn't afraid who knew about them." Lyssa traced patterns on the granite countertop. "She spoke up in your class a bunch of times about her Christian beliefs. Not just your class either."

"I remember. I goaded her into it sometimes, knowing she wouldn't be able to resist." Kirk set the plates down on the other side of the island and leaned on his elbows. "I mocked her. And not just her, but others."

"But not me."

True. But only because. . .

She met his gaze. "Kirk, I was a Christian then, but I was also a chicken. Still am. I'd grown up around someone brusque and confrontational. I couldn't handle any more of the ridicule and rejection it caused me back then."

He tried for a light tone. "That didn't stop you from telling me drinking soda was bad for me."

"It doesn't make sense, does it? Healthy food choices are an important issue to me, but, well, to be honest"—Lyssa took a deep breath—"being a Christian is more critical. I haven't been true to my beliefs by hiding that very vital side of me."

Oh man. He'd pushed her to this point. Kirk captured her hands against the countertop between them. "I'm sorry. If I hadn't been the guy who thought he knew everything—"

"It's not your fault." She tugged her hands free and folded them in her lap. "It's not even my dad's fault, though he embarrassed me half to death a thousand times when I was growing up. I made the choice to take the road of least resistance and simply kept my faith quiet and personal, not wanting people to laugh at me or ask questions I couldn't answer."

What could Kirk say? He would've laughed and poked. She knew it, and so did he.

"I couldn't imagine the prof I once knew sponsoring a church function, but I was too afraid to ask what had changed your mind, or even to let you know we'd met before."

Were those tears trembling at the ends of her lashes? Kirk rounded the island. "Lyssa. Don't cry. Please." If only she hadn't made it so clear she didn't want him to touch her. "I'm so sorry. I'll apologize to Jeannie, too, if she'll listen long enough to hear my words."

Lyssa's lips trembled. "Something happened to you. What?"

"Well, first it was Dale's wife." He took a deep breath, remembering. "There was just something about her. I could never hassle her like I did the students, but even when I did poke at her beliefs, she didn't take offense. Debbie didn't have a bunch of pat answers like some of the students. She didn't need them—she had light shining from her eyes." Kirk touched Lyssa's arm. "Like you."

She shook her head and swiped her eyes with the back of her hand. "Not me."

Kirk caught her chin, coaxing her to look up. "Yes, you." When she didn't fight him, he wiped her tears away with his thumb. "You've done nothing to apologize for. It's me who needs forgiveness."

She trembled under his touch. "What else happened?"

"That's the other thing." All he wanted was to gather her in his arms, but the rational voice in the back of his head warned him she wasn't ready. "I was back in Jefferson City yesterday and went for a run, trying to make sense of what had happened with you and your roommate. A guy stopped me on the sidewalk and asked me if I knew where I was going when I died."

Her shocked gaze met his. "Just like that?"

"Yeah, it was kind of brash, wasn't it? But I was ready to hear what he had to say. Ron—that's his name—sat me down and explained Jesus to me. Lyssa, I asked God to forgive me." He took a deep breath. "I hope you'll forgive me, too."

"Ron?" Her voice caught. "Did you say *Ron*?"

Kirk's eyebrows pulled together. Funny she should focus on the guy's name. "Yes. He's just a middle-aged man who works at the homeless shelter in Jefferson City. And preaches on the street corners, I guess. I've seen him around from time to time and always avoided him, but yesterday I was ready to hear what he had to say. Today I brought him home with me to meet my brother." That hadn't gone so well. He straightened and glanced around, frowning. Where had Ron gone?

"He's here?"

"Must be in the bathroom. He'll be out in a bit, I guess." Kirk focused on Lyssa's pale face. What had he said to upset her so? He'd expected her to be thrilled he'd found Jesus.

A little shuffling sound came from the hallway. Lyssa's head jerked up, and Kirk followed her sight line to Ron. Then back.

Kirk cleared his throat, wondering if he should introduce them to each other, but the stare they exchanged proved there was no need.

Ron spoke first. "Lyssa?"

Her response was barely a squeak. "Dad?"

Every emotion in the book flitted through Lyssa. Her father—the man who'd mortified her all her growing-up years—that man had confronted Kirk about his need of God? And Kirk had listened to him?

She wrenched her gaze from her father to the man standing beside her. "Kirk?"

Poor guy looked so perplexed.

"This man. . .this is my father." She'd rarely wanted to introduce him to anyone before.

Kirk glanced at her dad, who shuffled a few steps closer, then back at her. Questions filled his deep-blue eyes. "That's what I gathered. But there seems to be something wrong, unless I'm missing my guess."

Lyssa twisted her hands together. "I want to get something straight. You said you were out jogging and h–he just stopped you on the street and—and said what?" Because it couldn't be that simple. Boldness was one thing, but Dad had no manners to speak of.

"He asked if I knew where I was going when I died." Kirk shot a glance at her dad then lowered his voice. "I did know, and I wanted to change the destination."

She couldn't wrap her head around it. "What made you listen to some random guy off the street?"

"I was ready." Kirk sent a lopsided grin at her father, revealing that dimple on his right cheek. "God sent him to me."

Lyssa closed her eyes. *Oh God. Was it really so simple as all that?* Just trust Him to prepare people in advance, and let Him deal with the outcome?

"I mean—if it hadn't been for Debbie. . .if it hadn't been for you and Jeannie. . ." His voice dwindled for a moment. "I wouldn't have been ready. Not last year, or even last month."

Lyssa swiveled on the backless stool to look at her dad. "Thanks."

He looked so uncertain. So unlike himself. "Lyssa, I—"

She hadn't given him credit for listening to God's voice. All along she'd just seen him as a bumbling, loudmouthed fool. "No, Dad. It's me that needs to apologize. Today my pastor spoke about boldness, but he also mentioned that verse in First Corinthians where it talks about a series of people leading someone to Christ. My part isn't the same as yours, but I haven't been doing mine. I've been slacking."

He nodded, and his whole body relaxed. "It's true we're not all called to be the mouth. I forget that sometimes."

She nearly wanted to hug him. That would be a first. "Dad,

I tried to call you several times today, but you weren't home. You need a cell phone, or at least voice mail." She laughed, hearing the uncertainty in it. "I never expected to see you here. Happy Father's Day."

Her dad looked back and forth between them. The lines around his eyes crinkled. "Thanks. It looks to be one of the better ones."

In a few steps, Kirk stood behind Lyssa, his warm hands resting on her arms. She held her breath for an instant. There was nothing between them. No reason remained to push him away. She leaned back against him, reveling in his nearness.

Kirk cleared his throat. "Ron, I have a question for you."

Lyssa peered up at Kirk, and the shimmering emotion in his blue eyes glinted at her for an instant.

"Yes?"

"Your daughter is an awesome woman. We've gone out a few times over the past several weeks, but, well. . .you heard what's happened here today. Everything's on a whole new level." His hands slid up and down her arms, arousing tingles in her skin. "I'd like your blessing to court her."

Chapter 11

The doorbell rang.

Lyssa straightened her skirt and glanced at Jeannie. Her roommate didn't move out of the easy chair in the girls' living room. "A little late for you to be so nervous. Go invite the guy in. I'll let you know if I think he's worthy of you."

"My dad likes him," Lyssa tossed over her shoulder as she headed across the carpet. Didn't that matter more than Jeannie's opinion? It wouldn't have only a week before.

The door opened to a giant bouquet of roses obscuring Kirk's face.

Lyssa caught her breath as the heady scent flowed over her. "They're beautiful." No one had ever given her flowers before, let alone in such abundance.

Kirk swept the bouquet aside and reached for her, tugging her to him with one arm. He planted a light kiss on her mouth. "Not as beautiful as you are."

She blinked back tears of joy. "Come on in. I should get these in water." She didn't even have a pretty vase. What would she do with them?

"Taken care of. Where shall I put them?"

The table was set for three. "Here, on the end." She watched as he placed the arrangement in the vacant spot. How had she managed to find such an awesome guy?

He straightened and looked back at her. She could drown in those blue eyes, except for Jeannie clearing her throat behind Lyssa's back.

"I'd introduce you to my roommate, Jeannie, except that you've already met."

"Indeed we have." Kirk snugged Lyssa to his side for a moment as they turned toward the living room. "Nice to meet you again, Jeannie." He sounded a little cautious, and well he ought to.

"Hi, Kirk." If Jeannie's skin were capable of reddening, Lyssa guessed now might be the time. Jeannie got to her feet. "I have an apology to make."

"So do I. No other student got under my skin the way you did, and I'm sorry I baited you so often. God has forgiven me, but I'd really like it if you did, too."

"If you can forgive me for being so rude to you." Jeannie glanced at Lyssa, and a half grin formed on her face. "I don't want anyone to hurt Lys. She's the best friend I've ever had."

Kirk's hand tightened on Lyssa's waist. "I have no intention of hurting her. Not ever."

Silence held for a few seconds, and then Lyssa pulled out of his embrace. "If you'd like to have a seat and visit with Jeannie for a few minutes, I'll finish getting dinner on the table."

It looked like they could be trusted to remain civil. She could only hope.

"Nope, this time it's your turn to prove you can read lats and longs." Kirk waggled his eyebrows at Lyssa. "You've been making me do it every time. Do you still have what it takes or not?"

He'd been waiting for this day. Every time they'd been out geocaching lately—nearly every weekend—he'd been preparing to turn the tables on her.

She slapped his outstretched palm, accepting the challenge. "Oh, I am so up for it."

He jutted his chin at the GPS unit in her hand. "Show me how it's done. Read me the clue."

Lyssa turned it on. "Roses are pink, violets are blue. The treasure is close, and so are you." She cocked an eyebrow at Kirk. "Seriously?"

"Hey, I never said I was a poet."

"Roses are pink. Good grief, Kirk. That's only helpful if treasure hunters are here while the wild roses are in bloom."

No point telling her it was a one-use cache. She'd figure it out. "Anyone who does much hiking will recognize the bush whether there are blossoms on it or not."

"Point taken. So I'm warm?"

Kirk plopped down on a rock beside the stream, where he had a good view of the back trail. "I'll wait right here." The gurgling stream cooled the air beside him, and the flowers' heady scents filled the air. A bird chirped.

"Okay then. Three satellites in range, so the degree of accuracy is within ten meters." She wandered around the little clearing, mumbling to herself and watching the handheld.

Kirk scanned the forest. Ah, there she was. Jeannie waved at him from a shadowy spot down the trail. He wouldn't have seen her if she hadn't moved, with her dark skin and mossy-green clothes blending into the bushes. Kirk glanced at Lyssa as she circled the area then raised his hand in acknowledgment.

Jeannie nodded and trotted silently off. She'd been delighted to guard the cache for him this morning. He couldn't have done it without her.

Lyssa stopped in front of a rosebush clinging to the sandy soil along the stream bank. A few spent petals still dangled from the thorns. Little blue flowers sprouted between the rocks nearby. She planted her hands on her hips and turned to face Kirk. "These aren't violets."

He crossed his arms and winked at her. "Never said they were."

"There aren't any violets around here." She scowled. "So your poem doesn't make sense. If you can even call it that."

Surely there was a twinkle in those eyes. "Ever heard of poetic license?"

Definitely a sparkle. "So right here, then. Where there are both roses and...blue dayflowers."

Oh, so that's what those were called.

"What kind of container am I looking for?"

She'd never helped him find the first few but told him to figure it out himself. Payback was sweet. "You'll know it when you see it."

Maybe one day Dale would experience love again. The past few weeks he'd softened some, admitting he'd jumped too harshly on Lyssa. Now that they'd all spent a bit of time together, Dale had given his cautious approval. It meant a lot to have that much. Perhaps sometime Dale would even come to church with them.

Lyssa wiped her hair away from her eyes and got on her knees in front of the rosebushes. She leaned over and probed behind rocks and under deadfalls.

Kirk held his breath. Any second now...

She stilled, glancing at him before withdrawing a small wooden box from its dark crevice. "This one won't hold up to the elements for long." Her voice caught, and she turned to sit on a fallen log. She stroked the curved lid, biting her lip. Trembling?

"It isn't meant to." Kirk couldn't help himself. In four long strides he was beside her on the log. He slid his arm around her waist, filling his senses with her floral perfume. "Better open it and make sure it's the geocache."

Lyssa undid the clasp and tipped the lid on its brass hinges, revealing an envelope and a tiny brown leather box. *The* box.

He nuzzled her ear and drew her closer. "What did you find?"

Lyssa slit the envelope and pulled out his card. He'd labored over the inside, finally settling on the less-than-poetic *Roses are red/ Green is the tree/ I love you/ Will you marry me?* Her beautiful eyes shimmered as she met his gaze.

Kirk touched his finger to her lips then lifted out the box and opened it. He tilted it toward her, holding his breath. Not completely traditional, but neither was she. He hadn't been able to resist the symbolism.

Her trembling finger traced the diamond and the two small gems flanking it.

"Topazes," Kirk murmured against her cheek. "They're like your eyes, all brown, but lit up with sparkling gold."

She turned, leaning into his embrace.

"Lyssa?" Kirk smoothed the hair away from her face. "You haven't answered." He lifted the card from the log she'd set it on.

She threw her arms around his neck and buried her face against it. "Yes, please," she breathed against his ear. "I'll marry you. There's nothing I'd rather do."

His lips found her neck and traced a line up toward her ear, nudging her until she turned and met his mouth with hers.

A treasure more bountiful than he deserved.

Valerie Comer's life on a small farm in western Canada provides the seeds for stories of contemporary inspirational romance. Like many of her characters, Valerie grows much of her own food and is active in the local food movement as well as her church. She only hopes her imaginary friends enjoy their happily ever afters as much as she does hers, gardening and geocaching with her husband, adult kids, and adorable grandchildren. Check out her website and blog at http://valeriecomer.com.

BENEATH THE SURFACE

by Annalisa Daughety

Dedication

Thanks to Christine Lynxwiler and Jan Reynolds for reading this novella many times over and offering wonderful input. I couldn't have done it without you. To my mom, Vicky Daughety, thanks for always being my first reader. A special thanks to Megan Reynolds for listening to me talk endlessly about geocaching. Thanks to Kenny Pearle for insight about bass fishing and tournaments. Finally, thanks to Valerie, Nicole, and Cara for inviting me to be a part of this collection. Collaborating on this project was so much fun and definitely one of the highlights of my writing career.

For where your treasure is, there your heart will be also.
MATTHEW 6:21

Chapter 1

Even though she was alone in the car, Madison Wallace groaned loudly as she drove past the Camden County sign. It may as well have been flashing a "Welcome back home, Loser" message. She'd fought hard to keep this day from coming. Except for a couple of brief visits, she'd managed to spend the past twelve years flitting from city to city. First St. Louis, then Chicago, and most recently Atlanta.

And life had been great.

Mostly.

Until two weeks ago when the nonprofit she worked for had lost some expected grant money. As luck would have it, Madison's job as marketing coordinator had been one of the first to go. With no job in sight and the lease up on her apartment, there was only one thing to do. . .head back to her tiny, backwoods, Missouri hometown and regroup.

Her older sister, Brook, had been ecstatic. She'd promptly signed the two of them up for some two-month-long treasure hunt her church was sponsoring. *Geocaching* she'd called it. It sounded hopelessly dull to Madison.

Yet here she was, risking a speeding ticket to get to the opening session. She glanced at the clock on the dashboard of her Nissan Altima. She'd promised Brook she'd be there by now. Although it shouldn't be much of a surprise that she was late. Their mama used to say that Madison ran on her own time. She'd been born six days late and had been running behind ever since.

She careened into the church parking lot and slowed down as she searched for a place to park. The nearly full lot told her she was definitely late. An empty space beside an ancient green hatchback beckoned. She turned off the engine and checked herself in the mirror. Not bad, considering how many hours she'd been on the road. She dabbed on some lipstick and fluffed her dark-brown hair. If she ran into anyone she used to know, she wanted to look her best. No need for them to know that she was coming home a complete failure. Even if she wasn't the successful advertising executive she'd always aspired to be, she could still look the part.

She hurried toward the park across the street from the church, her high heels clacking against the pavement.

"Madison!" a voice called.

She whirled to see Brook, and her brother-in-law, Scott, hurrying toward her.

"Hey there, stranger." Madison embraced her sister, unable to hide her grin. She hated the idea of being back in her hometown but had to admit she looked forward to spending time with Brook.

"You look like a movie star," Brook said. "Couldn't you have cut us country bumpkins some slack?" She gestured from her own running shorts, faded T-shirt, and tennis shoes to Madison's dark-red dress and Jimmy Choos. "Of course, I'd fall flat on my face if I tried to wear those shoes."

"You look beautiful, hon." Scott pulled Brook to him and

planted a kiss on her cheek. "Just as pretty as the day I married you."

Madison rolled her eyes. If only spending time with Brook didn't mean being subjected to a nauseating lovefest all summer. Her brother-in-law had always bordered on cheesy, and it appeared not much had changed over the past few years. "Nice to see you again, Scott. Thanks for letting me stay."

He smiled warily. "You, too. We're glad for you to visit. Besides, with Joshua at my parents' house in Arkansas for most of the summer, we have an extra room."

Madison barely knew her six-year-old nephew. The plan had been for her to get to Osage Beach a couple of days earlier so she could spend time with him, but it hadn't panned out. "Sorry I missed seeing him. Packing took a lot longer than I expected." She'd put most of her earthly belongings in storage. There had certainly been no point in hauling them to Osage Beach. It would be a miracle if she lasted there the whole summer. *Please Lord, help me find a job, and get me out of here quickly.*

"We'd better hurry up." Brook ushered her toward the crowd. "They'll be giving out directions soon, and we don't want to miss it." She held up a box. "This is our GPS. I got it at Communication Location, a new shop in town. It was kind of expensive, but they offered a discount for Rainbow's End Treasure Hunt participants." She beamed. "This is going to be so much fun."

Madison raised an eyebrow but didn't say anything. Spending time with Brook sounded fun. Traipsing around the Ozarks looking for hidden treasure did not. "How've you been?" She and Brook fell into step next to each other and followed Scott toward the registration table.

"Wonderful. I'm teaching kindergarten now, and Scott is teaching sixth-grade science. We love it." She grinned. "Especially since we have summers off to spend together."

Brook and Scott were one of those couples who'd been joined at the hip since middle school. Madison could barely remember a time when Scott wasn't hanging around. "I'm sure that's fun."

They filled out the required paperwork at the registration table. *I feel like I'm signing my life away.*

"Thanks for your participation." The dark-haired girl manning the table grinned. "It should be a great summer. I'm Lyssa Quinn. If you have any questions about the treasure hunt, feel free to call me at the church office."

Brook smiled and took the paperwork Lyssa held out. "Thanks."

"And don't forget to come to the midpoint rally and the wrap-up party." She tapped the papers in Brook's hand. "The information is in there."

Madison scanned the crowd. No familiar faces. Thank goodness. Just being back in Camden County was enough of a walk down memory lane for one day. She was already dreading the inevitable visits with various family members she knew would be in her near future. "How's Grandma?"

Brook narrowed her eyes. "If you ever called her, you wouldn't even have to ask." She sighed. "But she's doing well. She gets around a lot better since her hip replacement last year."

"I sent flowers."

Brook shook her head, and her ponytail swished. "That's not the same as a call. Or a visit." She motioned toward the stage. "Looks like it's starting."

Madison listened as the guy onstage introduced himself and

went over the rules of the treasure hunt. Seemed like an awful lot of trouble, considering they weren't hunting real treasure, just trinkets. She tuned him out and continued to check out the crowd. There were a couple of people in the back who looked familiar. Maybe high school classmates, but she wasn't sure. It wasn't like she'd made it to her ten-year reunion.

Brook nudged her. "Did you hear what he said about Common Grounds offering coffee for participants? I love that place. I ran into Darcy Smith there the other day. She was excited when she found out you'd be here for the summer."

Madison frowned. "I guess I missed some of his announcements. I must be tired from the trip." She managed a tiny smile. "But that's nice about the coffee place and Darcy." She had a vague recollection of Darcy from the year she'd spent on yearbook staff during their junior year.

Brook's face lit up as she spotted someone in the crowd. "There's someone I want you to meet." She clutched Madison's arm and pulled her past a trio of geocachers huddled around their GPS. They looked as befuddled as Madison felt. *Glad I'm not the only one not sure what I'm doing here.*

Madison bristled as they walked through the throng of people. This had better not be some kind of matchmaking effort. Relief washed over her as they approached an elderly man sitting in a folding chair. She couldn't help but laugh at herself for worrying that Brook would try and set her up with a local. *I seriously need to learn to relax.*

The man looked up and grinned. "Well, well, well. It's my favorite neighbor." He stood up and clasped Brook's outstretched hand.

"Mr. Simmons, I'd like for you to meet my sister, Madison."

He nodded. "I've heard a lot about you, Miss Madison. Your

sister and grandmother speak highly of you."

Madison grinned. "It's nice to meet you." He reminded her a little bit of her grandpa. Even though he'd died when she was in junior high, her memories of him were still vivid and full of happiness.

Mr. Simmons hung on to her hand tightly after he shook it. "Have you been to see Clarice yet?"

Madison bit her lip. "No sir. I came straight here. But I will soon." She planned to stop by her grandma's house later. Maybe tomorrow. Or maybe Grandma would just come over to Brook's. That would be even better.

"Lookie who's finally here," Mr. Simmons said, dropping her hand. "I want you to meet my grandson, Grant."

Madison turned to see a tall guy walking toward them. Sauntering was more like it. Grant clearly thought he was hot stuff. His cargo shorts and faded camouflage T-shirt were a far cry from the business suits she was used to seeing on men. A baseball cap topped blond curls, and his blue eyes danced playfully as they landed on her.

She quickly looked away. He hadn't even opened his mouth, but she knew enough already.

Grant patted Mr. Simmons on the back. "Hey, Grandpa. Sorry I'm late." His mouth twisted into a grin. "I was tied up at the office and couldn't get away."

Mr. Simmons, Scott, and Brook burst into laughter.

Madison stared. She hated feeling like an outsider. "Did I miss something?"

Grant gazed into brown eyes the color of his grandpa's homemade root beer. He let his eyes travel from her dark, glossy hair down to her high heels. She was trouble. With a capital *T*. "I was out on the lake. Fishing." He shrugged. "My office."

She smiled thinly but not before he caught the flash of disdain on her pretty face.

He turned to Grandpa. "Are we all set for the treasure hunt?"

The older man nodded. "They gave a few instructions and a pep talk. I guess we're on our own now."

"Common Grounds is offering a free coffee hour for everyone participating in the hunt," Brook said. "Sounds kind of fun."

"I guess." Grant patted Grandpa on the shoulder. "If you like those frou-frou coffee drinks that are more sugar and milk than coffee. Me, I like my coffee black. No fuss."

"A little sugar never hurt anybody," Grandpa said with a wink.

Grant looked up to see the dark-haired girl watching him. She might be pretty—okay, downright beautiful—but he'd seen that I'm-better-than-you look before. He motioned toward the GPS in Brook's hand. "Y'all may as well just concede now. In fact, they should just cancel the whole thing." He draped his arm around Grandpa's shoulders. "Because Team Simmons is going to bring home the victory."

"Don't sell the Wallace sisters short," Scott warned. "These two might surprise you."

Grant grinned and turned his attention back to the brunette. He'd been so irritated that she seemed to think he was a mannerless lout that he was proving her right without meaning to. "Please excuse my manners. I'm Grant Simmons." He stuck out his hand. "I'm guessing you aren't from around here."

She eyed his hand for a moment as if she were trying to decide if he'd washed it since baiting a hook. She gingerly placed her dainty hand in his. "Madison Wallace. I'm Brook's sister. And I've been living in Atlanta for the past two years."

Her skin was soft. She probably spent an hour every day with her hands soaking in lotion or some other weird female ritual. "Well, welcome to the Ozarks, Madison Wallace." He realized he'd been shaking her hand for a moment too long and quickly let go.

Madison stiffened. "Thanks." She hoisted her oversized handbag onto her shoulder.

What could she possibly keep in that bag? For the millionth time, Grant wished he'd grown up with sisters. Maybe then he'd understand women better. Women just didn't make sense. In fact, they might as well be from another planet. He turned to Scott. "Are you part of the treasure-hunt team?" Scott and Brook looked in on Grandpa often, so he'd gotten to know the couple pretty well over the years.

Scott shook his head. "Nope. Brook and Madison are on their own." He grinned. "Although Brook and I have been doing some hiking to help her get ready."

Madison frowned. "You have?" she asked her sister. "I didn't know this was the kind of thing I needed to prepare for."

"You mean you haven't been studying the trails and maps each night?" Grant asked.

She looked at him with wide eyes. "No."

He chuckled. "Good. Us either. We're going to rely on natural talent."

"There's the guy who sold me the GPS," Brook said, motioning toward a tall guy standing at the edge of the crowd. "Let's go see if he can give us some tips on how to use it." She linked arms with Madison. "Good to see you, Grant. Maybe we'll see you out on the trails. And Mr. Simmons, why don't you come over for supper one night soon?"

Grandpa nodded. "You don't have to ask me twice. Just give me a call whenever you want me. Preferably when you make some of the chocolate cake I like so much." He chuckled.

Grant watched the sisters walk off, Scott trailing behind them. He turned to Grandpa, who was watching him curiously.

"She's a looker," Grandpa said.

Grant shrugged. "Yeah, but she's married."

Grandpa frowned. "I'm talking about Madison, and you know it."

"She might be a looker beneath that perfectly made-up exterior. It's hard to tell." Fancy clothes and a lot of makeup, plus those skyscraper heels, screamed high-maintenance. Grant had been down that road before.

And it wasn't an experience he planned to repeat.

Chapter 2

"You're sure you don't want to come?" Brook asked. "After all, he's your dad, too."

Madison shook her head. "I'm positive. I'll visit him sometime, but not today." She hadn't so much as spoken to her dad in six years. And even then it had just been small talk in the hospital waiting room while Brook was in labor.

Brook sighed. "Maddie, things have changed a lot. You might be surprised."

Madison bristled at the use of her hated childhood nickname. "Don't call me that. And people don't change."

Brook frowned but didn't say anything. She grabbed her purse from the kitchen table. "I won't be gone long. Maybe when I get back we can go find a cache."

Madison shrugged. "Whatever." She watched as Brook walked out the back door. Her sister had always been close to their dad. Even when they were kids, Brook was always Dad's favorite. Madison had been closer to Mama.

"It's not too late to catch her, you know," Scott said from the doorway. "I know she'd like for you to go with her."

Madison managed a half smile. "I'm fine here." She sat down at the kitchen table and leafed through yesterday's newspaper.

Scott sat down across from her. "It must be exhausting."

She froze at the coolness in his voice. "What's that?"

"Carrying around that giant chip on your shoulder. It's amazing that you can even walk upright."

Madison scowled. "I know you've never been a fan of mine, but don't you think you're being a little harsh?"

"Oh, this has nothing to do with me not being a fan of yours. It has to do with the fact that I've stood by and watched Brook make excuse after excuse for you. While you're off gallivanting around without a care in the world, Brook is here taking care of things. Who do you think takes your grandmother to her doctor visits? Who do you think sees to it that your dad has plenty of food to eat? Who do you think makes sure there are always flowers on your mama's grave?" Scott glowered. "And she does it without ever complaining that everything falls on her because you aren't grown-up enough to face what's going on here."

Madison pushed her chair back from the table and stood, fists clenched. "If Brook has a problem with me, then why did she insist I come and stay for the summer? I think it's *you* that has the problem. I thought you and I could play nice for a couple of months for Brook's sake, but clearly I was wrong." She turned on her heel and rushed outside. She blinked against the bright sunlight and the hot tears that threatened to spill.

She'd just wait until Brook came back before she went back inside. She didn't want to spend another second with Scott. She'd been stupid to come here. One of her friends from the church she attended in Atlanta had offered to let her move in while she job hunted, but she'd been afraid the job search would take too long. And Brook had begged her to come back to Missouri for the summer, so she'd caved.

At the edge of the driveway, she turned left. Maybe a nice walk would cool her down. Except that it was at least ninety degrees outside.

"Madison?" A voice called from across the street.

She looked up to see Mr. Simmons sitting on his front porch. She managed a smile. "Hi, Mr. Simmons."

He waved her over. "Have you and Brook found any geocaches yet? Grant and I logged our first one yesterday."

Brook had tried to get Madison to look for one yesterday, but Madison had spent the day working on her résumé. "No sir. But maybe later this afternoon."

He grinned. "We had a good time, but I'm afraid I'm beat today. I told Grant he might be on his own part of the time."

Madison nodded. Maybe Grant and Brook could hunt for the caches together since they were so gung ho. "That might be a good idea."

He motioned toward the house. "Would you like to come inside for a glass of lemonade? It sure is hot out here."

Brook could be gone for a while, and Madison had no intention of spending more time with Scott. "Sure." She followed the elderly man into his sparsely decorated living room. An ancient brown couch sat along one wall. A series of framed photos hung above it.

Madison peered at the pictures.

"That's me and Dorothy on our wedding day." Mr. Simmons pointed at a black-and-white picture. "It was the happiest day of my life."

She glanced at him and grinned. Even though she would never describe herself as a hopeless romantic, there was something very sweet about the old man's obvious devotion to his wife. "She was beautiful."

"Sure was. She went home to be with the Lord five years ago." He shook his head. "I always thought I'd go first. But He had other plans." He pointed to a picture of a small blond boy holding up a fish. "That was Grant's first catch."

Madison leaned forward to get a better look. "Wow, he's so little." Grant's blond curls framed his face, giving him an almost cherubic look. Although from the looks of him the other day, he'd outgrown his angel phase.

"He was four. His dad and I took him. 'Course when it came time to clean the fish and fry it, he had a fit. Cried and cried. I think he thought he could bring it home like a pet." He chuckled.

"Kids are funny." Madison followed him into a kitchen that made her feel like she'd stepped right into the sixties.

"How about you? Do you have a boyfriend?"

She shook her head. "No sir." Normally she would've been put off by someone she'd just met delving into her personal life, but she could tell Mr. Simmons wasn't being nosy.

"Brook talks about you a lot. It sounds like you live quite the exciting life." He poured lemonade into a glass and slid it across the counter to her.

"I don't know about exciting. But I travel a lot."

Mr. Simmons took a sip of lemonade. "Travel is good. But family is better."

First Scott, now Mr. Simmons. It seemed like everyone wanted to shove family down her throat. "I guess it depends on the family."

He leveled his gaze on her. "I knew your mom's parents. Your granddad and I were in the service together. Dorothy and Clarice were high school friends. We ended up living on the same street for a while." His wrinkled face broke into a smile.

"Those were happy times. Our kids went to school together."

"So you knew my mama?"

Mr. Simmons nodded. "You look a lot like her, you know. I remember how she used to give your grandparents fits, always wanting to go to the city. We all expected her to hit the road as soon as she graduated, but she stayed put."

It had been Mama's biggest regret. Staying in Roach, Missouri, and marrying the first boy she fell in love with. Madison had been determined not to make the same mistake, so she'd left and never looked back.

The back door flung open, startling Mr. Simmons. He steadied his lemonade to keep it from spilling.

"Hey, Gramps," Grant said with a grin. His gaze landed on Madison, and he furrowed his brow. "I didn't expect you'd have company. I was coming to check on you and make sure you'd recovered from yesterday's treasure hunting."

Mr. Simmons shook his head. "I'm taking it easy today."

Grant pulled the jug of lemonade out of the fridge and poured himself a glass. He leaned against the counter and eyed Madison curiously. "What brings you over?"

My brother-in-law thinks I'm pond scum, and I'm too chicken to go see my daddy. "Just a neighborly visit."

He wore the same cargo shorts he'd had on the other day, but this time he'd paired them with a T-shirt that was the same icy blue as his eyes. Without a hat, his blond hair was shaggy and curled up at the ends. The curls added a boyish contrast to his chiseled jaw. "Well, that's nice." He grinned. "Have you and Brook logged any geocaches yet?"

She shook her head. "We're still making a game plan."

He chuckled. "Why am I not surprised?" He turned to his grandfather. "So I guess I'm on my own today then?"

Mr. Simmons looked from Madison to Grant. "Why don't

you take Madison along? Show her the ropes." He grinned. "But don't give away too many of our treasure-hunting secrets."

The shadow that crossed Grant's face was unmistakable.

Madison jumped up. "Oh, that's not necessary. I should just wait for Brook." She could see that Grant didn't like the idea any better than she did. Which stung a little. She might not be interested in someone like him, but why should he be repulsed by her? She glanced down at the jersey-knit wrap dress she'd gotten at Ann Taylor just a few weeks ago. It was a cheery coral color, and she'd paired it with dark-brown wedge sandals. When she'd looked in the mirror that morning, she'd thought it was a winning combo. But Grant clearly didn't think so.

"Yeah, I don't want to get on Brook's bad side," Grant agreed. "But it was nice to see you again, Madison."

I know a dismissal when I hear one. She managed a smile in Mr. Simmons's direction. "Thank you for the lemonade. I'm sure I'll see you again soon." She brushed past Grant on her way out the door.

"'Bye," he called.

She waved over her shoulder and stepped out onto the front porch.

Brook's minivan was just pulling into the driveway across the street.

Perfect timing. As long as it meant a few hours out of the house and away from more of Scott's judgment, she'd be happy to go geocaching.

Lord, please let my résumé reach the right person so I can get out of here.

"That seemed a little rude of you." Grandpa sank into his old recliner and stared at Grant with steely gray eyes.

Grant shrugged. "Nah. I'm pretty sure she and I would kill each other if we tried to go treasure hunting together. Or anywhere else for that matter. Did you see those shoes? Besides, I signed up to spend time with you, not some hoity-toity girl who thinks she's better than the rest of us."

"Careful not to judge her. I happen to know a little bit about her past, and I dare say she might not be as tough as she seems."

Grant narrowed his eyes, but Grandpa didn't elaborate. He glanced up at the picture of himself that hung above the couch. "Don't you think you should take that down?"

Grandpa chuckled. "Now why would I do that? It was your grandmother's favorite. And besides, that was a good day. Changed the course of your whole life." He took a sip of lemonade. "Have you decided whether or not to enter the Big Bass Bash in the fall?" The yearly tournament that took place on the Lake of the Ozarks was one of the biggest of the year.

Grant shook his head. "You know I'm done fishing competitively. Being a guide is enough for me now." He'd walked away from the sport while at the top of his game, with sponsors clamoring for his business. Grandpa would never understand why, so there was no reason to even discuss it.

"I wish you'd reconsider. I'll bet that outdoor network would still be interested in you hosting a show for them. It isn't too late."

But it was too late. Grant had made the decision last year and hadn't looked back. At least not too much. "Nah. I'm happy with the way things are now. I'm home more, which means I can look in on you."

Grandpa grumbled. "I don't need a babysitter. And I certainly don't want you to give up a good opportunity because of me."

He should've known better than to use that excuse. "I really am happier this way. My life is much less stressful." He'd watched enough of his competitors over the years to know that once you reached the top of your game, there was only one way to go.

"If you're sure." Grandpa held out his glass. "While you're here you may as well make yourself useful."

Grant chuckled and took the glass into the kitchen for a refill. His gaze landed on Madison's lipstick-rimmed glass in the sink. He grabbed it and scrubbed the reddish stain from the side of the glass. As he scrubbed the glass, he realized he might be able to erase her from the kitchen, but he couldn't get her off his mind.

And that worried him a lot more than falling down in the fishing rankings ever had.

Chapter 3

The sound of voices brought Madison out of a deep sleep, and for a moment she wasn't sure where she was. The dream she'd been having about her mama had been so vivid, she could've sworn it was real and she was seven again, prancing barefoot in the backyard trying to catch lightning bugs while Mama laughed.

The ache of sadness washed over her as she came to her senses. Mama was gone and had been for a long time.

There was a soft tap on the door. Brook poked her head inside the room. "You up?"

Madison nodded and sat up. "Will be in a minute. Do I hear people out there?"

"Nothing to worry about. Get up and get dressed. It's nearly nine." Brook closed the door behind her.

Nearly nine? That wasn't so bad. It wasn't like she'd slept until noon or anything.

Thirty minutes later, Madison emerged from Joshua's tiny bedroom and walked into the kitchen. She needed coffee.

"Mornin', sleepyhead." Grant Simmons was perched on a barstool clutching a glass of orange juice.

Madison's eyes widened. She hadn't seen Grant since last

week at his grandpa's house. She was glad she'd taken the time to put on her makeup and get dressed for the day. She looked around the kitchen. Mr. Simmons sat with Brook at the table, a cat-that-ate-the-canary grin on his face. Scott was nowhere to be found. "I didn't know there was a party going on, or I would've gotten up earlier." She caught Grant's smirk and shot him a dirty look.

"Scott's mom called an hour ago," Brook said. "Joshua fell off the monkey bars at the playground this morning and broke his arm in two places." She sighed. "Scott thinks we should go right away. He's gone to get gas now. We're already packed."

Madison frowned. "I'm sorry. So will you be bringing Joshua back here?" She had enough trouble sleeping on the twin bed. If she ended up on the couch for the rest of the summer, she'd go crazy.

Brook shook her head. "No. Actually, we're going to stay there for a couple of weeks at least. We'd planned to go later in the summer, but now is as good a time as any." She frowned. "I'm just sorry it ruins our plans for the treasure hunt."

Madison shook her head. "Oh, don't worry about it. It's not a big deal." She and Brook had logged three caches so far. Madison hadn't admitted it to anyone, but it had actually been fun. There'd been a little poem that served as a clue for each cache, and once she'd figured out how to work the GPS, they'd been off and running. Of course, they'd chosen the easiest ones first. But still, she'd been proud to write her name in the little logbook and enter the information on the Rainbow's End website. "Besides, you remember that girl that we met the other day at the coffee shop? Hadley was her name. I think she's hunting alone, too. So I'll be fine."

"Actually, Mr. Simmons has an idea," Brook said.

The old man cleared his throat. "I still haven't recovered from our hike the other day." He gestured at Grant. "So since Brook has to bow out of the hunt, I think I'll do the same." He grinned widely. "And you and Grant can team up."

Madison met Grant's equally horrified gaze.

He shrugged.

"Don't even think about arguing. I don't want you traipsing around the trails alone," Brook said. "And Grant doesn't mind, do you?" She turned to look at him.

He grinned. "Of course not."

Liar. She could tell he was less than thrilled about the prospect of spending time with her. But it seemed like Brook and Mr. Simmons weren't going to take "no" for an answer. "Well, great. I guess you've got yourself a new partner."

He stood up and put his empty glass in the sink. "We should hit the ground running then. I have to work the next few days, so we should make the most of today." He took in her sundress and sandals. "I'll give you time to change and meet you back here in an hour." He turned to Mr. Simmons. "You ready?"

The old man rose slowly from the table. "Have a safe trip," he said to Brook. He grinned at Madison. "And I suspect I'll be seeing you around." He followed Grant out the door.

Madison poured herself a cup of coffee. She did not like this turn of events. At all.

"Sorry to spring it on you like that." Brook pulled a container of hazelnut-flavored coffee creamer from the fridge and set it on the counter. "Mr. Simmons was outside when I got the newspaper. I told him that we were going to be out of town for a while, and he immediately called Grant." She smiled. "I think he was looking for a way to get out of the hunt anyway. He only signed up to keep Grant involved with the church."

Madison nodded. "I just don't see us working well together."

"He's not a bad guy. He moved here about a year ago, but we've known him for a long time."

Just because they'd known him for a long time didn't mean he was someone Madison wanted to be forced to spend time with. But maybe she could play nice for a couple of days, and then they could go their separate ways. "I'm sorry about Joshua."

Brook nodded. "He's a little trooper. I knew when I found out I was having a boy that at some point there'd probably be a broken bone."

"I guess."

"But with me out of town, there are some things I'm going to need for you to do." She picked up a notepad from the counter. "I started making a list. Check to see if Grandma needs to go to the grocery store. And she has a doctor's appointment next Friday that you'll need to drive her to."

Madison nodded. She'd gone with Brook a couple of times to visit their grandmother, and it had been good to see her. Although all those pictures of Mama had probably been the reason for her dream last night. "Okay, I can do that. Maybe I'll take her to dinner one night or something."

Brook nodded. "She'd love it. Now that she doesn't drive, she doesn't get out much. She can ride the church van on Sunday, but it would be nice if you'd go pick her up instead."

"Of course."

Brook sighed. "And you're going to have to go and see Daddy. He knows you're in town."

Madison made a face.

"Come on, Maddie. He's not going to be around much longer. The doctor said there's nothing more that can be done for him. Do you really want to waste precious time holding some stupid grudge left over from when you were a teenager?"

"I'm not holding a grudge. And don't call me Maddie." Madison took a sip of coffee. "You weren't there. You were off at college. Do you know what it was like to live in that house after you and Mama were both gone?" Madison shook her head. "He didn't even know I existed most days. Before I could drive, he'd actually forget about me. Forget to come pick me up from football games or track meets. I was that poor kid who always had to catch a ride with someone. The kid no one cared about."

Brook shook her head. "It wasn't like that."

It had been exactly like that. Once Mama passed away, Daddy had started drinking and never stopped. Brook had gone off to college in Cape Girardeau and then got married. But Madison had been the one to suffer. In just a few short years, she'd lost every bit of stability she'd ever had. "He was awful to me," she whispered.

"He was a grieving widower who'd lost the center of his world. I know it seemed bad then, but don't you think you could cut him some slack now? Now that his kidneys are failing and there's nothing that can be done for him?"

Madison rubbed her temples. She and Brook would never see eye to eye on this. But she didn't want to argue anymore. "I'll go see him. Is there anything else?"

"No." Brook reached out and smoothed Madison's hair. "But you might try to get rid of some of that anger before it eats you up inside."

Madison's eyes filled with unexpected tears. Mama used to smooth her hair just like that when she was a little girl.

A horn honked in the driveway.

Brook peeked out the window. "It's Grant. If you want to run and change, I'll go out and tell him you'll be a minute."

Madison looked down at her sundress and leather flip-flops. "Oh, this will be fine. Don't you think? I mean, I'm not wearing heels or anything. And this dress is really casual."

"I'm not sure you should take off on a hiking trail in that."

Madison laughed. "I'll be okay. I wear dresses most of the time. Besides, maybe this way he'll go easy on me. I mean, the caches you and I found weren't on hiking trails. I'm sure there are more of those."

Brook sighed. "Have fun." She pulled Madison into a quick hug. "And call me if you need me or if you have any questions about anything here."

"I will." Madison grabbed her purse and headed out the door.

Grant stood in the driveway, the driver's side door open on what might be the oldest, rustiest truck she'd ever seen.

"You'll have to climb in through my side," he said. "The passenger side door doesn't open anymore."

You have got to be kidding me. She lifted her chin and climbed into the dirty pickup truck with as much dignity as she could muster.

Grant snickered but didn't say anything when she got her purse hung on the stick shift.

Madison buckled the rusty seat belt and cringed at the smear of dirt across her yellow dress.

He climbed inside and put the truck in reverse. The engine roared like a jet. "No worries," he said. "This truck has been running for a long time; it's not about to stop now."

It's probably been running ever since it came off the assembly line on the day trucks were invented. Madison shrugged. She'd just hope for the best. It seemed like she'd been doing a lot of that lately.

Grant forced his eyes to focus on the road and not drift over to Madison. She looked like she was heading to high tea instead of a geocaching hunt. She'd brought a purse instead of a backpack, and he'd be willing to bet his lucky fishing lure that she didn't have so much as a bottle of water in there. "I've already entered a few caches into the GPS. How about we go easy today and save the hiking for later in the week?"

"Suits me."

He cleared his throat. Most of the time not having a radio in his truck didn't bother him. But since he normally traveled alone or with Grandpa, there weren't awkward silences to worry about. "So what brings you here, anyway? You don't seem all that enthused about geocaching." He glanced at her from the corner of his eye.

"I've been in Atlanta working in marketing for a nonprofit that helps single moms find resources to aid in their success. It was kind of a catchall place. The organization does everything from providing cribs and car seats to résumé and interview workshops. But we rely on grants for funding, and this last go-around, we lost one of ours. Marketing is always one of the first things to get cut."

He could hear the pain in her voice beneath the matter-of-fact words. "Wow. Tough break. I'm sorry."

She shrugged. "I really enjoyed feeling like I was doing something to make a difference, but my dream is to get a marketing position for a big company."

That didn't surprise him. She struck him as the kind of person who'd want to be surrounded by the bright lights of a city. "So what's next?"

"I have my résumé out and am just hoping to find something soon. Brook and Scott invited me to stay with them rent-free while I'm looking, which is a huge blessing. Otherwise, I would've blown through my savings."

He nodded. "So you grew up here, then?"

"I grew up over in Roach. Population not many." She chuckled. "The place is so tiny we didn't even have a school. It's about twenty miles from where Brook lives now. When I went to college, I claimed Osage Beach as my hometown just because it sounded more glamorous."

He grinned. Madison definitely didn't seem like the kind of person who hailed from a place called Roach. "Wise decision." He slowed the truck down and flipped on the blinker. "So the first cache we're looking for is actually in a cemetery not far from Roach. I hope that doesn't freak you out."

She shook her head. "I thought this road looked familiar. I think I know where we're headed."

Grant parked the truck just off the road and grabbed the GPS. "I've got a cooler in the back of the truck with water, but this one shouldn't be much of a hike." He climbed out of the truck and waited for Madison.

"Okay, what does the clue say?" she asked once they were at the cemetery entrance.

He clicked a button on the GPS. "Here's the clue:

A place of peace
A place of rest
Find the prize
Just past a Test."

She stared at him for a long moment then burst out laughing. "At least this one kind of rhymes. The ones Brook and I did the other day sure didn't."

Grant grinned. "Yeah, the one Grandpa and I found didn't either." He clutched the device and began to walk.

Madison cleared her throat. "I haven't been here in a long time," she said softly. "Not since I was fifteen."

"Oh no. Let me guess. You and your friends used to hang out in cemeteries and tell scary stories." He'd grown up in a small town and remembered the lengths he and his friends had gone to entertain themselves.

She shook her head. "Actually, my mama is buried here."

Smooth, man. Very smooth. "I'm sorry. Hey, we can turn back if you want to. Or you can go sit in the truck, and I'll find the thing."

Madison forced a smile. "It's fine. I've been meaning to come out anyway. The last time I was here, the headstone wasn't up yet."

He concentrated on the GPS, unsure of what to say. Grandpa had mentioned that Madison had dealt with a lot, but he hadn't been specific. "We should be close," he said.

She pointed at an ancient stone. "Look at that. John Test." She grinned. "There's a bench just past his headstone."

Grant knelt down and pulled an ammunition box from underneath the bench. "And here it is." He held up his hand for a high five.

She slapped his hand. "Nicely done." She perched on the stone bench.

Grant sat down next to her and opened the box. He signed the logbook and passed it to her, all too aware of their close proximity.

"Okay, do we leave something in there or what?" she asked.

He grinned and reached into one of the pockets on his cargo shorts. "How about this?" He held up a fuzzy yellow fishing lure.

She laughed. "Perfect."

Grant had so many lures at his house, he'd decided to leave one in each cache box. A couple of years ago, one of his sponsors on the bass fishing tour circuit had been a lure manufacturer. He'd done a few commercials and print ads for them, and in return they'd sent him boxes and boxes of lures. "Okay, we have to put the box back exactly where we found it."

Madison grabbed the box and tucked it under the bench. "Would you mind. . ." she trailed off.

He understood immediately. "I'll wait here."

She nodded. "I won't be gone long."

Grant watched her walk away, suddenly struck by the urge to protect her from the pain he knew she was about to experience.

Chapter 4

Madison sank to her knees in front of Mama's grave. Her dress was already ruined by the rust smudges, so a little dirt wouldn't hurt it now. Her eyes filled with tears as she read the headstone:

Charlene Myers Wallace
Daughter, Wife, Mother, Friend
Matthew 6:21

She pulled her phone out of her purse and opened her favorite Bible app. Every Sunday she was always afraid the preacher would think she was texting in church, but really she loved being able to have the Bible with her everywhere she went. It even had a cool audio feature that allowed her to listen to the scriptures instead of reading them. Every time she had to fly, the soothing words calmed her nerves.

The verse in Matthew had been her Mama's favorite verse, one she'd quoted so many times when Madison was a little girl. "*'For where your treasure is, there your heart will be also.'*"

Madison traced her fingers over the birth and death years embossed on the stone. Mama had only been a few years older than Brook was now when she'd died of breast cancer. Madison remembered exactly how she'd felt the day the casket had been lowered into the grave. With Grandma on one side of her and Brook on the other, she had stood trembling, a fifteen-year-old about to become an adult overnight. Brook was a freshman in college who rarely came home, and Daddy spent the next three years lost at the bottom of a bottle.

Madison had fended for herself okay, but those milestones in a teenage girl's life—her first date, picking out a prom dress, applying to college—had been lonely reminders of what she'd lost. At first she'd tried to imagine what her mama would've said on each occasion, but soon it had become too painful.

She plucked a rose from the container that she guessed Brook had left at the base of the headstone. Was she selfish for staying away for so long? Or had that been the only way she could survive the pain?

"Mama, would you be proud of me? I did what you weren't able to—left this town and tried to make something of myself." Madison wanted to believe that her mama would've been happy with the way she'd turned out. But there'd been a niggling doubt about that ever since her conversation with Scott last week. He'd made no effort to hide his disapproval.

Lord, help me to face the past. Give me patience and wisdom as I deal with my daddy. She stood up and brushed the dirt from her knees. She hated that Grant had been with her for this. But at least he'd given her some privacy. She walked toward the bench where he sat. It wasn't that she thought he was a jerk or anything, but he was the kind of guy she'd made sure never to get involved with. The outdoorsy, no-ambition kind of guy who'd be content to stay in a rural town forever.

Just like her daddy.

So no matter how cute he was, with his blond curls and tanned skin, she'd just have to stay strong. She marched over to where he sat fiddling with the GPS. "We can go now," she announced.

He looked up. "Are you okay?"

At the concern in his voice and on his face, she almost faltered. But he wasn't the kind of guy she needed to confide in. She tossed her hair. "I'm fine." He'd seen her too vulnerable already. Time to toughen up. "What's next on the agenda?"

"How about we grab a bite to eat somewhere?" he asked as they headed toward the truck.

She wrinkled her nose. That seemed an awful lot like a date. "What did you have in mind?"

He opened the squeaky truck door and waited for her to slide in.

"Nowhere fancy. We can just grab fast food and eat on the way to the next cache." He fired up the engine. "If that's okay with you."

She shrugged. "Don't you think the truck is kind of. . .dirty to be eating inside of it?"

Grant rolled his eyes. "It might not be five-star like you're probably used to, but it would save us time." He raised an eyebrow. "But if you insist on going in somewhere and eating together, it's fine by me." He turned onto Highway 54 and headed toward Osage Beach.

His tone of voice irritated her. Like he'd be doing her a favor by gracing her with his presence at the lunch table. "You know what? Driving through for burgers is fine."

Grant slowed down as they approached a McDonalds. "This okay?"

"Fine."

He pulled into the parking lot. "It will probably be quicker if we order inside."

She was dying to use the restroom, so that was fine by her. "Okay." She slid across the seat and hopped out of the truck.

"You're an old pro at that now." He grinned.

Madison rolled her eyes and followed him inside. The cold air conditioning was a welcome relief from the heat. "Here's a five." She handed him a bill. "Just get me a burger and a chocolate shake." She hurried off to wash her hands and see if she could do anything about the splotches of rust and dirt on her dress.

Grant watched her go and shook his head. Just when he'd decided she was horrible and spoiled, she'd been a lot of fun as a geocaching partner. But then she'd been uptight again in the truck on the way here, acting like eating inside the vehicle was beneath her.

He wished she'd pick a side and stay there.

Grant quickly placed their order and waited at the counter.

"I'll stand here if you want to go wash up," Madison said.

He glanced at her. Her hair was freshly brushed, and it looked like she'd touched up her lipstick. "Sorry about the rusty spots." He nodded toward the skirt of her sundress.

She shrugged. "It's okay. I've had this for a long time."

Ten minutes later they were back in the truck.

Grant picked up the GPS and turned it on.

"Are there any other caches nearby?" she asked.

He scrolled down the list. "There's one on the way back to Brook's house. Are you up for one more?"

She nodded. "Sure."

"This is another easy one that we should just be able to park and grab. Not much hiking." He pulled onto the highway. "Did you ever go over to Ha Ha Tonka State Park when you were a kid?" The park, located just south of Camdenton, was one of his favorite places. In fact, the section of the Lake of the Ozarks that ran through there was where he liked to fish.

"Of course."

"There are several caches around there. I was thinking, maybe we can plan to spend all day there one day next week. I've got work to do the next two days, and I promised Grandpa I'd help him do some repair work at his house on Saturday. But maybe Monday?"

She nodded. "Monday works. I've got some stuff I need to do this week anyway."

"Just a hint though," he said, glancing over at her. "You might want to dress for hiking. Do you have sturdy shoes? Hiking boots?"

She furrowed her brows. "I'm sure I can find something suitable." She turned her attention back to her burger.

At least he'd made the suggestion. Whether she wanted to take it was up to her. But from what he could tell, some of the caches at Ha Ha Tonka would take some major hiking. And if she showed up in flip-flops on Monday, he didn't know what he'd do.

"Brook told me you just moved here a year ago." Madison glanced over at him. "Where had you been living before that?"

"I'm originally from a little town in Arkansas called Flippin. It's on Bull Shoals Lake. My dad worked for Ranger Boats until he retired."

"So that explains your love of fishing?" she asked.

He shrugged. "I guess. Grandpa and Dad took me fishing all the time when I was a kid." He wasn't ready to tell her that he'd been a professional bass fisherman for several years. He had a feeling she wouldn't be impressed by that, just like his ex-girlfriend hadn't been. In fact, his choice of career had eventually led to the demise of that relationship.

"I think my daddy was disappointed he didn't have boys to take fishing. Brook went with him, but I never did." Madison crumpled the wrapper from her burger and tossed it into the bag.

"Is your dad still around these parts?" he asked.

She nodded. "Yeah. He still lives in Roach."

"I guess he was glad to see you."

Madison didn't say anything for a long moment. "I haven't been to see him yet, actually." She cleared her throat. "He and I. . .well, we don't get along."

"I'm sorry." He flipped on the blinker and turned into the parking lot of the park where the next cache was supposed to be. Relationships were complicated, that was for sure. He and his parents had gone through some rocky times, but they'd remained close.

"Don't be. Those things happen. I'm going to visit him this week, and we'll see how it goes."

He knew forced cheerfulness when he heard it. "I'll pray that the reunion goes well." He turned off the engine and turned to look at her.

Madison widened her brown eyes. "Thanks," she said softly. "I can use all the prayers I can get."

"We all can." He climbed out of the truck and offered her his hand.

She hesitated then accepted his help.

And as soon as he felt the electricity pass between them, he immediately wished he'd not been so gallant.

Chapter 5

Madison smoothed her skirt and stood outside her childhood home. Just driving through the little community of Roach had been like going back in time. If she closed her eyes, she could practically smell the sweet honeysuckle perfume that Mama had worn and taste the fresh-picked peaches she and Brook had eaten as children.

She remembered when the now-rickety porch swing had been brand new. She and Brook would sit next to Mama and listen to her read Bible stories. The big oak tree in the front yard used to have a tire swing, and she and Brook had taken turns pushing each other. When Daddy would come home from work they'd both climb on, and he'd push them as high as he could until Mama called them all to the table.

Her childhood had been happy. It was too easy to forget that after the way everything had turned out. The realization made her take pause at the front door. Sure, they'd gone through some tough times. Her grandpa's illness and death had been difficult. And those long months when Daddy had been out of a job. But things hadn't actually fallen apart until Mama had been diagnosed with cancer.

At the time, Madison had expected that everything would

be okay. She couldn't imagine it any other way. But then Mama had taken a turn for the worse, and things had never been the same.

Madison rapped on the door and waited. She'd known this day was inevitable, but she hadn't expected to feel so many emotions.

The door slowly swung open, and for the first time in years, she stood face to face with her daddy.

"Hi," she said.

His weathered face broke into a smile. "Maddie," he said. He pulled her into his arms. "I've missed you so much."

She followed him into the house, not bothering to tell him not to use her old nickname. "The place looks exactly the same."

"Probably just like it did the day you left." He sat down in his old recliner. "Have a seat."

Madison sank onto the same couch she remembered as a kid. She and Brook had watched *Scooby-Doo* every Saturday morning while they ate their Cheerios. "I wish you'd have let me bring you something to eat. I could've picked something up."

Daddy shook his head. "Brook has put so many casseroles in the freezer, I think I could go for years without ever stepping foot into the grocery store." He smiled, but it didn't go all the way to his eyes.

Madison knew why. He didn't have years. According to Brook, he might only have months. "I'm sorry you're sick," she said softly.

He nodded. "At first the doctor thought the problem was just with one kidney. But pretty soon it became obvious both were failing. I'm on dialysis now."

"What about a transplant? Couldn't you get on the list or

something?" Madison wasn't totally sure how that worked, but surely there was something that could be done.

"I'm on the list. But it can take years for there to be a match." He shrugged. "And at this point, I don't have that luxury."

"But it could happen, right? I mean, they could call you with a kidney?"

He cleared his throat. "The chances are slim."

"What about. . .someone you're kin to?" From the way Brook had talked, Madison hadn't realized a transplant was even an option.

"Brook's already been tested. And your uncle Harold. Even Scott, though we aren't blood related. None of them are matches."

So that explained it. Scott's anger the other day had seemed a little out of place. The fact that Madison hadn't even known they were all being tested to be potential donors must've been too much for him to handle. "Why didn't anyone call me?" she asked quietly.

Daddy met her eyes. "I told them not to. Of all people, I could never let you do that. It's not like loaning someone a car or some money. And I knew if Brook called you, you'd get tested just because she wanted you to. And the truth is, I know I don't deserve for you to give me that kind of gift."

She opened her mouth to speak, but he cut her off. "Maddie, I messed up with you. A lot. The way I behaved after your mother's death is inexcusable."

Madison's eyes filled with tears. "You were grieving."

"So were you. And you were just a child. I want you to know that right after you left home, I got sober. Have been ever since."

"I'm glad." And she was. He hadn't been a big drinker

before Mama died, but it seemed like after that he just gave up on everything.

"I'm so sorry." His voice cracked. "I watched you scrimp and save so you'd have the money to buy a brand-new prom dress. And what did I do? Ruined it for you."

The pain came rushing back, fresh as it had been that day. When she'd finally gotten into her piggy bank to get the money out, just enough cash to buy the dress she'd had her eye on all year, the bank was empty. She'd ended up wearing a hand-me-down from a girl at church. Instead of feeling like a princess, she'd felt like a pauper. "That's all in the past now." His taking the dress money to buy booze had been the last straw. Madison had spent the weeks between prom and graduation living with her grandparents. She'd left Roach the morning after graduation.

Daddy put his head in his hands. "And then not showing up to your graduation. And you the valedictorian. Just like your mama had been." He wiped his eyes. "There's no excuse."

At the time, his excuse had been that he was passed out in his truck outside some seedy bar. "We really don't need to re-hash this. I'm fine now. Everything is fine." She wasn't sure if it was, though. Thinking about those incidents brought her so much sorrow. But seeing the pain on Daddy's face didn't give her the satisfaction she'd always expected it to. Instead, it made her feel worse. Both of them had wounds that ran deep. And now he needed a kidney.

"I've tried to make up for it though." Daddy reached over and took a thick book from the coffee table. He handed it to her. "I've been keeping up with you."

She frowned and flipped through a few pages. "These are press releases." She looked at him with wide eyes. "Press releases that I wrote."

He nodded. "Brook taught me how to use the computer. I've been keeping up with everything you do. Ads you write, events your companies have participated in, and a few times I've found announcements in the newspaper when you've gotten promoted." He grinned. "Whenever I start to feel like a complete failure, I flip through that book and just think to myself that by the grace of God and the good influence of your mama, you've somehow landed on your feet. Despite all I did to screw up."

Madison closed the book and placed it carefully on the coffee table. "It's really sweet that you've kept track of me." Sweet and surprising.

"I love you. I never said it enough. But I guess when you're facing the end, you start to realize what's really important."

Madison stood. She couldn't handle much more, and she wasn't sure he could either. "I should go now. You look tired."

"It's amazing how just a little bit of conversation takes my energy these days." He rose from the recliner. "I remember when I could work twelve-hour days and still come home and have enough energy to chase you girls around the yard."

She nodded. "Get some rest." She reached up and kissed him on the cheek. "I'll come back again soon."

He walked her to the door and watched as she got in the car.

As she pulled out of the driveway, she could still see him waving. Tears filled her eyes until she couldn't see the road ahead. She slowed the car down and pulled blindly onto the side of the road as she gave into the sobs.

She knew they couldn't get back the years they'd lost. And only the Lord knew how much more time they had. But somehow she had to find it in herself to forgive and forget.

"Thanks for the generous offer," Grant said into the phone as he paced the length of his small living room. "But I have no plans to compete in the fall."

"We'd love to have you," Mr. Richards said. "Now that you're a hometown boy, you'd be a great addition to the tournament. If you change your mind, you know how to reach me."

Grant ended the call and tossed the phone onto his scarred coffee table. He'd pulled the worn table out of a Dumpster a couple of years ago, expecting it to be a temporary addition to his house, but had never gotten around to replacing it. It kind of matched his decor scheme anyway.

Mr. Richards directed the fall bass tournament and had been calling monthly for the past three months. Grant turned him down every time, but the man didn't want to take no for an answer.

He sank onto the couch and looked around his sparsely furnished cabin. *Madison would hate this place.* The way his mind kept drifting to her was really starting to irritate him. Yesterday he'd taken an older couple out on the lake, and the woman had squealed every time she came close to a worm. He'd laughed and imagined how it would be to take Madison fishing.

Except that he knew she'd never go for that. And the last time he'd been involved with a woman who viewed his lifestyle with disdain, it had only caused him heartache.

Grant stood and grabbed his tackle box. *No point in sitting around here dwelling on it.* He'd have to face Madison tomorrow for a day of caching. But this afternoon, it would be just him

and the great outdoors.
     Solitary.
     Just like he wanted.

Chapter 6

Madison dug through Brook's closet. They might be the same size, but their taste couldn't be more different. She was going to have to give Brook a lesson on the travesty of mom jeans as soon as she returned from Arkansas.

She held up a faded Hillbilly BBQ Cook-Off T-shirt and threw it back in the drawer. No way could she stomach that. But after the rust stain had relegated her yellow sundress to the rag pile, she didn't want to get anything else messed up. For a second she imagined Grant's response if she called to cancel because she didn't have anything to wear. After the way he'd suggested she dress appropriately for hiking, she didn't want to give him any more reason to judge her.

She finally settled on something from her own suitcase: her favorite black Nike running skirt paired with a hot-pink tank. She pulled on white ankle socks and her running shoes to complete the outfit. She might not be outdoorsy, but she had a gym membership. And the day she'd joined the gym, she'd bought some cute workout clothes. Looked like they'd finally come in handy.

Just as she finished putting on her makeup, she heard the

unmistakable roar of Grant's truck pulling into the driveway. She swept her hair up into a high ponytail. *I might be pushing thirty, but today I can pass for a cheerleader. At least from a distance.*

A loud honk from the driveway brought her primping to an end. She hurried down the stairs and grabbed her purse from the counter.

"Mornin'," Grant said as he hopped out of the truck. "I was beginning to think you'd backed out of our little outing."

She shook her head. "Not a chance."

"No flip-flops today, I see." He leaned against the truck and grinned.

Madison narrowed her eyes. "I believe you said sturdy shoes were in order." She held up a foot encased in pristine white tennis shoes with a hot-pink Nike swoosh that perfectly matched her tank top and her fingernails. "These are sturdy."

He chuckled as she slid across to the passenger seat. "Have you ever even worn those outside?"

She silently buckled her seat belt. It looked like the passenger seat had been wiped clean, because last week's offending dirt was gone. "Does it matter?"

He grinned as he backed the truck out the driveway. "You do know we aren't headed to a tennis match, right? Some of the caches at Ha Ha Tonka might be off the beaten path. You gonna be okay if you get a little dirt on your shoes?"

She lifted her chin and didn't say anything. Why did he have to make fun of her? She'd tried to come prepared for the hike. Just because she wasn't decked out in ugly boots and those hideous cargo shorts didn't mean she couldn't maneuver along a hiking trail. At least she hoped not.

"Don't sulk." He shot her a dimpled smile. "I'm only kidding. Workout wear is a step in the right direction. Before the summer is out, maybe we'll have you in real hiking gear."

"Maybe. I wonder if Prada makes hiking clothes."

Grant groaned. "You're impossible." He turned the truck onto Highway 54 and headed toward Camdenton. "How'd the last week go? Any job leads?"

She'd actually sent in résumés for a couple of jobs that seemed perfect, but she saw no need to share that with him. "I'm still looking."

"I'm sure you'll find something soon." He slowed down as they got behind a tractor. "Bet you're not used to this anymore, huh?" He motioned at the green tractor in front of them.

Madison shook her head. "Not exactly." She grinned. "But would you believe that I know how to drive one of those?"

Grant veered around the tractor and waved at the driver. "No way," he said once they were safely back in the right lane. "You?"

She grinned. "My grandpa had farmland. When I was a little girl, he used to let me ride with him on the tractor." She had a sudden memory of coming in from the field and sitting on her grandparents' porch, eating fresh watermelon and not caring about the sticky juice running down her bare legs. She might've grown up and left her rural roots behind, but she hadn't forgotten the simple joys of childhood summers in a small town. "When I got a little older, he taught me how to drive it."

"I'll keep that in mind in case I ever buy some land." He chuckled. "Maybe you could give up your big-city job and become a farmer."

She raised an eyebrow. "Laugh all you want. I might have grown up and moved away, but I haven't forgotten my roots." Not for lack of trying, though. Twelve years in the big city and she hadn't quite been able to break free. But the last résumé she'd sent out had been to a PR firm in New York. If anything could allow her to leave her past behind once and for all, it would be that. She'd always seen New York as the brass ring.

"So how about we come up with a game plan for today?" Grant asked. "I read up on the caches at Ha Ha Tonka, and it looks like they're a little different than the others."

Madison wrinkled her nose. "What do you mean?"

"I guess the organizers want to mix things up a little, because in addition to finding and logging the caches, we have to take a picture at each site and upload it to the Rainbow's End website." He slowed down and flipped on his left blinker. "Hey, we're close to your hometown, aren't we?"

She nodded. "If we stayed on this road for another ten minutes, we'd be smack dab in the middle of Roach."

Grant glanced at her. "Does your dad live in the house you grew up in?"

She nodded. "He does." At the thought of Daddy, she grew sad. "I went to visit him last week."

"How'd it go?" He turned left and headed toward the park entrance.

Madison sighed. "Considering it was the first time I'd seen him in six years, I guess it went okay."

Grant let out a low whistle. "Six years. That must've been an awkward reunion."

"Not really. Just. . ." She trailed off, unsure of how much to share. She preferred to keep people at a distance, so the idea of opening up to Grant threw her off her game. "He has some health problems. I don't think the prognosis is good."

"I'm sorry." He gestured at the park visitor center. "I'm pretty familiar with this place, so we don't need to stop for maps or anything unless you want to."

Madison was thankful for the change of subject. Another minute and she might spill her guts about the angst she felt over Daddy's need for a kidney transplant. She'd been researching kidney donation for the past few days but hadn't decided how to handle the situation. His parents had been dead for years, and if Uncle Harold and Brook had already been tested, that left Madison as his last hope. "I don't need to stop. We have the GPS, and my smartphone has a map app in case we need it." She let out a tiny laugh. "Actually, there is a geocaching app, too. I didn't know it until a couple of days ago. I guess Brook didn't realize it when she bought the GPS."

Grant chuckled. "I didn't know either. I haven't upgraded my phone yet. The way I see it, my phone is for making calls, and even then I leave it in my truck sometimes when I don't want to be bothered. I prefer the no-frills way of life."

"No kidding." She glanced down at the truck floorboard. "I mean, if that rust gets any worse, we'll have to Fred Flintstone it home."

He laughed out loud. "It's not that bad."

She smiled. "If you say so."

Grant pulled into a parking lot and cut the engine. He shot her a mischievous grin. "You sure you're prepared for this? We might see lizards and snakes." He hopped out of the truck.

"I'm not a complete wimp just because I prefer city pavement to dirt roads." She slid across the seat, thankful he didn't offer his hand again. The less contact she had with him the better. She walked around to the back of the truck where he was spraying bug repellent on his legs and arms. "About those snakes. . .are they big ones?" she asked.

Grant burst out laughing. "Not a wimp, huh?"

Madison scowled and grabbed the repellent from his out-stretched hand. This was going to be a very long day.

Grant knew he should be ashamed of himself for trying to scare her a little. But she was so much fun to mess with. "I've got water in my backpack." He grinned. "I figured you'd be armed with that big old purse of yours that's probably full of beauty products, so I packed our supplies."

Her glare told him he was pushing it.

"Anyway, you can leave your purse in the truck. Just cram it underneath the seat."

She wrinkled her nose. "This bag cost four hundred dollars. I'm not going to just leave it under the seat. Someone might steal it."

Grant rolled his eyes. Four hundred dollars? He'd never heard anything so ridiculous. "The upside to having a truck as old as mine is that it isn't exactly a target for thieves. I feel certain your overpriced bag will be fine for a couple of hours. Besides, you don't want to lug that thing around."

She didn't say anything as she tucked her purse underneath the driver's seat. She slammed the door and walked over to where he stood. "So what's our plan?"

He held up the GPS. "We're going to head down the Spring Trail. There are two caches down there. The other two caches are in different areas of the park. I think these might be a little easier though, so I thought we could start here first. Is that okay with you?"

She nodded. "Lead the way."

They started off down the trail.

"How far do we have to go for the first one?" Madison asked after they'd been walking for a few minutes.

He stopped and consulted the GPS. "It shouldn't be too much farther until we get to the first one. Here's the clue:

The place you seek
Was full of flour
Once it used
The spring as power."

Madison burst out laughing. "I think I know where we're headed."

"I'm clueless on this one. Care to share?"

She grinned. "What's this? Mr. Outdoor World is asking me for help?"

"First time for everything."

"It's got to be near the old gristmill. I remember it from when I was a kid. We didn't do a lot of hiking or anything, but believe it or not, I've been down this trail once before to see the springs. And my grandma made sure we stopped at the site of the old mill so she could explain to us how it used to work."

He liked the way her brown eyes lit up as she talked about her childhood. Something awful must've happened for her to turn her back on her family. Something more than just her mom's early death. The fact that he wanted to know her secrets caught him by surprise. Ever since he and Samantha had broken things off, he'd closed himself off to getting to know anyone new. "It sounds like you're probably right then." He looked at the GPS again. "We should be close."

Ten minutes later they came to the site of the old mill. "Cool," Grant said. "I can't believe I've never been down this trail before."

"They burned the mill in the 1930s to make room for the

Lake of the Ozarks. My grandma wasn't born yet, but her parents told her about it burning."

Grant consulted the GPS and checked the coordinates of the cache. "Looks like it should be right over here." He walked toward a rustic shelter that housed an interpretative display. "Check underneath this little table."

Madison came up with the ammunition box. "Here it is," she said with a grin.

She snapped a picture with her phone and then signed the logbook. "You have one of those fishing lures with you?" she asked.

He grinned. "Yep." He pulled a bright-pink lure from his cargo pocket. "Look, it matches your shoes."

Madison giggled. "I guess you know what lure I'll choose if I ever go fishing."

"That'll be the day." Grant tucked the cache back where it came from then hoisted his backpack over his shoulder. "I'm sure you'd just be a regular Bill Dance."

She frowned. "Who?"

He shook his head. "Never mind." He'd grown up watching Bill Dance's bass fishing show on TV and had even gotten to meet him a few times over the years, but Madison would never understand. "Okay. It looks like the next cache is down the trail and closer to the springs." He grinned. "You ready to keep going, or do you need to rest?"

Madison tossed her dark ponytail. "I'm fine, thanks." She grinned. "In fact, this time you can follow me."

He set out down the trail after her, trying to keep his eyes off her long, tanned legs. She might not consider herself outdoorsy, but she obviously worked out. And even though he still thought she was way too prissy for his taste, he had to admit that her beauty wasn't lost on him. In fact, his attraction to her seemed to grow by the hour. "How about if I take the lead? Scare off any snakes."

She stopped and motioned for him to go around her. "Good call."

They rounded a corner, and the paved trail turned into a wooden boardwalk. "Here's an overlook." Grant motioned toward an interpretative panel that gave more information about the spring. From their vantage point, they could see the water. "Isn't it beautiful?"

"Wow." Madison stood next to him, and her bare arm brushed against his. "It's so pretty."

He gave her a sideways glance. "Sure is," he whispered. *Get a grip.* "So it looks like if we just keep going down the path, we'll find another cache."

"What's the clue on this one?"

Grant groaned. "Whoever wrote this one isn't much of a poet. It doesn't even rhyme."

"Let me see." She grabbed the GPS and scrolled to read.

"Two rocks meet
But never touch.
To find the treat
You'll have to climb."

Madison consulted the GPS. "Let's just keep going and see if we figure it out once we're at the right coordinates." She motioned for him to follow.

"I can tell we're getting close to the spring because it's getting cooler."

She stopped suddenly, and he ran into her.

Grant put his hands on her waist to keep them both from tumbling. "Sorry," he breathed. He was close enough to smell her shampoo. He let go of her and stepped back. "You okay?"

Madison glanced over her shoulder with a grin. "I didn't mean to stop like that. But look." She pointed ahead at two large rocks with just enough space between them for a person to fit through. "I think that must be the first part of the clue."

He followed her through the opening. "You're right. Two rocks meet but never touch. It's got to be these."

Madison stopped in front of a tree. "Okay, according to the GPS, we're here." She pointed upward. "And now we have to climb." She laughed. "Well one of us does. And I nominate you."

Grant smiled and shrugged the backpack from his shoulders. He grasped a low limb and shook it to see how sturdy it was. "I haven't climbed a tree since I was a kid."

"Were you good at it?"

He made a face. "Only broken bone I ever had was from a tree climb gone wrong." He shimmied onto the first limb and looked up. The box was right above him. "But this isn't bad at all. Guess they didn't really want us to get too far off the ground." He grabbed the box and held it out for Madison to take.

She snapped a picture of the box and then opened it. "Isn't this cute? A little plastic castle."

"Yes, so cute," he said mockingly once he was on the ground.

She rolled her eyes and passed him the logbook and box. "Don't forget the fishing lure."

Grant held up a bright-turquoise lure. "Of course not." He closed the box and hurried to put it back in place.

"Check this out," Madison called.

He made his way to where she stood in front of a trail sign.

"I'm glad this is the last cache on the trail." She pointed at the sign. "Because otherwise we'd be climbing 316 stairs. And they look pretty steep."

"Sounds fun to me."

She shot him a dirty look.

He held up his hands in surrender. "But maybe on another day when we don't have two more caches to find."

She glanced at him. "How about you come back another day without me? You can send me a postcard and let me know how the climb goes."

He nodded. "Right." He kept forgetting that she'd be leaving soon. Off to the bright lights of the big city where she could find some guy who wore business suits and drove a fancy car.

But the sooner she was gone, the sooner he could get back to his old routine.

Somehow that didn't make him feel any better.

Chapter 7

O kay, where to next?" Madison asked once they were back in the truck.

"The castle ruins. Ever been there?"

She shook her head. "I've seen it from the overlook, but never actually gone to the ruins." Even though she'd never visited the ruins, she still knew the story behind the spot. In the early 1900s a businessman from Kansas City visited the area and found it so beautiful he immediately bought 5,000 acres and began construction on a European-style castle. A year later, he was killed in a car accident, and construction stopped, but his sons stepped in and finished the project. Eventually the castle was turned into a hotel, but in the 1940s a fire broke out and gutted the insides. Thirty years later, the area became a state park, including the castle ruins.

"I've been to the overlook, too. Grandpa wanted to go a couple of years ago, and I took him. But we didn't go to the ruins, either. I always think what a sad story surrounds the place. That guy who wanted to live there never got to. It just seems like tragedy went with the place, you know?"

She nodded. "Is it a long hike?"

"I think it should only be about half a mile from the parking lot." He pulled into a space. "Ready?"

"Yep."

She followed him down a wooded path. "What's the clue?"

He stopped and checked the GPS. "They just get worse and worse," he said with a grin.

"It's time to stop
And get your fill
Take your bottle
Try not to spill."

Madison returned his smile. "Okay, obviously we're looking for water." The thrill of solving a clue and finding hidden treasure was a lot more fun than she'd expected it to be. Of course, she'd gone through a phase as a child when she wanted to be Nancy Drew.

She glanced at Grant. He concentrated on the trail, glancing every now and then at the GPS. Maybe he had something to do with her sudden change of heart about geocaching, too. He wasn't as much of a Neanderthal as she'd expected him to be. In fact, if he were to put on a coat and tie and trim his curls a little bit, he could probably fit in anywhere. She quickly pushed the thought out of her mind. He probably didn't own a tie. And he certainly didn't seem too interested when she talked about her life in the city.

"Check it out." He stopped as they came into a clearing. "A water fountain."

She grinned. "That's got to be it, don't you think?"

"Only one way to find out." He walked over to the fountain and looked around it. "Here it is." He knelt behind the fountain and pulled out a small box.

"Smile," she said, holding up her phone and snapping a picture.

Grant opened the box. "Another little plastic castle." He grinned and dropped a yellow fishing lure in the box.

"You sure do have a lot of those lures." She raised her eyebrows at him. "Don't you use them?"

He shrugged and quickly signed the logbook. "I've got plenty at home."

Madison put the box back where it came from. "Oh yeah. I've been meaning to ask. Where exactly do you live?"

An unmistakable shadow crossed his face. "Actually, not far from here. I live in a little cabin on the Niangua River. That's the branch of the Lake of the Ozarks that runs by the park here."

"Cool. So we're kind of in your neck of the woods then?" He grinned. "Something like that. A lot of the time when I work as a fishing guide, I like to fish the Niangua. I've had a lot of luck there." He raked his fingers through his hair. "You want to go on to the castle while we're here? Or would you rather turn back, since we've already found the cache?"

"I definitely think we should go to the ruins. I mean, if you want to." She met his eyes and was struck again by how blue they were.

Grant nodded. "Let's go."

They walked side by side toward the looming castle ruins. Just as they reached them, a boom of thunder ricocheted around them.

Madison jumped and grabbed hold of Grant's arm.

A jagged streak of lightning flashed across the sky, followed by another boom of thunder.

Grant pulled her close. "The rain is coming. I should've checked the weather." He looked around the castle ruins. "Do you want to wait it out here or make a run for it?"

The nearness of him clouded her ability to think straight.

What she wanted right that second was for him to hold on to her and never let go. But that wasn't an option.

"Let's run."

He grabbed her hand, and they took off toward the truck just as the bottom fell out of the sky.

Grant let go of her hand so he could unlock the door. He flung it open, and a soaked-to-the-bone Madison jumped in and slid across the seat.

He climbed in behind her and closed the door. The rain pounded so hard against the truck, it sounded like a million tiny hammers. "You okay?" He glanced at her.

Water dripped off of Madison like she'd just climbed out of a swimming pool. She managed a smile. "I kind of need a towel."

He'd been afraid she would freak out at the prospect of being soaked through. "I'm glad you're a good sport." He turned the key, and the truck roared to life. "Let's go to my place and dry off. Maybe by then the storm will have passed."

She nodded. "Dry sounds good."

Grant carefully exited the park. Even with the windshield wipers on high, he could barely see. "It's not far, I promise."

Madison flicked water from her arm. "Okay."

Two turns later, and they were parked in front of his rustic cabin. "You want to sit here and see if it calms down or make another run for it?" he asked.

She grinned. "I see no reason to wait it out now. We look like drowned rats. Besides, all this water might rust out your floorboards right before our very eyes."

He chuckled. "Smarty-pants." He got his house key ready

and opened the truck door. He took off running toward the door and stuck the key in the lock.

Madison squealed all the way to the door. "Hurry, hurry, hurry!" She raced inside after him and slid when her wet shoes hit the hardwood floor. She grabbed him to steady herself.

Grant instinctively slipped his arms around her. "Whoa." His face was so close to hers, he could see the water dripping off her eyelashes. He grinned. "Way to make an entrance."

She laughed. "What can I say, I'm a little dramatic."

He realized he was still holding on to her and quickly let go. "So welcome to my humble abode." He waved an arm around the wood-paneled living room.

"It's. . .cozy." She looked around the small room. "Do you have a towel or something?"

"Sure. Hang on a sec." He went into his bedroom and grabbed a T-shirt and a pair of running shorts out of a drawer. "These will have to do," he said, walking back in the living room.

She took the clothes and eyed them suspiciously. "Thanks."

"The bathroom is the second door on the left. There are towels in the cabinet."

He quickly changed into dry clothes and flipped on the TV to check the weather.

"This is so not my style." Madison emerged from the bathroom in his T-shirt and shorts, holding her soaked tennis shoes in her hand. Her face had been scrubbed free of makeup, and her wet hair was drying in loose waves.

Grant couldn't believe his eyes. He'd known she was beautiful all made up and wearing her fancy clothes. But he'd had no idea just how naturally pretty she was. "You look amazing."

Her cheeks turned pink. "Shut up. I look scary, and you know it." She put her tennis shoes on the mat next to the door and sat down on the couch.

Grant shook his head. "I'm serious. You always look nice and well put together and all that. But right now you're on a completely different level."

She ducked her head and smiled. "Thanks," she said quietly.

He knew he was playing with fire by telling her what he thought, but he got the feeling she thought she was nothing without her designer clothes and expensive makeup. "So I guess the storm has kind of messed up the day."

Madison shrugged. "Do you think we really have a shot at winning the treasure hunt anyway? There are some people who are seriously hunting all the time. I looked at the website last night, and there are a couple of groups way ahead of us."

"I think we make a great team." He grinned. "Besides, I was looking over the rules. Maybe we'll find that Rainbow's End geocoin thing. It would give us extra points."

She looked at him blankly.

Grant chuckled. "I take it you didn't read the rules?"

She made a face. "I sort of relied on Brook for that. Sorry if that makes me a loser teammate."

"Hey. . .don't talk about my partner like that." He grinned. "The deal with the coin is that you get five points if you find it. And you can either keep it and prevent anyone else from finding it or turn it in at the church, and it will be rehidden."

"You can do either one?"

"Yep." He raised an eyebrow. "Which would you want to do? Provided we found it."

Madison sighed. "I'd probably turn it in."

"Look how nice you are."

She shook her head. "Not really. I was actually thinking that maybe we'd end up finding it again and getting even more points."

He burst out laughing. "You're so cutthroat."

She shrugged. "Just makes good sense to me."

He met her gaze. "You know what doesn't make sense to me?"

"What's that?" Madison turned toward him on the couch.

"Why are you in such a hurry to leave here? What is it about home that you can't stand?"

Her eyes widened in surprise. "Wow. Right for the personal questions, huh?"

Grant raked his fingers through his wet curls. "Better than just sitting here watching it rain." He looked at her seriously. "Besides, I really want to know."

Madison twirled a damp strand of hair. "It's not that I can't stand home. It's that it makes me so unbelievably sad to be here, that I like to stay as far away as I can."

Grant listened as she explained her mother's illness and her daddy's downward spiral. By the end of her story, he wanted more than anything to pull her into his arms and promise her the rest of her life wouldn't be as traumatic. Except he knew from experience that no matter how well you thought you had your life planned, sometimes things didn't quite work out that way. "I'm so sorry. What about now? You visited your dad. Did that go well?"

"He needs a kidney transplant. No one in the family is an acceptable donor." She met his gaze. "I'm his last shot."

"Are you a match?"

She sighed. "I'm not sure yet. He doesn't want me to even consider it." She shook her head. "But even though he wasn't always the man I needed him to be, I don't think I could live with myself if I didn't at least give it a shot."

"That's a lot to deal with, huh?" He could see the pain in her eyes.

"I've been consumed by anger toward him for so many years. But now. . .I guess I have a new perspective."

He reached over and rubbed her shoulder. "You'll figure it out."

She gave him a tiny smile. "I hope so. I've been praying about it a lot."

"Sometimes that's the only thing you can do."

Chapter 8

Madison couldn't believe it was already the Fourth of July. The summer was really flying past. She'd kind of hoped Brook would be back home by now, but they'd spoken the night before last, and it sounded like she and Scott were planning to stay in Arkansas for at least another couple of weeks.

And after a really promising phone interview last week, she was positive that she'd be offered a new position any day now. Which would mean moving far away from the Ozarks.

Funny how that didn't sound nearly as wonderful as she'd expected it to. She flipped through Joshua's tiny closet where her clothes hung. Ever since the big rainstorm, she'd been thinking about what Grant had said to her about how clothes didn't make her who she was.

For so many years, she'd let her identity be tied to the label in her sweater and the name inside her shoes. She'd fought to straighten her wavy hair because she thought it made her look more polished. And she'd spent a small fortune at Sephora so her face was always perfectly made up.

These past weeks, coming home to the quiet of Brook's house, Madison had spent a lot of time thinking. Had she forgotten who she was? Had years of trying to forget her past made her lose important pieces of herself?

She couldn't be sure.

And now she'd agreed to go out with Grant. On a real date, not just some geocaching excursion. When he'd asked her out to dinner, she'd been hesitant. Was she playing with fire? Even though he wasn't the kind of guy she normally dated, she couldn't ignore the fact that she liked spending time with him. And even harder to ignore was the little spark that seemed to have ignited between them.

She pulled on a pair of denim capris and a green polo shirt. She and Grandma had visited the outlet mall last week, and she'd picked up a few new things. It had been so nice to spend time with her grandmother over the past weeks. Grandma had asked her point-blank if she'd consider sticking around for a little while, but Madison had put her off with a blanket sentence about not knowing what the future held. *I might not know what the future holds, but I'm pretty sure it doesn't hold me staying here.*

The ringing doorbell brought her back to reality. She took one last look in the mirror and grinned. She'd let her hair dry naturally, so it hung in loose waves. Grant had been such a fan after the rainstorm, she'd figured it would be a good move for their date. He hadn't mentioned what he had planned, just that it included dinner and watching the fireworks.

She paused at the door, surprised by her growing excitement. They'd spent tons of time together over the past weeks searching for geocaches, but this would be different.

She flung the door open.

Grant stood on the porch, a bouquet of daisies in his hand. "For you," he said with a grin.

She couldn't hide her smile. "Thanks."

Ten minutes later they were loaded up in the truck. "After dinner we're going to go watch the fireworks over the lake," he explained. "And I'm out of bug spray." He glanced at her with a grin. "I don't guess you have any in that big purse of yours."

She unzipped her purse. "I have gum, peanut butter crackers, a notepad, my e-book reader, and a stun gun." She ticked them off on her hand. "But no bug spray. Can you believe that?"

He laughed. "That's a wide assortment of things, I'll give you that."

"I'm more prepared for the city, I guess." She'd laughed a couple of years ago when Grandma had bought her a stun gun for Christmas and had it shipped to her house in Atlanta. But it did make her feel a little safer.

"There's a little sporting goods store up ahead," Grant said. "I'll run in and grab some." He slowed down and flipped on his blinker. "We're lucky they're still open. They must be having a Fourth of July sale or something." He turned into the parking lot and killed the engine. "You can just wait here."

She grinned. "What's wrong? You think I might faint if I see live bait?"

A look she couldn't identify flashed across his face. "No. But it won't take me but a second."

The sun was already heating up the old truck. "It's too hot to wait out here, even for a second. I'll just go with you." She slid across the seat and followed him into the store. A huge banner advertising some kind of bass fishing tournament was draped across the back wall. Mounted fish lined one wall, and deer heads lined the other. "Whoa. That's a lot of dead stuff."

Grant chuckled. "What, you mean you didn't have a stuffed deer head on your wall back in Atlanta?"

"Um. . .that would be a big no. I'm pretty sure I would have nightmares if I had a Bambi head staring at me all the time like that." She shook her head. "My grandpa used to have one, but Grandma made him keep it out back in his workshop. She said she felt like its eyes followed her everywhere she went."

"Here are the keys if you want to go back to the truck." He held up the keys.

She shook her head. "I'm fine."

"Okay. Wait for me right here. I'll go grab the repellent." He hurried off.

She wandered down the first aisle. Every kind of rod and reel imaginable must be on display. She turned the corner and came face-to-face with Grant.

A cardboard cutout of Grant, holding up a giant fish in one hand and a fishing lure in the other. She backed away from the cutout and collided with a display of children's fishing poles. They clattered to the ground with a bang, and Madison scurried to pick them up. Her face grew hot as other customers stopped to stare.

"Clumsy," Grant said as he walked up with a smile on his face. "Did you run into a stuffed deer?"

She leveled her gaze on him. "Not exactly." She stood up and walked to the cardboard cutout. "I ran into *you*."

Grant's face turned white beneath his tan. "I thought all those had been taken down."

"I'm a little confused." She waited on an explanation.

His jaw tensed. "I guess I should've told you," he started.

"Grant Simmons," a man said, hurrying over. "I thought that was you when you walked in." A huge smile spread over the man's round face. "My son is your biggest fan ever since we saw you with that fifteen-pound bass at a tournament in Tennessee.

We were at the weigh-in, and Bobby talked about that fish for months." He chuckled. "He's gonna want to meet you—hang on." He hurried off.

Madison looked at Grant. "So, what? You're some kind of fishing celebrity?"

He frowned. "It's not like that."

"Here he is," the man said, a young boy in tow. "Grant Simmons."

The little boy grinned, displaying two missing front teeth. "Hi," he said shyly.

Grant knelt down to the child. "What's your name?"

"Bobby."

"Do you like to fish, Bobby?"

The child nodded. "Yes sir. When I grow up I want to be a bass fisherman just like you."

If she hadn't been so shell-shocked, Madison would've thought the whole exchange was adorable.

Grant grinned. "You just keep fishing, Bobby. You never know what the future holds." He reached into the pocket of his cargo shorts and pulled out a bright-blue lure. "Here you go."

Bobby's face lit up. "Thanks."

His dad smiled. "Best of luck to you, Mr. Simmons." He put an arm around Bobby, and the two of them walked off.

Madison turned on her heel. "I'll be outside."

She knew she had no right to be upset. But she'd thought she and Grant had developed a close friendship. So why had he kept something that was obviously a huge part of his life from her?

Madison stepped out into the muggy July heat. She hated to be kept in the dark about things. It took her back to when she was fourteen and Mama had been diagnosed with cancer. Everyone in the family knew except for Madison. By the time her family decided it was time for her to learn the truth, Mama didn't have much time left.

And even though Grant's withholding of information wasn't in the same category, it still felt oddly like a betrayal.

Grant tossed the bug spray back on the counter and hurried out the door. He could understand that coming face-to-face with a cardboard cutout of him had probably freaked her out a little.

Madison stood next to the truck, arms crossed.

Lord, give me the right words.

She stepped aside so he could unlock the door.

He swung the creaky door open, and she climbed inside without saying a word. Grant started the engine and glanced over at her. She didn't look mad, exactly. Just stoic. Okay, maybe mad. "Let me explain."

"You don't owe me an explanation. It's not a big deal. I mean, I'm just temporarily in your life and all."

The plans he'd made for tonight weren't looking so good. He'd thought this would be a real date, and he could finally tell her how he felt. But this might be something he couldn't come back from. "I think I need to show you something."

She looked over at him with one eyebrow raised. "What... are you on a billboard, too?"

"No—well maybe once, but that was a couple of years ago." He smiled at her as he backed out of the parking lot.

Madison didn't respond. Clearly, she wasn't impressed with his notoriety.

Grant headed somewhere he hadn't been to in a long time. He pulled the old truck into the long driveway of a multistory brick house.

Madison shot him a questioning look.

"Just wait." He hit the button on a garage door opener that was clipped to the driver's side sun visor. The spacious garage door opened, and he drove his truck inside.

"Wasn't there a for sale sign out front?" she asked once he turned the engine off and closed the garage door behind them.

He nodded. "Yep." He climbed out of the truck and held out his hand. "Come on."

She hesitated for a moment then grabbed his hand and jumped down from the truck.

Grant closed the door, and they were surrounded by the dark coolness of the enclosed space. He kept a firm grasp on her hand and led her to the door that opened to the kitchen.

"Where are we?" she asked once they were inside. "Is this just an empty house?"

He nodded. "It sure is. But come look at the view." He walked into the living room where floor-to-ceiling windows looked out over the lake. "This is the reason I bought this place."

Madison looked at him with wide eyes. "You own this place? I thought you lived at the cabin." She frowned.

Grant pressed his lips together, wondering where to start. "Let's go sit out on the deck, and I'll explain."

She followed him outside, and they sat on the top step of the deck. "I think you'd better start from the beginning," she said. "Because I'm beginning to think you're not the guy I thought you were."

"I went to college in Arkansas," he explained. "Classes were fine, but mostly I wanted to be out fishing. I majored in parks and recreation and worked for a year as a park ranger in a state park."

"I can totally see you as a park ranger."

Grant grinned, hoping that her commentary meant she'd cooled down some since they were at the store. "I enjoyed it. But not as much as I enjoyed fishing. Grandpa encouraged me to enter a tournament, and that turned into my biggest hobby. Pretty soon I'd won some big ones, and the logical thing to do was to turn pro."

"Hence the cardboard cutout?"

"Yeah. And the abundance of fishing lures." He gazed out over the lake. "I got some sponsorships, and pretty soon I was doing well as a professional bass angler." He turned to face her. "Really well." He motioned at the house. "I bought this place after I won my first major tournament."

She glanced around. "It's amazing. But why don't you live here?"

He sighed. "This isn't the kind of place for a bachelor. I mean, there are five bedrooms." He shrugged. "It just ended up that I didn't need so much space."

"So. . .you didn't expect to be a bachelor when you moved in?"

He hated to talk about one of the darkest parts of his life, but he knew Madison deserved the truth. "I was engaged. Her name was Samantha."

Madison's eyes widened at his revelation. "Engaged. Wow. What happened?"

"We met at a charity event in Little Rock. I fell head over heels for her, even though she hated what I did for a living. She wanted me to go into business with her daddy." He shook his head. "I tried everything in the world to make her understand why I loved fishing, but she always said it was the one thing about me that she considered a deal breaker."

"So the two of you broke up?"

He chewed on his bottom lip. "You have to understand that I was convinced we could make it work even though sometimes it felt like we were from totally different planets. Eventually I proposed, and she accepted." He sighed. "I thought that was the big hurdle. The proposal."

"But it wasn't."

He shook his head. "I'd bought this place a year earlier, before we even met. I thought this would be a wonderful place to raise a family; plus it was near the water. I'd grown up visiting my grandparents here and had just fallen in love with the area."

Madison nodded. "I can see that you would."

"Anyway, I guess Samantha kept thinking I would just change. She tried buying me new clothes and dragging me to fancy restaurants. She refused to ride in my truck and wouldn't even come look at the house. She said it wouldn't be her style, and we could just find a place together somewhere in the city."

Madison met his gaze. Her brown eyes reflected sympathy. "I'm sorry."

"It came time for the wedding rehearsal. I knew as soon as I saw her that night that there was something terribly wrong. Her daddy walked her down the aisle, and she just started crying. She stood there in front of our family and friends and told me that she'd fallen in love with a coworker. That the two of them saw eye to eye on things, and she knew he was her soul mate. She handed me the ring back, and that was it."

Madison reached over and grasped his arm. "You're better off without her. It sounds like the two of you would've been in for a world of trouble. But that probably didn't make it any easier."

He nodded. "It was tough. Partly just my stupid pride. Some of my buddies from the fishing circuit were there that night. I didn't want to face any of them again." He shrugged. "That's when I decided to take a break. I moved here, bought the cabin, and started working as a guide." He raked his fingers through his hair. "I thought I'd sort of hide out for a little while then go back to fishing competitively. But I actually enjoyed working as a guide."

"So do you think you'll ever go back?"

He shook his head. "I doubt it. Taking some time off gave me a little perspective. It seemed like once I started getting sponsorships and trying to win big tournaments, it kind of sucked the fun out of fishing."

"I guess I can see how that would happen."

"The one thing that used to be so relaxing had become a chore. I'd always planned on becoming a guide once I retired. I just did it a little earlier than I thought I would." He grinned.

She leaned over and bumped against him. "So why didn't you tell me all of that before?"

"When we first met, you looked at me the same way Samantha had. I could tell you wouldn't hold my career as an outdoorsman in high esteem, professional or not. Besides, you've made no effort to hide your disdain for the area ever since you got here." It seemed harsh, but he figured at this point, honesty was the best policy.

Chapter 9

Contrary to what you might think, I loved growing up in Roach." She leaned back against the deck. "I didn't especially like telling people where I was from, though, because they'd make fun. But these past weeks, I've started remembering just how wonderful my life here was." At first she'd been surprised by the happy memories. But soon, she'd started to remember more and more. "The good times definitely outweighed the bad."

"I'm glad you came to that conclusion."

"Can you guess why I'm named Madison?"

He shook his head. "Family name? Descendant of James and Dolly?"

She grinned. "No. Because of Madison Avenue. My mama's biggest dream when she was young was to go to New York and work on Madison Avenue in an office that overlooked the city."

"She told you that?"

"Yeah. Just before she died, she told me she hoped I'd do all the things she wasn't going to get to do. When I was a senior in high school and trying to figure out what to do with my life, I found her diary from her own senior year. She wanted to go to New York and work in advertising."

"But she stayed here."

Madison nodded. "She met Daddy that summer, and they were married by the fall. She didn't even go away to college. Just stayed here and raised us." A stray tear dripped down her cheek.

Grant reached out and tenderly wiped it away. "Please tell me you aren't off chasing someone else's dream."

"I owe her that much. She never got to live in the city. She never got to do anything except stay here and be a wife and mother."

He took her hand, and she tried to ignore the way it made her heart beat faster. "But how do you know that didn't mean more to her than living in the big city ever would? And why would you think that being a wife and mother had to be the end of her ambition? Maybe she chose to stay here."

Madison shook her head. "No way. Even your grandpa told me that he remembered how much she always wanted to head off to the city."

Grant frowned. "She was in high school. Everyone says that kind of stuff when they're sixteen. I know I did."

"Seriously? You?" She couldn't hide her surprise.

He grinned. "Yes. I went through a phase where I wanted to be a lawyer and move to a city where no one knew me."

Madison burst out laughing. "You wanted to be a lawyer?"

"Don't make fun. I could've been if I'd have wanted to." He smiled. "But actually I was just going through my John Grisham phase." He shrugged. "Eventually I figured out what I really wanted."

"So do you ever regret giving up professional fishing?"

"Now and then I'll see one of my old buddies on TV and wonder what would've happened if I'd stuck with it. When I stopped doing it competitively, I was at the top. I even got an offer to host a show on one of those outdoor networks."

"No way! You'd be great at that. And you're sure you don't want to give it a shot?"

Grant shook his head. "I'm positive. I enjoy working as a guide. I even run a camp in the spring where I teach kids how to fish. So I'm happy with the way things have turned out." He grinned. "Plus it means I have the time to be here, taking care of Grandpa and geocaching with you."

"I've met your grandpa. I don't think he needs much taking care of." She met his gaze. "But I am glad you're here to do the geocaching with me."

"So you admit that you kind of enjoy it."

She pushed a stray hair from her face. "Maybe."

He chuckled. "How about we head to dinner?" He stood up and pulled her to her feet. "Then maybe we can come back here to watch the fireworks. Unless you'd rather be with a crowd."

Her stomach lurched. She knew she should opt for watching the fireworks with the crowd. The more time she spent alone with Grant, the harder it was going to be to walk away. But given the choice, she'd much rather it just be the two of them. "I think the deck is fine."

Grant couldn't remember when he'd had a better time. Even though the day had started out a little rocky, what with that stupid cardboard cutout at the store, he was glad to have everything out in the open.

"Dinner was delicious." Madison slid into the truck.

He nodded. "I'm glad you liked it. I was afraid barbecue might be too hokey for you."

She laughed. "It was perfect. One of my favorites, actually."

"So do you still want to go watch the fireworks from my lake house?" He wanted her all to himself, but didn't want to press the issue.

She nodded. "Yes, please. That house is too fantastic. The deck should definitely be used for a viewing party."

He slowed the truck down as he neared the driveway. "This might be my only Fourth of July at the house. I bought it thinking I'd have these wonderful cookouts and invite tons of people over." He hit the garage button.

"Do you think you're making a mistake? I mean, maybe you should move in and give it a try before you sell it."

Grant shook his head as he turned off the motor. "I've thought about it. But don't you think it'd be weird for one person to live in a house this big?" They walked into the kitchen, and he flipped on the light.

"It's your dream house. Right?"

He nodded and looked around the kitchen. "It is. I got a really good deal on it, too. It will be hard to let it go." He met her gaze. "It's hard letting go of something you want so badly."

"Then don't."

He motioned for her to follow him outside. "Sorry I don't have chairs out here."

She laughed. "You don't have to keep apologizing. I'm actually not the high-maintenance girl I can appear to be."

He reached over and took her hand. "I know. I think I may have been way off the mark about you. There's a lot more substance beneath that city-girl exterior than I expected there to be."

"You're admitting you're wrong about something?" She squeezed his hand.

Grant laughed. "Every now and then."

"Well I might've judged you a little, too. I mean, that first day you showed up you barely looked at me. And then when I was visiting your grandpa, you made it pretty clear you wanted me to leave."

He traced his finger along the back of her hand. "I expected you to be like Samantha. A city girl who looked down on me."

"I don't look down on you," she whispered. "In fact, I think you having been a professional fisherman is kind of cool." She smiled. "You might be the only person I know who's been captured in a cardboard cutout."

He laughed. "You know, I actually have a couple of those in storage if you want one."

She squeezed his hand. "Now, that would make for some interesting wall art." She smirked. "But only if it's autographed, of course."

The sky lit up with brilliant flashes of light.

"So pretty," Madison whispered.

He glanced at her upturned face. "Beautiful."

She caught his gaze and smiled.

Grant tipped her chin and leaned down to kiss her. "I've wanted to do this for a long time," he whispered just before their lips met.

And there, underneath the fireworks on the deck of his dream house, Grant knew he was in trouble.

But there was no turning back.

The girl in his arms had captured a piece of his heart.

Chapter 10

"Madison Wallace?" an unfamiliar voice asked.

Madison pressed the phone closer to her ear. "This is she." She glanced at the clock. If she wasn't careful, she'd be late for the big Rainbow's End Treasure Hunt rally that was taking place at the park. "Can I help you?"

"It's Mr. Swanson with Swanson Group."

Madison swallowed hard. It was the PR firm from New York. She'd had a phone interview a few weeks ago and a Skype interview last week. "Yes sir?"

"We'd like to invite you to come to New York for the final round of interviews," he explained. "We're working on a short time frame, though. Can you be here day after tomorrow?"

Day after tomorrow? She and Grant had planned to go back to Ha Ha Tonka and get the final cache. And she'd promised Grandma that they'd go to the grocery store and stop for dinner at the new barbecue place. But this was her future. "Of course."

"Good, good. I'll have my assistant e-mail you to confirm your travel plans. We're looking forward to seeing you, Madison. Everyone here has been very impressed with your body of work."

She thanked him and clicked off the phone. An interview in New York. It was almost too much to process. She sank onto the bed, thankful she'd planned to meet Grant at the park. It would give her time to figure out how to tell him he was about to be minus a geocaching partner.

Twenty minutes later she left her car in the lot and hurried across the street to the park. She waved at Hadley and a couple of the other geocachers who'd already settled into chairs.

"Glad you're here," Grant said from behind her. "So we'll get our full participation points."

She turned to face him. His yellow T-shirt and khaki shorts showed off his deep tan. When they met, she'd thought his curls were unkempt. But today she wanted to reach up and touch them. "Wouldn't miss it." She frowned. She needed to tell him about New York.

"Let's go sit down. I think they're about to get started." He grabbed her hand and led her toward a row of chairs.

She pulled her hand away. "Actually, I need to talk to you."

He turned to face her. "Is everything okay? Is it your dad?"

"No. It's just. . ." She glanced around. "There's a bench in the back. Let's go there. Maybe we can still catch some of the announcements." She led the way, trying to muster up her courage as she walked.

"What's up? Have you mapped out some caches for the rest of the week or something?" He grinned. "I know there are a couple of groups ahead of us, but we could still beat them, especially if we find the Rainbow's End coin."

She stopped walking and turned to face him. "No. Nothing like that." She avoided his eyes. "Actually, it looks like you're going to be on your own for a little while."

"I don't understand."

She bit her lip. "There's a PR firm in New York that I've done a phone interview and a Skype interview with. They called this morning." She looked down at her hands. "They want me there in two days for the final round of interviews."

"New York," he said. "Is that really what you want?"

She swallowed. "You know that's always been my plan." She waited for him to try and talk her out of it, but he didn't.

"So you're leaving. Just like that."

She shrugged. "Well it's not a done deal or anything. They might hate me."

Grant's lips turned up in the slightest hint of a smile. "They won't."

Madison remembered how his lips felt on hers. Like they'd been made especially to fit her. But there was no turning back now. "I hope not. This is what I've always wanted."

Grant stood. "So this is good-bye then?"

"I'm sure I'll be back." Madison stood and faced him.

He smirked. "Right. In six more years."

She frowned. This wasn't going like she'd expected. "We can stay in touch though, right? E-mail or Facebook or something."

"Sure, sure." He cleared his throat. "Listen, they're about to start the rally. I want to hear the announcements." He pulled her into an awkward hug. "Bye, Madison." He walked away without another look back.

She stayed rooted to the spot and watched him go. Maybe she hadn't meant as much to him as she'd thought.

Twenty minutes later, she pulled into the driveway at Grandma's house. It was funny. At the beginning of the summer, she'd avoided the place because the memories made her too sad. But over these past weeks, she'd spent more and more time here. She and Grandma had years of catching up to do, and last week she'd finally learned how to make biscuits from scratch.

She rapped on the door and turned the knob. "Grandma?" she called as she walked inside.

"Madison," Grandma said, shuffling into the living room. "What are you doing here? I thought you'd be at the rally."

Madison sighed. "Yeah. I was, but I needed to come talk to you."

Grandma settled into her rocking chair. "What's wrong, dear?"

Madison perched on the couch. She quickly explained about the interview. "I think it's a really great opportunity."

Grandma didn't look convinced. "New York. That's so far from here. And you won't know anyone."

"I'm sure I'll make friends. It's always been my dream, you know."

"Your mama's dream, you mean."

Madison didn't respond.

"I want you to look at something." Grandma picked up a faded blue photo album from the table next to her chair. She flipped through the yellowed pages until she found the one she was looking for. "You see this?"

Madison walked over to look at the photo Grandma pointed at. "Wow. I haven't seen that in years." Mama and Daddy stood on the porch, holding hands. Madison and Brook were in front of them in matching dresses.

"It was Easter Sunday, and y'all had come over here after church. You and Brook both had new dresses."

Madison smiled. "Mama made them. She let us choose the colors."

"And look at your parents." Grandma pointed at them. "What do you see?"

Madison leaned close to the album. "They're laughing."

Grandma nodded. "They were always laughing. Even when times were tough, they had each other, and they had you girls, and that was enough."

"What are you saying?"

Grandma closed the album and grabbed Madison's hand. "You've spent your whole adult life running away, saying you didn't want to turn out like your Mama—stuck in a small town." She shook her head. "But she didn't feel that way. She wouldn't have wanted to be anywhere else but right here. And deep down, I think you know that."

Madison's eyes filled with tears. Trying to chase her mother's dream had been her purpose in life. If she gave that up, what would she have left? "I should go. I need to pack and check on my travel arrangements."

Grandma rose slowly from her chair. "I've seen you with the Simmons boy. You have the same spark your mama had around your daddy." She cocked her head. "Make sure you know what you're throwing away."

"I do," Madison whispered. Grant hadn't even cared enough to try to talk her out of going. She had her answer there.

"And what about your daddy? I guess this pushes you into making a decision quickly."

Madison had finally let go of the anger toward her dad. It had taken most of the summer, but she could at least see that holding on to the bad feelings was like poison. "I can get tested as easily in New York as I can here. I'll go by the house and tell him when I'm on my way out of town."

Grandma pulled her into a hug. "I love you, dear. But you might be even more stubborn than your mama was."

Madison kissed her on the cheek. "I'll call you soon." She hurried outside and climbed into the car. There was one more stop she needed to make before she went back to Brook's. And it might be the hardest good-bye yet.

She parked her Altima in the same spot Grant had parked his truck on their very first day of geocaching. That seemed like so long ago. She hurried through the cemetery gate, past the bench where they'd found the cache, and stopped at her mama's grave.

"I got an interview in New York, Mama." Madison sank to her knees. "I'm pretty sure it's just a formality. Can you believe it?" She traced the words on the headstone and stopped on the Bible verse. *For where your treasure is, there your heart will be also.*

Mama's treasure had been Madison and Brook and Daddy. It had been her parents down the road and a church full of people who'd prayed for her when she got sick. Mama's heart had always been here. Not in New York.

Madison's eyes filled with tears. She'd wasted so many years separated from the people who loved her and whom she loved. And why?

"I thought you might be here," a voice said from behind her.

She turned to look at Grant. "What are you doing here?"

"Sorry for being so abrupt earlier. I had to process things." He knelt down next to her. "You saying good-bye?"

She swallowed against the lump in her throat. "That's why I came."

He took her hand. "You have every right to follow whatever path you want to, but I'm not going to let my pride keep me from telling you how much I've grown to care about you."

She looked at him, and he flushed. "How much I've grown to love you. Might as well say it. I'd have never believed it was possible, but how I feel about you makes me realize that Samantha did me a big favor by leaving me at the altar."

"Really?" She could barely choke out the one word.

He nodded and grinned, even though the pain was evident in his eyes. "If I'm going to be mourning the one who got away for the rest of my life, I want it to be the real deal and not just hurt pride." He tightened his grip on her hand. "Stay or go, Maddie. But as far as I'm concerned, you're the real deal."

She turned her tear-filled eyes back to the tombstone and willed her heart to quit slamming so wildly against her ribs. Funny how coming from Grant, her old nickname didn't sound so bad. In fact, she kind of liked it. "I came here to say good-bye. But right before you walked up, I realized something."

"What's that?"

Madison pointed at the verse on Mama's headstone. "That was her favorite verse."

"It's a good one." He smiled. "I know it by heart."

"I realized that Mama was right where she wanted to be. She loved Daddy more than she loved the idea of moving to the city. And she wouldn't have traded the years she had with me and Brook for all the high-powered jobs in the world."

Grant nodded. "Of course not."

Madison swallowed. "I'm not going to the interview," she said quietly. "I was going for all the wrong reasons."

"Are you sure?"

She nodded. "My heart is here. With you."

He pulled her to him and hugged her tightly. "I didn't dare even dream you'd say that."

"It's true. I don't want to leave. I want to see where this goes." She smiled. "And I want to let Grandma teach me to bake, and spend time with Brook and her family." She stood. "And get tested to see if I can donate a kidney to Daddy. He and I have some lost time to make up for."

Grant stood up and pulled her to her feet. He leaned down and kissed her lightly on the lips. "And you'll keep hunting geocaches with me?"

She laughed. "Of course."

He put an arm around her, and they walked toward the parking lot.

Madison felt more peace than she'd felt in years. She knew there were challenging times ahead, but with Grant and her family at her side, she could face them. *Thank you, Lord, for showing me the way back home.*

Annalisa Daughety, a graduate of Freed-Hardeman University, writes contemporary fiction set in historic locations. Annalisa lives in Arkansas with two spoiled dogs and is hard at work on her next book. She loves to connect with her readers through social media sites like Facebook and Twitter. More information about Annalisa can be found at her website, www.annalisadaughety.com.

LOVE'S PRIZE

by Cara C. Putman

Dedication

To my prize, Eric.

God placed us together twenty years ago and I can't imagine my life without you. You have encouraged my dreams, endured the way I take on too much, and have gifted me with support and love I couldn't imagine. I love you.

Chapter 1

Reagan Graham pressed against her brother's side, trying to avoid the crush of bodies. When Garrett had invited her to spend the summer on this crazy geocaching adventure, she hadn't considered it because it sounded crowded. She needed time and space to recover from the chaos, stress, and intensity of tax season. Spending an extended vacation with hundreds of strangers did not strike her as a good time. At all.

But when an unwanted admirer showed up at her condo hidden in the shadows, accompanying her brother to Osage Beach seemed like a good idea. No, make that a great idea. If the police hadn't arrived when they did. . . She shuddered at how close the stalker had gotten.

Her brother tightened his grip on her. She glanced at him, his athletic frame lending her comfort. He would do anything he could to keep her safe. She knew that. Then her glance landed on his roommate.

Colton Ryan was an enigma. Gorgeous, but an enigma. He seemed friendly, yet after a week she knew less about him than the day they'd met.

He stood apart from them, yet watchful, his gray eyes constantly surveying the crowd. He stood an inch or so shorter than Garrett, but erect and alert. And the way his dark hair curled around his ears made her fingers itch to brush it in place.

Colton was her age, a few years older than Garrett. He planned to start classes at Washington University School of Law in the fall along with Garrett. He called enrolling in law school "seeing the light." She called it a sign that he still hadn't decided what he wanted to be when he grew up if he was changing course a few years into his engineering career. He and Garrett had met through the admissions office and decided to room together during the year. But now he'd attached himself to their summer plans. She hadn't wanted him as a tagalong for her summer away, but there he stood.

She didn't need the complication.

His presence in the smaller, neighboring condo couldn't be called anything but a complication.

All she wanted was a couple of months to forget about the fright that crowded her back home. A shiver shook her at the thought. If she got to do it with a camera in her hand, all the better. She'd leave spreadsheets behind and focus on finding God's beauty and creativity in the midst of the Ozarks.

She sucked in a calming breath and closed her eyes. The crowd noise rolled over her until someone grabbed the microphone and started talking. Even then, she tuned out, the sun warm on her face. Garrett could take notes for both of them.

In fact, she'd let Garrett and Colton plot all kinds of strategies to win the race. She'd focus on her camera. Relax as she saw the world through the narrow focus of her lens. Avoid all the pressures and stresses of a life out of control. For two months she'd pretend she was someone else. Someone without a constant shadow.

The thought brought a smile to her face.

She'd try to relax and return to St. Louis ready to reenter her career. As long as she fixed real food a couple of times a week, Garrett would be thrilled. And if he didn't let the condo disintegrate to a bachelor pad's level of cleanliness, she'd make do.

She opened her eyes as the speaker stepped away from the microphone.

That's all she had to do to survive the summer. Slip under her stalker's radar and return home in August, ready to resume her life. Hopefully, she'd find herself energized from the time in nature, exercising her creative muscles. She touched the camera dangling around her neck. Maybe she should snap some photos of the crowd. She could document the entire hunt. A snicker slipped out at the thought of handing Garrett a photo book at the end of the summer.

"What's up?" His eyebrows arched over clear blue eyes as he studied her.

"Nothing important. You ready to find your first cache?"

"Only if Colton gets that gizmo figured out. You'd think I could make it work without help from my buddy the engineer. Noooo." Garrett rolled his eyes. "Should've known."

Reagan had to laugh. Her brother had the simplest cell phone because he chose to remain "technology adverse," as he called it. Yet he'd rushed out to buy an iPad the moment Apple released them. She couldn't make sense of his quirk. Then her gaze landed on Colton. His eyebrows met over his nose as he studied the small GPS unit.

He must have sensed her gaze, because he looked up and smiled, the kind of smile that could stop the heart of a lesser woman, one hunting for romance. With his rugged movie-star looks, it wouldn't be hard to lose perspective when he flashed the dimple in his chin.

Too bad for him, she didn't want anything to do with men other than her brother right now. Not if there was the iota of a chance Colton could move into position as the next weirdo who fixated on her. She shivered at the thought of inviting anyone into her life right now.

Nope, it was safer to stay far away. His smile shifted as if he could read her thoughts.

What she wouldn't do to get that adorable dimple back in place. . .if only.

Colton shook off his disappointment as he hit the power button on the GPS unit he'd picked up at the Communication Location. He still wasn't convinced it was worth all the coin to buy it, but Garrett had bought the sales pitch. Too bad his soon-to-be roommate didn't have any interest in figuring out how to operate the complicated device.

Guess he'd do that instead.

His gaze traveled back to Reagan.

Garrett's sister wasn't at all what he'd expected, and she left him decidedly feeling like a third wheel. Odd man out. The interloper on her summer. No matter what he did, she gave him a very cold shoulder.

It didn't help that they'd spend practically every moment together except when they slept. His tiny condo barely had room to turn around, let alone cook the kind of meals he liked to prepare. Had Garrett filled her in that Colton hoped to eat many of his meals with them? Even cook, if he could talk them into it?

When Garrett requested he come to Osage Beach to help

protect Reagan, Colton had agreed. Guess Garrett wasn't convinced the small town was far enough from St. Louis, but it was all he could come up with to get his sister out of the city for a couple of months. He had to admire Garrett and his commitment to protecting her, whether or not she wanted it.

Two months.

Colton fiddled with a couple more buttons, waiting for the machine to acquire a satellite signal.

The summer would extend like an eternity if he couldn't break through Reagan's reserve. It didn't matter that Garrett said not to sweat it. It bothered him that she always seemed on edge. That wasn't the way for either of them to live over the summer. With law school coming, he'd decided to invest the money to relax and recharge before the intensity of school hit. Now it looked like he'd have a summer of feeling on the spot, trying to balance Reagan's expectations with his plans.

That's the vibe he got off her.

The machine finally acquired a signal. Maybe Garrett hadn't picked up a dud after all. He glanced up as Garrett and Reagan approached. There was something about her, something almost hidden that intrigued him. He could wait patiently for her to accept him if it meant he could uncover that spark.

The youth pastor stepped down from the stage.

Colton had to admit the hunt appealed to him. He loved the idea of competing with others to find a few secreted goodies. Sure, most of them would be silly trinkets. He had a pocketful of his own St. Louis Rams magnets to leave behind. His little mark that he'd arrived at each cache.

The crowd started to disperse, and Colton approached Garrett and Reagan. "Here you go, dude. Fully fired up."

Garrett held his hands up in front of him. "I think you

should operate that little doodad."

Reagan shook her head. "Who are you trying to kid, Garrett?" She took it from Colton, pressed a couple of buttons, and turned it back to him. "Nothing to it. Here are the downloaded coordinates for the first cache you wanted to tackle."

"Too bad we have to wait for tomorrow." Garrett's gaze followed a cute girl in short shorts and layered tanks. The baseball cap pulled over her ponytail couldn't hide her bright-green eyes. "I'll catch up with you later."

"What about. . ." Colton tried to grab his attention, but the kid kept moving. Guess Garrett thought Reagan was safe if one of them was close. Well, the police did have a suspect they were talking to, so maybe Garrett was right. Who would follow her this far from the city even if he knew she'd left? He glanced at Reagan. "Want to grab a bite?"

She studied him, her sky-blue eyes seeing inside him. He resisted the urge to squirm under her directness. "Okay. We need to find a grocery store."

"After we get food." He patted his stomach. "Have to feed the beast first."

She chuckled and fell into step next to him. "I've heard there's a great custard place, Randy's."

"Does that qualify as food?"

"Every day, twice a day. Don't tell me. You didn't have sisters."

"Nope. Grew up in a house of boys."

"Then you missed the therapeutic effects of ice cream. Covers a host of woes. That and nature."

He knew he liked this woman. "Lead the way."

They left the park, and after a few minutes he spotted a five-foot ice-cream cone posted above the sidewalk. "Let me guess. . .that's our destination."

"Of course." Reagan's pace picked up as she approached the small, green-roofed building.

A family of painted turtles marched across the front windows. Reagan pointed to the words underneath. "Think I'll try the Ozark Turtle."

"Size?"

"Small."

Of course. The gal might want her custard, but he shouldn't expect it to be supersized. He placed their order and, a few minutes later, carried two sundaes to the park bench where Reagan waited. A grin spread across her face as she accepted the caramel- and walnut-topped treat. He'd buy her an Ozark Turtle every day if she'd keep smiling at him like that.

This summer would be amazing if he could keep that smile on her face and the shadows at bay. Add in the Rainbow's End Treasure Hunt with following GPS coordinates to remote locations around town to find the hidden caches, and he'd return to St. Louis rested and ready for school.

Reagan glanced at him, a shy smile turning his insides to goo. Yep, this could be a great summer.

Chapter 2

With her alarm blaring before the sun brightened the sky, Reagan wondered why she'd agreed to start the search first thing. She popped the snooze button then pulled the pillow over her head. It wasn't like any of the caches would disappear if they waited until a reasonable hour like, say, ten.

"Reagan?" Garrett pounded on her door, and it popped open. No matter that he didn't want it locked in case she needed him, she'd bolt it tonight. "Time to get up and at 'em."

"What are you? My drill sergeant?" she grumbled.

He laughed, making her want to throw the clock at him. If it happened to find his chest, oh well. Maybe then he'd let her sleep. "Come on, Sleeping Beauty."

"I'm getting up." Sheesh, what happened to the baby brother she'd had to drag out of bed in the morning to do anything? She'd like him back right about now. With a groan, she threw back the covers and headed to her small bathroom. Ten minutes later she joined Garrett in the kitchen but skidded to a halt when she noticed Colton standing at the stove, flipping an omelet. "I thought you had your own condo."

"Your kitchen is nicer." He smirked at her. Yes, smirked.

This early in the morning? She knew there was a reason she didn't want to like the guy. Too bad the food smelled amazing, with the scent of ham and onion floating toward her. "What would you like on yours?"

"Whatever Garrett's having."

His eyebrows spiked. "Really?"

"Wait. Unless he's having you lace it with jalapeños. Nix the spicy."

"All right." He went to work cracking eggs and whipping them before filling the frying pan with a layer of egg, then cheese, onion, ham, and red pepper. Maybe she could get used to this. It sure beat her normal bowl of microwaved oatmeal. In short order he handed her a plate with a steaming omelet. "Madam."

Her mouth watered as she accepted it. "Thanks."

"We ready to hike?" Garrett rubbed his belly then pushed his empty plate away. It looked clean enough to put back in the cupboard. The boy must have been starved.

"How far today?" Reagan wanted to think she could tackle a long hike the first day, but reality remained. The calendar was too close to tax season for her to be back in non-tax-season shape.

Unless you considered round a shape.

Which she had until Mr. Omelet Chef showed up. He looked like he could hike twelve miles without breaking a sweat. She tugged at her waistband, evidence she'd spent too many hours glued to her chair and computer this year. Maybe she'd start exercising discipline by leaving a few bites on her plate. At least that was one form of discipline that didn't involve sweat or hideous gym clothes.

Colton turned to the map Garrett had taped to the pantry door. "Four miles."

"Round trip?" Please, God.

"Each way."

"Oookaay." She could do this. Especially if she stopped somewhere along the trail and let them get her on the way back. Would Garrett go for that? She could only hope so.

"Is that a problem, Grandma?" Garrett's grin let her know he poked at her, even as she heard his serious tone.

Fine. She'd match him step for step. "Let's do it."

Colton held up a hand. "Don't forget to grab a couple water bottles each. The humidity is more than we're used to."

"We're only a few hours from home." Garrett grabbed one with a frown. "Do we really need it?

"Trust me."

"We have to carry it?" She wrinkled her nose.

"Better than carrying you."

True enough.

Could Reagan be any cuter when her nose wrinkled like that? Colton knew the answer. She struck him as the bookish type who didn't realize she turned heads with her quiet charm and beauty. He'd love to change that about her. Help her see the amazing person God had created.

He'd have to take it slow. She'd warmed up since their custard run last night, but had looked less than pleased to see him in the kitchen.

While he waited for her to do whatever women do first thing, he sank onto the couch and tightened his pristine hiking boots. Hoped he didn't regret wearing them without an initial test hike. The last thing he needed at the beginning of a long competition like this was a series of blisters. Not his idea of fun.

Maybe the extra layer of socks would provide the protection the salesman promised. "How long does this usually take?"

Garrett looked up from the business magazine he held. "Depends on her mood. Might as well settle in and wait."

"It can't take that long."

"You'd be surprised."

Finished with his boots, Colton knew he couldn't idle and decided to work on the kitchen. He'd never been great at waiting. Maybe it came from being the oldest son in a family of doers, but sitting didn't feel right. Like he must be missing something. Something he should be doing, achieving. Soon the dishwasher stood loaded with the breakfast dishes. Then he grabbed a couple of bottles of water for each of them from the fridge. Added reusable bottles to his mental list. No sense filling a landfill while they worked their way around the lake.

He pictured it in his mind's eye. The lake looked more like a caterpillar squiggling along the area, dozens of inlets fingering out from it. Those inlets probably provided some excellent hiding places for caches.

Last night he'd spent time reading through the locations, trying to map them out on the GPS. After awhile, he'd given up on entering all of them but had a decent sample for them to pull from. That is, if they ever left the condo. Didn't Reagan know daylight wasted while they sat here?

He wiped the counter with a swipe that dislodged most of the crumbs. Crossing his arms, he leaned against it. What now?

A door closed, and a minute later Reagan stood in the doorway, looking ready for a day of photography with a large camera around her neck. Her long ponytail flipped over her shoulder as she tossed her chin. "Ready?"

She spun and headed to the front door, and he caught

Garrett's gaze with a question. Hadn't they been waiting on her?

Garrett drove as Colton watched the blinking dot on the GPS. He glanced back at Reagan. She watched the terrain out the window, seeming not to really see anything.

"Turn right in two hundred feet," the mechanical voice grated.

"Maybe there's another voice." Colton flipped through screens and hit buttons.

"Turn right in fifty feet." The male voice was even worse.

Garrett laughed. "Turn it back. I'd rather listen to the woman."

Colton turned down the GPS's volume. They skimmed the edge of the lake and crossed the bridge on State Highway MM.

"Turn left now." The quiet instruction reinforced the blinking dot.

Garrett slowed, but Colton couldn't see on the screen where he should turn. "Hmm. Maybe this expensive gadget isn't working right."

A feminine snort reached him from the backseat. He turned and pinned Reagan with a stare. "Suggestions?"

"You might put the gadget down and look."

Garrett slowed down even more. "I don't see a turnoff."

"Up there." Reagan pointed to a break in the trees.

"You want me to take my car in there?"

"I guess we could hike."

Garrett pulled as far to the edge of the road as possible then parked. As the boys hopped out, Reagan adjusted her camera then made sure she had extra batteries in her pocket. She held the camera to her eye and pointed it out the window toward a cardinal sitting on a tree branch. Examining the screen, she smiled at the sharp image then deleted the picture.

After climbing from the car, she took a photo of Garrett and Colton as Colton adjusted his backpack. He'd filled it with enough water bottles and snacks to fuel a hungry Girl Scout troop. Colton turned as she pushed the shutter, and his grin stole her breath. He practically sparkled with excitement as he tossed her a water bottle.

"Hang on to this, and be sure to take sips as we go. Dehydration can sneak up on you."

Reagan dropped the camera on its strap as she grabbed the water bottle. "All right."

He could stop acting like she'd never ventured outdoors. Maybe she should mention she'd been a Girl Scout. Nah, she'd let her comfort with the outdoors surprise him. She might be deskbound now, but that had sneaked up after college.

Twenty minutes later, when she swiped yet another tree branch from in front of her face, she decided maybe it had sneaked a little further than she anticipated. Her breath came in short gasps, and she could hardly look around to notice any of the beauty. Keeping up with the guys and their longer legs just might do her in.

As another branch snapped back, she ducked under it then stopped. "Hey, guys."

Both turned toward her, and Colton frowned. "What?"

"You mind slowing it down a bit? Last I checked this was more a marathon than a sprint."

Garrett grinned at her. "Sorry, sis. Didn't mean to leave you in the dust."

Oh, she'd like to dust him after comments like that. Instead, she unscrewed her bottle cap and took a nice, long swallow of water. Maybe Colton hadn't been crazy to shove so much water in his backpack.

"Can we continue?" He quirked an eyebrow.

"Fine." This could be a long summer.

An hour turned into two before they finally reached a clearing with a picnic table. The car had better be waiting when they finally returned to the road because she was not hiking back to the apartment. Reagan inhaled a cleansing breath, pushing her frustrations with the two macho men in front of her out with the carbon dioxide. They'd barely stopped as they pushed toward the prize. If she'd needed any proof that men were goal oriented, she had it in spades.

"So we're here?" Garrett sounded skeptical as he studied the small clearing with its lone picnic table. "You've got to really want a table to hike here."

"Yeah." Colton clicked a button on his gizmo. "Okay, here's what the note says:

The bread of life
Cuts like a knife
No meal, but find the cache
At its base."

He frowned. "That doesn't rhyme. At all."

Reagan walked past him to the picnic table. "No, but there's your cache." She pointed at the ammunition box tucked in the darkness under the table.

After plopping it on the table, Colton opened the case and pulled out the logbook. The guys entered their names while she snapped a series of photos. Colton handed it to her. "Your turn."

"No thanks." Only a handful of people knew she'd traveled here. No way would she enter the information in a logbook anyone could find, especially one not well hidden. No reason to give her stalker a road map to where she was in case he decided to follow.

Nope, she preferred anonymity. Lots of it.

Chapter 3

Reagan had some spunk—Colton had to give her that as he watched her sit down and rub her feet. He'd avoided blisters the other day with thick socks, but she hadn't fared as well. The hitch in her steps illustrated how much her heels must cry for relief. Yet she hadn't asked to stop. Garrett plopped down next to her, disinterest on his face. He already looked bored with the hunt, something Garrett had talked Reagan and Colton into.

Had Colton pushed too hard?

Based on the entries on the website, he didn't think so. They were in the hunt, but barely. Some Hadley girl must be living and breathing the treasure hunt. The number of caches she'd entered online boggled him.

Maybe they'd have to settle for second, but he wouldn't concede in the first week. His dad always said life was a long ball game, and this hunt lasted almost two months. That gave them plenty of time for Hadley whats-her-name to flare out.

If her experience mirrored Reagan's, she'd give up soon enough.

Until then, he'd keep pushing.

Maybe not. Reagan carried her camera every day, but he

hadn't noticed her taking many pictures. Instead, the camera hung around her neck like a weight rather than a tool to capture images of the area.

She raised it and clicked in his direction.

Maybe she'd gotten more shots than he'd noticed. Might as well pose. He tilted his chin and planted his hands on his hips. Maybe he'd look like a conquering prince. Wouldn't mind if she thought of him that way. A hero. He'd never had anyone call him that.

A giggle escaped her lips as she clicked. "You ham."

"Yep, that's me." He shook free of his thoughts. That was a road he didn't need to travel. Especially with his law school roommate's sister.

She cocked her head as if trying to get inside his thoughts. "You okay?"

"Fine and dandy." He adjusted his pack. "Come on, Garrett, daylight's wasting."

His friend groaned good-naturedly. "I picked this hunt so we could have fun, not hike every last inch around the lake."

Colton turned toward the lake, picking out the brilliant blue water through the trees. "I can think of worse ways to spend our summers before sacrificing our lives to law books."

"When you put it that way..." Garrett pulled on his backpack as Reagan laughed. The sound was magical, a tinkle of fairies.

Yeah, he could get used to this.

Reagan watched Colton follow Garrett as they moved down a trail. He pushed hard to hit at least two caches a day, but it was okay. Her muscles didn't protest as much today as they had a couple of days ago, and she didn't mind feeling more toned.

She even found her thoughts straying to her stalker fewer times as the days progressed. Maybe she could shake him off permanently. She'd thought Garrett was overprotective when he decided to spirit her away from St. Louis for the summer. Now she thought he might be a genius.

Her steps felt lighter, her load less burdensome, as each day she delayed the need to look over her shoulder.

Her shadow had disappeared.

It would be hard not to soak in the peace when she spent her days out in creation. The sound of the wind whispering through the leaves soothed her as the play of the light through the branches intrigued her. The constant chatter of birds alerting others to their unwanted intrusion brought a smile to her lips. This is what she'd needed.

She couldn't wait to get home with a few hundred or thousand photos capturing the various spots they'd visited. The guys might care about the hunt, while she relished the time exploring.

"Still with us?" Garrett's teasing tone pulled Reagan's gaze to his. He pointed to the trail. "Let's get moving again. Shouldn't be far now, according to that little machine."

"Right behind you." She raised the camera, adjusted the lens, and snapped a shot of an Eastern bluebird on a limb of a flowering dogwood. She checked the viewfinder then raised the camera and snapped another one. That's better. The camera dropped, and she picked up her pace.

"Come on." Garrett motioned her forward. "I've got a coffee date this afternoon at Common Grounds."

"A date? For free coffee?" Colton shook his head with a sneer. "Not sure that qualifies. Usually, you have to lay out some coin."

"Not when I'll soon be a starving student." Garrett patted his back pocket. "I might have to snag a part-time job to last the summer."

Reagan quickened her pace until she walked behind Colton. "Don't believe him. Grandma left each of us a trust fund for school. Why do you think he's refused to join the real world like us poor slaves?" They walked in silence a minute before Reagan slanted a glance toward Colton. She knew why Garrett had decided to go back to school. The more she learned about Colton, the more she wondered what would prompt him to make a change. "Why head to school now?"

Colton glanced at her as if trying to gauge her interest. A clump of dark hair had fallen into his eye, and her fingers itched to brush it free. Her breath caught at the thought, and she stepped back.

"I guess engineering stopped being enough. I used to love the challenge of checking structures for problems, but it stopped giving me a sense of fulfillment. I want to make a difference. Law seems like a good way to do that."

"Right the wrongs of the world?"

"Something like that."

"That's a change from engineering."

"Yes. I guess it is." Colton shrugged. "It's one of those times where the decision just felt right. It'll be interesting to see what God does with this."

Reagan nodded, letting his words soak in. "Garrett's motivation isn't quite so altruistic."

Garrett hooked his hands on his backpack. "Not me. I want to make money. Corporate law all the way. I'll leave the bleeding heart cases to you, Colton."

"Sounds like you two would make good partners."

Colton studied Garrett then shook his head. "Nah. I can't imagine combining my cases with corporate law. That area sounds mind-numbing."

"Like accounting." Garrett needled her with a grin.

"You have no idea. I like being a CPA." Reagan slipped in front of the men. "There's something amazing about getting numbers to cooperate and tell a cohesive story."

Colton quirked an eyebrow. "I'll leave that to you."

A couple of hours later, they returned to the condos with two more caches added to the list. "Meet you out front in an hour to head to Common Grounds?" Colton asked as he left the others at their door.

"I'd rather head to the outlet mall." Reagan batted her eyes then froze as if she caught herself. "Since Garrett's abandoning me for his 'date,'"—she put quotes around the word with her fingers—"I need someone else to go with me."

She said the words with a light touch, but he could hear her uncertainty. Maybe she wasn't as over the stalking as she appeared. No other reason she'd insist on company to go shop.

Could he do it? It didn't sound relaxing at all. Not when he'd rather collapse in front of his television for a few hours. Is this what women did in their spare time? His mother didn't like shopping much or had learned quickly she was better off without dragging her boys along.

Reagan's eyes clouded, the light disappearing.

"Sure. I'd be glad to take you." How bad could it be?

Two hours later, all he wanted to do was wring Garrett's neck. He should be the one walking beside Reagan as she entered every store they passed. She even spent time in a store that sold only sunglasses. Seriously! A store filled with hundreds of pairs of glasses, and she felt the need to try on at least half.

He stifled a groan when she entered a children's clothing store. "Looking for anything in particular?"

Quiet longing filled her eyes as she touched an impossibly tiny outfit. "I never know when another friend is going to get pregnant." She sighed as she picked up a pink frilly thing. "Isn't this adorable?"

"I guess."

"You guess? This would make some little girl look like a princess. And this." She tugged out a blue-and-white outfit decorated with baseballs. "This is perfect for a little baseball player in training." She brushed a piece of lint from the sleeve.

"If you say so."

"Guess your mom does all your gift shopping."

"Guys aren't expected to buy baby gifts." He shifted his feet as he wondered how much longer he'd have to wait.

She rolled her eyes and replaced the outfit. "Fine. We can leave."

"Wait." If it was that important to her, he could endure a bit more. "How about I wait for you in the Nike store?"

"Never mind." She sagged as she pushed the door open. The humid air hit him like a blanket as he hurried to follow her.

Once outside, he touched her shoulder, and she stopped. "Reagan, help me out. Remember, I don't have sisters. What just happened? I want to understand."

A soft smile touched her lips as she looked up at him. "Shopping isn't fun alone."

He'd do anything to make her smile genuine. "I'll go back in with you."

Her cheeks flushed as if she was embarrassed that she needed anyone with her. "No way. You don't want to look, so we won't. We can hit the Nike store. I shouldn't have expected you to ooh and ah over baby clothes. Garrett wouldn't have even gone in."

Colton nodded. The Nike store would work. It'd qualify as shopping with a purpose since he needed a couple more T-shirts. As they walked, her shoulder brushed his arm, and a shock of electricity zinged from that spot. He paused and stared at her.

She slowed to a stop and looked at him with a quizzical expression. "What?"

"Nothing." Nothing other than the fact that the last thing he needed right now was to be interested in a woman. No matter how gorgeous or perfect she seemed. No, he couldn't do that. Not with something as all-consuming as law school starting in a matter of weeks.

He squared his shoulders and urged his brain to forget the rush of attraction.

Too bad it refused.

Chapter 4

A couple of mornings later, Colton left his efficiency early. The morning air was damp and cool as he crossed to Garrett and Reagan's condo. He stilled when he approached.

Reagan sat in a rocking chair on the porch. She wore a pair of capris and a T-shirt, her hair pulled back in its customary ponytail. What would it look like if she ever wore it down? He itched to tug it free and find out.

She must have heard his approach, because she looked up with a smile. "Good morning."

"Hey." Hey? That was the great opener he came up with? He resisted slapping his forehead. He glanced at the stack of pictures in her lap. "What are those?"

"Just a few photos."

"Yours?"

She nodded, a soft look falling on her features.

"May I see?"

"Sure." She straightened the pile and handed them over.

Colton flipped through them slowly. Some shots showed Garrett and him in various stages of the hunt. His intense look in a few surprised him. Maybe he'd taken this whole game thing more seriously than he intended. He'd have to do something about that. Relax a bit.

Reagan cleared her throat. "Well. . . ?"

"You've got quite an eye."

"What does that mean?"

"I'm impressed." He tapped a photo of a bird clinging to a branch, beak open in midsong. "I can almost hear this guy."

"Actually that's a female."

"Wow. How do you know that?"

She blushed and looked away. "I picked up a bird book. Wanted to make sure I knew what I was photographing. Hard to scrapbook it when all you can say is 'here's another bird.'" Her voice rose in a funny way as she said the last words.

He laughed and handed the photos back. "I'm glad you're taking these. They really capture what it's like out here."

"A far cry from the city."

"You could say that." The thought of heading to the Washington U campus didn't exactly excite him anymore. He'd gotten spoiled by a couple of weeks spending time outdoors every day. "You going to the Fourth of July shindig?"

"Shindig? Seems like a little more than that." Reagan counted off on her fingers. "The Elden Family Day events are on the third. Followed by six sets of fireworks on the Fourth. I have a feeling I won't want to see or hear fireworks for at least a year after that." She studied him.

Yeah, he'd kept his distance the last couple of days. If he didn't make plans with her, would she slip out on her own? He didn't think so but decided to be certain. "Garrett taking you?"

"No." She looked past him as if worried. "He has plans but won't tell me what they are." She shrugged. "Guess I'll stay home."

"On the Fourth?" That seemed wrong. It would be terrible to sit alone listening to the good times. One night wouldn't matter. He could spend it with her. . .and remind himself every five minutes they couldn't be more than friends. Surely that would work. "Let's go. Maybe we can find a spot on the beach to watch the fireworks."

Her eyes brightened, and she sat up. "I could pack a picnic."

"Okay." More than he'd intended, but at least he could protect her.

"It's a date."

A date? Did she really just say that? Reagan stared at Colton as he strolled back to his condo. She didn't mean it the way it sounded. But he'd turned and left before she could clarify. A date clearly indicated a romantic overtone.

She couldn't let that happen. No, not until she could rest, knowing the stalker was behind her. Otherwise, it would be too easy to spend her dates wondering if anyone was watching and what the ramifications might be.

With his first year of law school set to start in weeks, Colton had other things on his mind anyway. And with the stress of school, he didn't need a girlfriend who had to worry about the shadows. Sure, things seemed calm, but she wasn't in St. Louis. She couldn't help wondering if she'd truly shaken her stalker or if he'd gone dormant until she returned. A ripple of fear coursed through her.

She picked up the photos and shuffled through them. A couple she'd snapped from the parking lot in front of the condos. Her temporary home was the kind of place she wouldn't mind coming back to in the future. It was small but comfortable. As she studied one of the pictures, something caught her attention. She squinted and pulled the picture closer. Could she blow it up? Not without her laptop. . .but maybe a photo store could.

She squinted harder. Had something been scribbled on her back window?

She couldn't quite make it out. Yet she was certain she'd never noticed a message. She shook the thought free then tucked the photo back in the pile.

The events of the spring had her on edge. Imagining something where there wasn't anything.

She was safe in Osage Beach.

Her stalker wouldn't follow her. Why would he? It was such a small place that even with all the visitors and extra bodies for the Rainbow's End hunt, she would still notice if someone lurked in the background.

She had to believe it, or she'd go crazy wondering. Besides, she had two men watching over her.

Everything would be fine if she didn't let her imagination run wild. This is why she preferred orderly rows of numbers. Numbers were objective. There was nothing to dispute about how they added up. Two plus three was always five. No ifs, ands, or buts.

Why couldn't life mirror an accounting program? Orderly, easy to interpret. No matter how complex, she could bring numbers into submission.

She bowed her head. When her heart got this stirred up, there was only one thing she could do. Pray for God's peace to overwhelm her. After a moment, she felt her nerves ease.

The door banged open next to her, and she didn't even jump. "Good morning, Garrett."

He stretched into a big X then turned and grinned. "It's

going to be a great day. One hunt and then a break."

"You'd better double-check with your buddy on that." Reagan shook her head. "I think he's determined to win this thing."

"Nah. He likes to put on the show that he wants to win. It's all good fun."

"If you say so."

"I do. We'll take the next two days off to enjoy the festivities. Got to celebrate the birthday." He made it sound like a required event. She couldn't resist smiling at his enthusiasm. "Ready in fifteen?"

"Sure, Garrett." She slipped into the condo and walked to the kitchen. The scent of french vanilla coffee filled the small space. She inhaled deeply then grabbed a mug. After lacing it with some sweetener and cream, she headed back to her room. He didn't really mean fifteen minutes.

Colton entered the last few caches in the online database. He'd given up waiting for Reagan to get ready and told Garrett they could find him in his condo when they were finally ready to leave.

He studied the rankings. No matter how many caches he pushed Garrett and Reagan to hit in a day, someone else stayed in front of them. Who led the pack changed from day to day, but these people must be highly motivated. Maybe Garrett was right. Colton should quit pushing so hard and enjoy the summer. Hit a cache every once in a while, but let it be enjoyable.

Nah, that wasn't him.

He couldn't participate without at least trying to win. Anything less wasn't in his makeup. Garrett might as well learn that now—he planned to be a grueling study partner once classes started. Colton's goal was to hit honors from the first semester if there was anything he could do to make it happen.

Garrett didn't give off the same intense vibe.

It'd be Colton's luck that Garrett was one who could read something once and know it for life. Skate by on a great memory. That would be just perfect.

A knock on his front door made him turn from the laptop. "Come in."

Reagan slipped through the door. "Hey. Garrett wants to know if you're ready."

"Garrett?" His frustration at the delay smoldered below the surface. He hoped she couldn't see it.

"I know. He's decided to start pushing. . .no idea why." Her gaze moved around the condo. It didn't reflect who he was, but how could it when none of the furniture was his? Wasn't worth the effort to move anything big here with only a few weeks before they'd head back to St. Louis. "Nice place."

"Yeah. Identical to yours."

"Just smaller. Must have the same designer." The smirk looked good on her.

"Know where you want to go today?"

"Wherever you guys go. I figure I'm still the tagalong."

Something about the way she said it had him turning his laptop toward her, earlier annoyance gone. Maybe she thought the guys weren't letting her participate in the game enough. If she didn't carry the camera everywhere, it might help, but still, he could include her more often in some of the decisions. He clicked a couple of buttons then motioned for her to take a seat. "Here's the list. The caches with green check marks are the ones we've already found. If you click this button, you can see the sites superimposed on a map. Any appeal to you?"

She set her chin in her palm, fingers curled by her lips, and studied the screen. "How about that one?" She pointed at one that looked like it was nearby in town.

"Why that one?"

"It's close. And if I were going to hide the bonus token, I'd keep it close."

"Ah, the token." He grinned. Maybe she was in this to win, too.

Her eyes sparkled as she smiled back. "I also think we should check the one at the outlet mall. How many people would search for that one?"

"All the women?"

"Sure. And how many of them will be able to drag men along with them?"

"Not very many."

"Exactly. So it's a nice way to get you a bonus log in."

"I like the way you think."

"Just methodical." She shrugged. "That's how accountants are wired. I'll tell Garrett you'll be ready in a few." She slipped out the door, and Colton watched her go. There was something about her that was like watching a dance in progress. One that captivated his attention and made him want more.

He had to shake free of that. In less than two months, law school and his studies would consume his life. He hadn't worked hard to save for his tuition just so he could be distracted by a relationship. He wasn't even sure he'd have time for friends. He definitely needed to rein in his thoughts.

Reagan could be a good friend. One he'd stay in touch with via e-mail and Facebook. But that was it. His life didn't have room for more. Not now.

Chapter 5

I'm headed to the mall," Reagan yelled toward the bathroom as she grabbed Garrett's keys off the kitchen island. She wanted to slip out before he could get out of the shower.

It might be insane, but she needed a few minutes. Leaving when he couldn't stop her seemed the best way to accomplish that. Otherwise, he'd have an argument for why it still wasn't safe. She'd grown weary of that disagreement as the days passed without the hint of fright. But she also knew her chances of beating him in a squabble were nonexistent. The kid had practiced his linguistic skills on her since he was six. He'd parry circles around her while she tried to craft her first thrust.

And she didn't want to ask Colton to come along, not after making him miserable last time. Nothing would happen.

She unlocked the car and drove the couple of miles to the outlet mall. She didn't need anything but freedom. Wonder which store sold that? She slipped the car into a vacant spot and pulled her purse strap over her shoulder.

Soon she stood in front of the directory. The board listed dozens of options, but nothing appealed. Walking and ducking into the occasional store would work. As she stepped into a funky clothing store, she felt herself relax. Without the boys around to remind her of the haunting spring, it was easy to breathe like no one watched or cared.

Time slipped away, and she acquired a few bags as she walked down sidewalks.

This trip felt different. Lonely.

Who would have thought having a reluctant guy along would make the excursion more fun?

Colton had let her know he thought the stores ridiculous, but she'd enjoyed tweaking his nose as she prolonged her trips in the stores that annoyed him most. He was too fun to play with.

His intensity had disappeared for a bit. And she'd enjoyed getting to know the man left behind. She entered Eddie Bauer, her eye drawn to a bucket hat that looked perfect for Colton. His neck had gotten scorched a time or two. The brim would protect it on future hikes. If he'd wear it. . .

She grinned at the thought of him wearing the hat. Chances were he'd think it ridiculous, but still, the sunburn had to hurt.

"I'll take this." She handed the hat to the clerk then added a festive scarf to her purchase and a few minutes later exited the store.

A cloud crossed in front of the sun, and Reagan shivered in the sudden chill. The hair on her neck tingled, and she glanced behind her. Nothing seemed out of the ordinary. Just other tourists and shoppers on the hunt for steals and deals.

Still, her pace picked up as she moved to the next store.

"Reagan." She skidded to a stop, frantically looking for a place to hide. Nobody knew her here. Nobody.

She hurried down a hallway that led to restrooms.

"Reagan." The male voice was louder, but the competing noise of a group of women passing kept the tone garbled. Her pace increased until she opened the door to the ladies' room and hoped whoever it was wouldn't follow. Then again, when had a bathroom sign stopped someone intent on causing harm?

She dragged in a shallow breath. Her heart pounded, and she could hardly stand under the sudden pressure.

Think. She had to think. How could a relaxing afternoon evaporate in an instant? One word. That's how. Her name on the lips of somebody who couldn't know her. No one should know her here. She'd worked so hard to stay in the shadows. Making sure no one really noticed her even though she was there.

She'd started to believe she was safe and now this.

The door to the ladies' room banged open. She screamed as she backed her way to the corner.

"Are you okay, dear?" An elderly lady with a visor resting atop her white curls eyed her.

"Was anyone out there when you came inside?" Reagan's voice trembled as she squeezed the words past the tightness in her throat.

"Only a young man." The woman squinted and stepped closer. "He could be your brother."

Reagan exhaled in a whoosh. Garrett. She should have considered he'd come after her. "Thank you."

She pushed out the door and straight into Colton. He steadied her and grimaced.

"What are you doing here?" She punctuated the question by stabbing his chest with her pointer finger. "You scared me to death. Ruined my perfectly nice time. And where is Garrett?"

Colton held up his hands and pushed her back a step, getting out of poking range. "Hey, hold up. You left the apartment in such a rush, you scared him."

"I. Scared. Him?" She was going to kill that meddling

brother of hers before he could do something like this again. There he was, the coward, leaning against a vending machine. Was he munching a candy bar? She grabbed the half-eaten bar from his hand, took a bite, and chewed. "I didn't think the three musketeers intentionally scared each other."

"Keep that in mind next time you take off like that." Garrett's eyes hardened.

"An hour. I just wanted time to myself."

"Check your watch."

"What?"

"Check your watch." Garrett stabbed at her wrist. "More than an hour disappeared while I tried to reach you on your phone. Make sure you were okay. All I knew is you were headed here. What if something happened?"

"All that happened is you scared me to death." She dug through her purse. Not there. She must have left her phone in the car. "My phone's in the car. No one ever calls me anyway." She shoved one of her bags at Colton. "Here. I got this for you." She let go, spun on her heel, and left the guys standing there.

Colton had kept his mouth shut even as he wanted to insert himself into the sibling spat. As Reagan thrust the sack at him, he caught it, stunned to watch her spin and take off. "Is she usually this independent?"

He liked that about her. Really, he did. It just made it hard to keep an eye on her, though the longer they were here, the less necessary that seemed.

"She was until everything started this spring. It made her an easy target. She doesn't need anyone. Mom always said she was that way as a toddler, too."

The image of a short-legged, pig-tailed, absolutely adorable three-year-old Reagan made Colton grin. He could only imagine what her daughter would look like some day. Adorable as her mom.

Garrett rubbed his eyes. "Guess we'd better follow."

"You go back. I'll make it up to her. She was terrified when she came out."

"Good." Garrett locked his fists on his hips. "I'd rather have her terrified and angry than hurt."

"Want my car?"

"Nope. I need to walk this off." Garrett struck off toward the entrance before Colton could stop him.

Make that two stubborn siblings. Both adamant he or she was right and the other wrong.

Colton sighed and took off after the prettier sibling.

When mad, the woman marched with conviction. He would have laughed if it hadn't bothered him that he was one of the people who'd ticked her off. He'd have to do something to make things better again. The scent of fresh pretzels reached him. Who didn't like an Auntie Anne's special?

It didn't seem like the most effective way to apologize, but it sure couldn't hurt anything.

He picked up his pace until he walked next to her. "Can I buy you a pretzel?"

"Did somebody tell you that's an effective pickup line? They lied."

"Come on." He touched her arm, and she stilled. "I really am sorry. I don't see a five-star restaurant, but I can get you a warm treat."

"Add a slushie?"

"Sure." A minute later, they sat on a park bench, shoulder

to shoulder. In minutes, her tongue would turn cherry red thanks to her slurps on the slushie, while he sipped a flavored lemonade.

The price tag reminded him why he didn't date. Way too expensive for a law student. Better to keep that part of his life free and clear, though he had to admit he liked the connection developing between them. "I really am sorry we scared you."

"Scared me? Try petrified." Reagan's slim shoulders shivered. "I'll thank you not to do that again."

"Then don't run off without us."

"A girl needs some alone time. At least I picked a public place."

"True." He tore a piece from the large salty pretzel. "Still, bad things happen in public."

"I just want the danger to disappear. Go back to living my life the way I did before." She studied him. "It's been so quiet here. Why can't I go to the mall by myself?"

"I don't know. I guess Garrett wants to be certain." She seemed to accept his answer, but her shoulders didn't relax. Maybe she sensed he couldn't really promise she was safe. "Hey…" He tipped her chin up, until her clear blue eyes stared into his. A strand of her loose blond hair brushed his hand. Focus, Colton. "Um, I'm sorry we ruined your day."

She swallowed hard, and his thoughts locked up. She looked so soft and vulnerable, her recent worry clear in her posture and the way she leaned into his touch. Did she have any idea how much he wanted to protect her when she did that? Going shopping with his new friend had transformed into a deep need to make sure she lost her bewildered expression. He wanted her to adopt the freedom that comes from walking without fright.

"Anything else you want to look for?"

She glanced down at his bag. "Not until I know if you like your present."

"Hmmm." He pulled the bag onto his lap. It was so light there couldn't be much in it. A pair of socks maybe? Some type of gag gift? He pulled out a khaki blob of fabric.

Reagan started laughing, the sound melodious and perfect. "Don't you see?"

"See what? Fabric?"

She snatched it from his hand, adjusted it, then plopped it on his head. "No, silly. A hat. To keep you from frying."

"A hat." He could hardly contain his enthusiasm.

"Yep. Can't have you walking around with a perpetually red neck. Consider the skin problems this will prevent." She tweaked the brim. "Looks like I imagined."

The words sounded innocent, but the look in her eyes was pure delighted mirth.

But if she'd keep laughing like that, he'd wear the ridiculous hat. And as he swept it off for a closer look, he decided it wasn't too bad. At least not for a sixty-year-old fisherman.

"Try it on again." She snorted. "It's the perfect touch."

"Sure it is." He grinned then leaned closer to her as he smashed it on his head. "I'll wear it for you. . .but next time get something a little more debonair."

"Debonair." She breathed the word then snorted again. "I didn't think you'd know a word like that."

"Minx." He tugged her close with one arm, in a lopsided hug that felt so natural and right.

Chapter 6

The morning of the fourth dawned clear. . .and hot. When he pulled up the data on his phone, Colton saw it had already climbed to ninety degrees.

One hunt. That's all they'd do this morning. They'd already found the easy, close caches. This hunt would take them farther away from the condos and Osage Beach. The good news was that new possibilities showed up on the Rainbow's End website each week. Maybe the organizers would add some closer spots soon.

When he hit law school next month, his body would go into shock with the sudden inactivity. Campus wouldn't compare to the months spent at Lake of the Ozarks. No way to fairly measure the two against each other.

He laced his hiking boots and headed to the Grahams' door. He stood, hand raised to knock, when the door opened.

Reagan took his breath away. Today she'd added a patriotic flair to her hiking ensemble with a red, white, and blue scarf holding her hair back. Her smile reached her eyes as she took in his ridiculous hat. Guess it was official. He'd do anything for her.

"Garrett said to go without him."

"Not up to the hunt?"

She snickered. "Out too late last night with the festivities. He's always loved fireworks, so I can't be too surprised that he stayed out for all of them."

"Those ended at ten thirty."

"I know. Guess he found someone to spend time with after that." She shrugged. "I know he thinks I pay too much attention to his life, but that's what sisters are for. Anyway, he's a big boy. If he wants to miss the hunt, that's his choice."

"Ready?"

She dangled the keys in one hand and a backpack with water bottles tucked in outside pockets in the other. "Yep. Let's get going."

She handed him the keys, and he followed the mechanical instructions from the GPS as they wound along the lake to the latest destination. An hour later, they worked their way around a small clearing.

"We're on top of the cache."

Reagan plopped her hands on her hips and glared at him as she puffed a strand of hair out of her face. "If I had a dime for every time you were certain the GPS had us right next to the cache. . ."

Colton glared at the device and clicked a button. Then he thrust it at her. "See? Right here."

"It's wrong." She sighed then reached for it. "Maybe there aren't as many satellites here. Let me read the clue. Maybe it'll make sense this time." He handed it over and watched as she read.

"Bird on the stand.
Bird in the bush.
You'll want a hand

To beat the rush."

She groaned and handed it back to him. "What rubbish. Whoever wrote these is not a poet."

"It has the right number of syllables and rhymes."

"But it doesn't make sense!"

"Poetry makes sense?"

"Well-written poems do." She turned slowly around, repeating the clue as her gaze traveled to the trees.

"It refers to bushes," he said.

"Only because that rhymes with 'rush.'" She pointed toward a pine. "Do you see something in those branches? Two-thirds of the way up?"

Colton stood next to her and followed her finger. "Maybe." But how to get up there? Whoever climbed up there would break an ankle if he fell. "Maybe this is one we'll leave behind."

"Nope. We're here. We are definitely getting the credit." Reagan tugged on a couple of branches then climbed the tree.

All he could see were branches swaying as she scooted up. A minute later she shimmied down with another artillery box tucked under her arm.

After they signed in, she tucked the box inside a bush. "Now the next group won't have to risk the climb to find it."

"I think it's supposed to go back in place."

"But now it matches the clue." She thrust her chin out, and he held his hands up. Maybe he could return and put it back in the tree later. It would be easy to get here now. She must have read his intent. "Fine." She grabbed the box and a few minutes later had it tucked back in the pine. When she climbed down, he pulled a few needles from her hair. She stilled then looked away. "My spot was better."

He plucked another pine needle, enjoying the feel of her

silky hair. "Let's go back and get ready for the fireworks."

Reagan took a step back before he could find anything else in her hair. Didn't he feel the fireworks when they were together?

Maybe it was because of the holiday, but she had a strong suspicion the sensation would remain after Independence Day disappeared for another year.

They'd watched the fireworks from the park last night. Would tonight be any different? If it were just the two of them, it would. In ways that scared and excited her. "Okay."

Her answer must not have met his expectations, because he frowned at her.

"What?" she asked.

"I won't force you to come."

She forced a smile past her nerves. "I'm looking forward to tonight, Colton. Truly."

He frowned then nodded. "All right then."

The walk back to the car passed in silence, a silence that was mirrored on the drive. By the time she walked into the condo, all Reagan wanted was a bottle of aspirin, a nap, and to forget she'd agreed to spend the evening with Mr. Silent. Instead, she spent the time giving her toes a pedicure so they wouldn't scare anyone who spied them through her sandals. No hiking boots tonight.

Throughout the afternoon, she didn't see Garrett. Wherever he'd disappeared, he hadn't bothered to leave a note. She'd bet anything a young lady associated with the hunt had captured his attention.

Maybe he was ready to consider a future match. Nah, this was her baby brother.

She left a note on the island for Garrett and sat in the rocking chair on the porch, waiting for Colton to collect her. She bit back a whistle as he approached. He wore khakis and a navy polo. Boat shoes completed the relaxed yet sharp summer image. He looked like he'd stepped off the cover of a Ralph Lauren flier, a good look for him. His skin had the healthy glow of someone who'd spent the summer outside but avoided the overdone red hue it had carried earlier. The hat had been a great idea.

"What's got you grinning?"

"You're missing one thing."

"A beautiful woman on my arm?" He raised a rakish brow.

Color flooded her cheeks, color she hoped her tan concealed. "No. The hat."

He rolled his eyes. "I like my answer better."

She stood, and he offered his arm as he escorted her to his compact car. A wonderful aroma filled the vehicle's interior. "What do you have in here?"

"Supper. A little birdie told me you like fried chicken."

"That must have been Garrett."

"Yep."

"Too bad he's not observant enough to notice I really don't enjoy chicken." Reagan felt a teeny bit bad as Colton squirmed. "But if there's a breast in there, I'll take it."

"I think there are a couple."

"Perfect. Where are we eating this feast?"

"The lake shore. Figure we'll find a spot to enjoy ourselves until the show."

There was an odd glint in his eyes as he glanced her way.

"Okay. Did you send Garrett to hold it for us? That would explain why he disappeared."

"Didn't think of that." As they neared the lake, she wondered if they'd get within a mile of the beach. Then Colton turned toward the pier. She bit her lip to keep from asking what he was up to. She'd already ruined one of his surprises. If it killed her, she'd keep her mouth shut on any more.

They found a small open square, big enough for the picnic blanket Colton had brought, and soon he had the basket unpacked. He handed her a plate loaded with a perfectly fried chicken breast, potato salad, a biscuit, and warm berry cobbler. She almost asked if she could bypass the rest and eat the cobbler. Instead, she picked at the chicken until she took a bite and decided it was delicious.

After the cobbler, Colton surprised her by packing everything up.

"Aren't we staying here?"

"Nope. I've got a better vantage point for the fireworks."

Reagan glanced around. Sure, they could be closer to the beach, but it wasn't a bad location. And the area between them and the water overflowed with other people parked to watch the fireworks.

"Let me take the basket and blanket back to the car." He laid a jacket on the ground where the blanket had been a minute before. "You wait here, and I'll be right back."

She nodded and sank on the jacket.

After awhile he returned with a big grin. "Follow me, mademoiselle."

"Yes sir."

He walked her toward the Grand Glaize Bridge and to a pier. "Colton?"

"I decided the best place to watch the fireworks was the lake. So I got us tickets on the *Queen of the Ozarks*, that yacht down there." He pointed at the yacht with such pride, she almost believed he owned the vessel.

"I've never done anything like this before."

"Even in St. Louis?"

She shook her head. The romance of the moment as they walked onto the boat almost swept her breath away. If she didn't know better, she'd let herself believe Colton Ryan, the man who fascinated her, wanted to woo her. But he'd been honest from the beginning that he didn't have time for a relationship, not with the new direction his life would take in August.

Until that moment, she'd been content with friendship.

Goodness, she hadn't wanted to trust anyone but Garrett when they'd left St. Louis. Somehow in the intervening weeks, Colton had slid beneath her protective barriers. She needed to rebuild them quickly. Before he stole her heart with no intention of keeping it. If he kept planning amazing nights like this, she might not be able to keep her mind from agreeing with her heart that Colton Ryan was her Prince Charming.

Chapter 7

The engines of the yacht powered the boat away from the pier.

People crowded the boat, each eager to watch the fireworks from the unique perspective of the lake. Reagan tried to find the same excitement. Instead, her stomach churned, whether from too much chicken or the thought of spending several hours on the boat with this man, she wasn't sure.

She wanted to relax and enjoy the moment. Garrett must not have told Colton what happened the one and only time she'd been on a boat ride. The thought of how sick she'd been made her shudder.

It would be okay this time.

It had to be, since she refused to leave that kind of impression with Colton.

Maybe if she didn't watch the water rush by. Or if she had a glass of ginger ale in her hand. Something had to distract her enough to keep her stomach in its place.

"You okay?" Concern laced Colton's words.

"Absolutely." She glanced toward the cabin. "Looks like there's food in there."

"Why not wait? We just ate, after all."

She bit her lower lip and pressed a hand into her stomach. "A glass of Sprite would be wonderful."

Understanding crossed his face. "Gee, I'm sorry, Reagan. I never thought to ask if you handled boats well. I bet the staff has Dramamine. Let me get some for you and some Sprite. I'll be right back."

Reagan nodded and sank onto a bench. The soft spray coated her face, and she focused on how good the water felt. Water wasn't all bad since it could cool her feverish skin.

She lost track of time as she watched the others and waited for Colton. A country band played in a corner of the *Queen*. The affected twang of the songs made her smile. Then the group launched into a string of patriotic songs that made her want to stand up with her hand over her heart.

"Here you go." Colton handed her two small pills and a glass filled with sparkling soda as he sat down next to her.

"Thanks." She swallowed the pills gratefully. "How long does it take for these to kick in?"

"I've never needed them."

"I'll try not to hate you for that."

He shrugged. "Not much I can do about my iron stomach." He thumped the offending organ then turned serious. "Sure you'll be okay?"

She nodded. "Absolutely. I've got my friends the sparkling bubbles here. Combined with the wonder drug, I'll be in great shape."

"Then how about we take a quick stroll around the boat, see what we can spy from here?"

"I don't think there's a cache onboard," she said.

"There isn't."

She cocked an eyebrow, and he grinned mischievously. "I checked."

"Why doesn't that surprise me, Mr. Competitive?"

"Hey, you say that like it's a bad thing." He offered her his hand and helped her to her feet. She focused on him as he led her around the boat.

"Tell me this. . .would you turn in the bonus chip if you collected it?"

He opened his mouth then closed it.

"Exactly." She grinned at him. "You're in to win."

"Nothing wrong with that."

"Right. Don't forget to enjoy your vacation, too."

She leaned against the railing. Wow, this drug was effective. Her stomach didn't dare rebel with Dramamine winging through her. Then it flipped as Colton eased toward her.

"Oh, I'm enjoying myself."

She waited to see if he'd distance himself, retract the words, give any indication he didn't mean them. That they'd been uttered as a mistake. Instead, he leaned closer, almost as if he wanted to seal them with a kiss.

Someone bumped against Colton, knocking him into Reagan. His lips brushed her cheek, and he pulled back with a frown.

He growled and looked around. It was impossible to tell who had hit him. He turned back to Reagan. "That's not quite what I had in mind."

As he stroked her cheek, Reagan leaned into the touch. At the moment, the rest of the world disappeared, even whoever'd bumped Colton. They were the only two on the boat, the placid water of the Lake of the Ozarks like glass beneath them. She should pull back, put distance between them, but all she wanted was to sink into the moment, wrap it around her like a blanket.

"Look!" The excited squeal broke the moment.

Reagan didn't know whether to cry or thank the tween who pointed at the sky where the first fireworks broke through. It hadn't completed its transformation to black velvet, yet the pinpricks of swirling light in red and cream drew oohhs and aahhs from those on the boat.

Colton drew her against him. As he wrapped his arms around her, she relaxed for a moment. It wouldn't hurt to enjoy knowing someone cared for a few minutes. He tensed, and Reagan pulled away. She turned to see his face.

"What?" A shiver of fear crept up her spine, destroying the relaxation she'd just felt.

"That guy over there." He nudged his chin to the left. "He's been staring at you for a while." Colton focused on the mystery man, jaw tight, gaze focused.

Maybe he should keep his mouth shut. Why ruin the evening? One that had gone so well, better than he'd hoped when they started out. Yet, if his instinct was right, he needed to make sure she was aware. He took a breath. "Don't you think it's strange, he's focused on you when everyone else is watching the fireworks?"

The color leeched from Reagan's tanned face, and lines tightened around her eyes. He hated causing her distress. She swallowed hard then turned toward the cabin. "I need to get away." She stumbled toward the doors.

Colton waited a moment, tempted to confront the man. But if he did that would the man disappear before Colton could know his intentions? Would the man follow Reagan? Colton kept his gaze slightly off him as he memorized what the man looked like. Average height and build with sandy, mussed hair, a little long. He had the pale complexion tinged with pink of someone who worked inside and wasn't used to time outside. He wore khaki cargo shorts and a T-shirt, with battered high-tops.

Could this be Reagan's stalker?

If so, how had the man found them?

Reagan hadn't told anyone where she planned to spend the summer. He was almost certain. That would defeat the purpose of disappearing.

When Reagan didn't return and the man took a step in her direction, Colton hurried inside.

A blast of cold air smacked him as he entered the cabin. Reagan huddled in a corner, arms wrapped tightly around her middle. "You okay?"

"Trying to tell myself he's a random guy." She gulped.

"How's that working?"

"Not well." Reagan turned from him, her profile reflected in the window against a dark sky punctuated with fireworks. "He couldn't have followed me, could he?"

Colton shrugged, wishing he could tell her something different. "I don't know. Don't the police have a suspect in custody?"

"I thought so. Guess I'll call the detective tomorrow. The problem is I never got a good look at the man outside my apartment, so I don't know if that's him out there. What now?"

"Enjoy the fireworks. If it's the guy, he won't try anything here. We'll slip away once we're on shore. Hopefully, he doesn't know my car, so we should be okay."

"But how did he find me here?" Reagan's voice tremored. "He had to follow us from somewhere, and the most logical place is the condo. There's no way he just happened to luck out."

She rubbed her forehead, a strained look staining her features.

Colton tugged her to him. He couldn't discount her words, but they couldn't stay on the boat forever either. If only he could ditch the guy. Didn't want to give the man a calling card for his car on the off chance he hadn't followed them from the condo. He had to keep the creep from knowing where Reagan lived. At least until they could figure out if their imaginations had run crazy. "We'll leave with the rush, try to get to the front of the crowd. Then we'll drive around awhile. Maybe get you some custard." The words sounded empty, but he didn't know what else to do.

"If this is the man who stalked me in St. Louis, time won't keep him away. He'll keep returning." Reagan stayed stiff in his arms, as if her mind ran to her fears. What could he do to assure her she was safe? And could he promise that?

Several months ago her nemesis had slashed her tires and sent dead roses to her at home and work. It was the note accompanying the roses that had caused Garrett to threaten yanking her out of town. *Pretty flowers for a pretty lady who belongs to me.*

Not a threat, but definitely disturbing. Still she'd resisted Garrett's pleas.

Garrett said Reagan hadn't seemed really frightened until her cat died. Poisoned, according to the vet. Then she'd packed a bag and shown up on her brother's doorstep.

What if that maniac had found her here? Colton didn't want to imagine what Garrett would say. All he knew was that at this moment his condo seemed too far away. She shivered, as if reading his thoughts, and he tightened his hold. A silent promise that he wouldn't let anything happen to her. He couldn't.

Goose bumps erupted on her arms. He rubbed his hands

along her skin, trying to warm her. She shuddered.

"Will I be okay?"

"Absolutely. We don't know it's him, but we'll play it safe. And you've got two brawny guys here to take care of you and 911 a call away. What could go wrong?"

She tipped up her chin and tried to smile, a weak shadow of its normal glory.

"I promise I won't let anything happen. Trust me."

Because he'd never forgive himself if anything happened to the woman in his arms.

Chapter 8

The next morning, Reagan lay in bed wondering where the truck had gone that hit her. After a night spent tossing and turning, she might as well have stayed up. Her thoughts were muddied and slow. Images of bright lights exploding against a midnight sky had disappeared in terror, haunted by masked faces.

They'd slipped off the boat as soon as it tied on to the pier, getting ahead of the crowd. As Colton led her at a fast clip to his car, she'd felt safe with her hand tucked in his. She'd longed to forget about the man behind them and focus on the man with her. To slip back into the easy camaraderie they'd shared. Then reality had hit, as Colton slammed the car into reverse and drove around the lake for an hour before heading home. The problem was they didn't know the vehicle of the person on the boat, so she couldn't tell if he waited at the condo. So he haunted her dreams all night, turning them into nightmares.

She pulled the comforter under her chin and curled into a ball.

The morning light couldn't quite penetrate the blinds, leaving odd shadows in the corners of her room. She needed to get up.

Yet she pressed into the mattress.

Safe. She felt safe here in her room with the door closed and the blinds drawn. Her camera and lenses sat on the dresser, reminding her she should get ready for today's hunt. She'd left St. Louis to abandon the feeling someone watched her every move. Would she let her hard-found freedom evaporate in a moment because someone had looked at her?

She wanted to laugh at the idea, but her lungs locked up. She snuggled lower into her pillow.

Bam bam bam.

"Go away, Garrett."

"It's Colton." *Bam bam bam.* "Come on, Reagan. I'm not letting you hide in your room."

What right did he have to disturb her? And why wasn't he in his condo? Her skin remembered his touch. Still, banging on her door wasn't the right way to woo her. "Go away."

"Nope. You have a call to make, and then we have more caches to find."

Colton and his drive to win. "Have you shot up in the standings?"

"It's not over until it's over." Silence settled for a moment. "I'm giving you one minute to give me audible sounds of movement, or I'm sending Garrett in there."

"You wouldn't!"

"Wanna try me?"

Reagan gasped then thrust aside the covers and launched from the bed. She opened and slammed a drawer on the dresser. "I'm up, I'm up."

"You've got ten minutes to join us for omelets in the kitchen."

Reagan glared at the door. How dare he? She didn't like

anyone telling her what to do, even after a night like last night. Still, she didn't dare push him. He seemed pretty intent on getting her moving. She grabbed a pair of shorts and a clean T-shirt and headed into the bathroom.

Eleven minutes later she walked into the kitchen, damp hair pulled back in a ponytail, baseball cap slammed on her head.

"Morning, princess." Garrett's eyes hid in shadows as he watched her. "How you feeling?"

"Hunky-dory. Every girl loves being pounded out of bed." She glared at Colton, but he turned back to the stove. Infuriating man.

"Want the usual?"

How could she stay mad with a man who made delicious breakfasts? She sank into a chair at the small table. "Yes."

Garrett leaned close and whispered, "Sellout."

"Absolutely."

Colton plated an omelet and walked it to her. "Here." He sat next to her and started eating his.

"So the plan?" she asked, but he kept eating. "I mean, you must have one since you got me up."

"Eat." He gestured at her untouched omelet. "They're better hot. Then we'll call the detective, get an update, and get back to what we're here to do. Win."

"All right." Reagan glanced at Garrett, noting his tightened expression. "That your plan?"

"Your stalker shouldn't be here."

Reagan sucked in a breath and held it a minute. Imagined the tension leaving as she exhaled. "If I talk to Detective Myers, we'll know where his suspect is. If he's in jail, then we were paranoid last night. If he's not. . ."

"We stay cautious." Colton pushed his empty plate back.

"Nobody followed us from the beach, at least not that we could tell. So maybe he doesn't know where you are. Both condos are in my name, and there's no way he knows me. Maybe he got lucky and followed us from somewhere else."

Garrett nodded. "Glad we took that extra step."

"Me, too." Reagan studied her fingernails, not wanting to catch the pity in Colton's expression. She stood and walked away from the table and her niggling doubt. They'd gone to the celebration from the condo. The odds of him stumbling onto her at the crowded Fourth of July events were too small to be possible. "I'll make that call."

She returned to her bedroom and left the door open. No sense closing it when Colton would enter anyway. He leaned against the doorway and watched as she pulled out her cell phone and clicked through to the detective's number. The phone rang until she expected voice mail.

"Myers."

"Detective, this is Reagan Graham."

"Graham." The sound of rustling papers reached her. "Yes, I've meant to call."

"That doesn't sound good."

"Our suspect in your matter alibied out."

A weight sunk in her stomach. "You're sure it's not him."

"Certain as we can be." The detective sighed. "The guy's scum, but not your scum. We'll get him on something later."

"He might have found us here." Reagan explained what happened the prior night.

"Be careful."

"Yes sir." Reagan's hands trembled as she shut the phone.

"Bad news?"

"They don't have a suspect." She shuddered then pushed to

her feet. "Well, let's get out to that cache."

"You sure?"

"I'm not hiding. If that man was the stalker, he knows where I live. Staying here won't do me any good. It's better if I keep moving." She prayed she was right, because she was tired of shadows. She wanted the freedom to walk in the light.

"Okay, then let's head to the park."

"Which one?"

"Where the kickoff rally was. I'm pretty sure that matches the coordinates I downloaded. We'll stick close today. Maybe pick up another one this afternoon."

"Okay." Reagan pulled on some shoes and followed the guys to Colton's car.

A few minutes later, they pulled into the park's lot. The sun punched through a thin layer of clouds, the humidity wrapping around them. Even with the heat, she shivered as she exited the car. Colton headed toward the middle of the park then stopped.

"Here we are. There's not much." He turned around, taking in the empty field with a few scattered picnic tables. She had to agree. Without all the people and the stage that crowded the park during the rally, the space was wide open. Not many hiding places.

Garrett pulled his cap lower and slouched. "So read the clue already."

Reagan frowned at his tone but had to acknowledge he had a reason for his off-attitude with the gloom the detective had cast. Well, she for one refused to spend the rest of the summer out of sorts or living in dread. She had these two guys and a beautiful day to enjoy. *God has not given us a spirit of fear, but of power, love, and of self-discipline.* God had made it clear she wasn't to live in fear, so she would choose a different approach.

These weeks had been too good to allow anything to destroy it.

She forced the fear from her mind and pivoted, trying to predict where the cache could be hidden. "I'm picking that collection of picnic tables. Garrett?"

Her brother shrugged then pointed toward a stand of trees. "I'll take that spot." He sauntered toward it.

"That confident?" Colton chuckled.

"You bet. I feel it."

Colton shook his head. "I don't have any clue where this one is. It's weird. It's like the GPS can't get a read on it."

"We're ready." The words were right, but Reagan still looked poised to jump at the least sound. Colton would do anything to erase the tension in her stance, help her relax. She'd brought her camera but hadn't once brought it to her eye to frame a shot. Instead, she worried the strap with her fingers then stilled them. As if sensing his gaze, she met it and visibly relaxed. She cleared her throat, and he glanced at the GPS.

"It's an odd one." He squinted at the screen, trying to make out the words in the glare.

"First day, sat on a gazelle's perch
Those dimples made his stomach lurch
Spotlight from God framed her face
How long would she make him chase?"

Garrett rolled his eyes. "Sounds like whoever wrote that one needs some serious help. Bet his girl didn't get all gooey-eyed when she read this."

"Gooey-eyed?" Reagan laughed, the first real laugh since last night. For that alone he could thank the terrible, lovelorn poet. "I think you need to leave high school behind, Garrett.

Maybe the clue is the writer's way of trying to let someone special know how he feels. Wonder if it worked?"

Colton shrugged. "We'll never know. Let's find the cache."

"The clue's too easy, and we were all wrong." Reagan glanced around the park then pointed at a rock formation. "It's got to be over there. I can't see another gazelle perch."

Garrett pretended to gag. "I'll wait by the car. This should have come with sugar warnings."

Reagan grinned at him and headed toward the rocks. "We'll find it in no time."

As they walked across the park, Colton glanced at her. "You okay?"

"Yes." Her voice was firm, and he almost believed her. "God and I had a little talk." She said it like it was the most natural thing. "I can't live in fear. Especially when there's nothing I can do about the shadows. Who knows? Maybe last night wasn't anything."

"Maybe. But you can't pretend the stalker isn't real."

"Sure." She nodded. "But at the same time, I can live smart and trust God. So let's find this cache and go from there. We have a lot of ground to make up if we're going to win."

As he watched her climb on the rocks, he decided he didn't care if he won, as long as Reagan emerged unscathed.

Chapter 9

The next few days passed in a blur of hunting for more caches. Colton kept watching behind them as they went from place to place. The clues were getting tougher, the hunts more challenging, and the fear more tenuous.

Then one morning, he found a note tucked on Garrett's car.

Peekaboo. I see you. You can't hide from me.

He refolded the note and paced next to the car. Should he show it to Reagan? She was living in such a good spot, really shaking off the fear—he hated to reignite it. But if something happened, and he hadn't shown it to her. . .

"Whatcha doin'?" Garrett came alongside him.

"I just found this."

Garrett studied the piece of paper like it might turn into a snake and bite him. "Is that what I think it is?"

"Yep. Proof the stalker's here." Colton pinched the sheet between two fingers. "What do we do?"

"Call the detective." Garrett looked ready to pass out. "Let him notify the local police, and then we get Reagan out of here."

"Do we tell her?"

Garrett ran his hands over his short hair. "What else can we do?"

"You're right. Make the call, and I'll tell her."

Reagan took the news better than he expected. "You shouldn't be surprised. Now we have proof he's here."

"Garrett's calling Detective Myers now."

Reagan nodded. "Okay. What next?"

"We'll take a day off. Go rent a boat. Give the police a chance to work."

Garrett entered the apartment and held his phone out to Reagan. "Detective Myers wants to talk to you."

She walked to a corner, put a finger to her ear, and started talking. Colton only caught sporadic phrases. Things like she didn't have any ideas. That's what bugged him. He'd peeled his eyes for a week and still had no idea where the stalker hid. Whoever he was, he knew how to hide, stick to the edges, stay out of view.

The waves rocked the boat as it shot across the lake. Garrett seemed to believe speed would protect her. She was glad she'd left the camera behind. The spray could ruin it.

She closed her eyes, grateful for the Dramamine that kept her stomach settled. She tipped her face to the sky, letting the sun kiss her face. Detective Myers had promised to call the Osage Beach police, but the force was too small to spend resources looking for her mystery man. She shuddered, remembering the message. *Peekaboo.*

God, help me push away the fear.

She let the prayer whisper through her mind over and over until it sank in. When the fear started to lift, she breathed a thanks. God was making it so clear she wasn't supposed to stay in her fear. She could be alert and on guard without giving in to a paralyzing fear.

Colton had relaxed the second they stepped into the rented boat. They hadn't gotten skis, but that was okay. With the picnic lunch he'd brought, they could still spend the day on the water, relaxing. She'd sensed the moment he didn't have to worry who might sneak up behind them.

After awhile, Garrett slowed the boat. They sat in the middle of an expanse of water so blue it almost hurt her eyes. The occasional bird flew overhead, but other than the sound of other boat engines and Jet Skis, peace settled.

"You know what we should try next?"

Reagan startled from her reverie and turned to look at Colton. "What?"

"We haven't looked for any of the caches near the caves. There are caves all over this area. We can't leave here in a couple weeks without checking a few out."

Garrett nodded. "I'd love to go spelunking."

"I'm not sure how much I'd like tight, dark spaces, but I'm game to at least go look around them." Reagan would try it if Colton wanted to go. "Do you have any in mind?"

"A couple. There's one that's supposed to be near Camdenton. That's only thirteen or so miles according to the GPS."

"Want to go now?" Garrett started turning the wheel as if to steer the boat back toward shore.

"Nope, we'll enjoy today, head back to the condos, and go caving tomorrow."

Colton turning down a cache? Reagan hadn't thought that day would come, even if he was trying to keep her safe.

The next morning, the three were in Colton's car bright and early. If they pushed, they might reach three caves before the end of the day. Reagan looked a bit sunburned after the time on the lake, but relaxed and ready for the next adventure, even after her brief conversation with the police chief in the area. The police hadn't found anything, and she seemed determined to not worry.

Colton glanced in the rearview mirror and noted her camera in her lap. Yep, his girl was back and ready to capture every moment of the trip. She met his gaze and quirked an eyebrow. "What?"

"Ready to try out some caves?"

She mock shivered, only making his grin grow. "At the first bat, I'm outta there."

"Don't worry, sis. I'll protect you."

"That's exactly what I'm afraid of."

The miles passed quickly, and soon the GPS alerted them to turn into the parking lot at Bridal Cave. Garrett frowned. "This is pretty commercial."

Colton hadn't expected that either. "Guess I should have done more homework. Well, we're here. Shall we go in?"

"Of course." Reagan placed the camera's strap around her neck and headed for the entrance before Colton could get the key out of the ignition. When he arrived at the ticket counter, she was telling the agent all about their hunt. "So is there a discount or waived entry fee for the Rainbow's End hunters?"

"Let me check." The teenage girl picked up a phone and had a quiet conversation. "The manager says to go on in. The church arranged payment. Enjoy the cave."

Once they were inside, Reagan held the camera to her eye, framing shots over and over. Too bad she couldn't take photos and would have to rely on postcards. She eased away from the guys then glanced at Colton.

"I'm not going far."

"I know." He wouldn't let that happen. He pulled the clue up on the GPS. "So here's the clue:

Where the bride's veil meets the rocks
You'll find a place that mocks.
Look deeper, deeper still.
Until you find your fill."

Reagan wrinkled her nose and glanced around. "Find your fill?"

"These folks aren't professionals." Garrett thrust his hands on his hips and frowned. "I'm about ready to pack it in. Bride's veil? Come on, that's what this whole place is."

"We'll find it." Colton knew they would. They always did. "Maybe we have to hunt. Nothing wrong with that."

Reagan looked around. "This looks interesting over here."

Garrett looked the direction she pointed and frowned. "Not to me."

Before Colton could say anything or present a plan, Garrett took off. Guess the guy was ready to be done. Odd, since it had originally been his idea. Hope his attention span lasted longer in law school, or that could be a long ordeal.

Colton turned back to Reagan.

Just in time to watch someone pull her into the shadows.

"Scream and your brother dies." The low voice filled Reagan with the certainty that whoever this was would do exactly what he said.

She nodded but kept silent as he pulled her off the marked path into the depths of a cavern. Surreal images played in the light and darkness, and she willed Colton to turn around, to see her before she disappeared. The man jerked her around a corner. Had Colton turned in time? She prayed he had.

Fear should scream in her veins. Instead, she felt cold but certain. Now she'd unmask her shadow.

He tugged her closer and kept pulling her backward. Her shoes slipped on the damp rock, and she struggled to stay on her feet. Would it be better to let herself fall and then try to run? Or should she wait?

God, help me.

The whispered words filled her mind, a steady refrain as the man's progress slowed. He bumped into something, and his grip loosened a moment as an oomph escaped. Garlic-tinged breath overwhelmed her, and she tried not to gag.

"Let me go."

"Not yet." Good. Maybe that meant he didn't mean to harm her, just scare her. As a tremble coursed through her, she decided he was very good at that.

"Who are you?" *Keep him talking. Learn something about him in case he suddenly disappears again.*

"A friend." The word held an overtone that was anything but friendly.

"Friends don't do things like this."

"They do when it's the only way to get your attention. You've missed all my messages."

"Messages?" She frowned and thought back over the summer. "I only got a couple."

"Peekaboo. I've watched you all summer. Garrett thought he was so smart. Taking you away from St. Louis so we couldn't threaten him through you. He thinks he's smart, but when he comes to find you, he'll learn how serious we are."

His words didn't make any sense. "Garrett?"

"Your precious baby brother has a side you don't know. He likes to play the games. You know where he's gone all summer? He's been driving to Boonville."

"No, he's never even mentioned Boonville."

"Ask him about the Isle of Capri."

"The what?"

"It's a fun little place where his debts have multiplied rather than dwindled. He had a run of beginner's luck and never learned to stop. Now he has to pay. You're the bait."

Garrett gambling? She didn't believe it, but did she know the signs? He'd disappeared several times—at least once a week. Always exhausted the next morning. He never introduced the mystery girl he supposedly spent time with. Why would he start gambling? It didn't make sense.

His hold tightened on her, and Reagan collapsed, trying to bring him down. She had to get away. He cursed and scrambled to tighten his hold. She scurried to her feet and ran as fast as she could in the dimness that hung like a veil. A shadow in the rock caught her attention, and she aimed for it. Nothing. She slid down the side of the cavern, her hand searching for a break. There! She felt a gap and lunged for it, praying she could disappear into the darkness before he found her.

Chapter 10

"Where is she?" Panic edged Garrett's voice as he joined Colton.

"Someone pulled her that way." Colton took off in that direction as he tried to understand where the man came from. He'd been certain no one followed them. He'd done everything he'd ever seen in the movies to try to lose a tail—well, except turning massive figure eight patterns. The highways didn't work that way around the lake. Still he hadn't noticed any cars or trucks.

Had this guy put a transmitter on his car?

He'd have to check later. Now he had to find Reagan.

Garrett caught up with Colton, grabbed his arm, and spun Colton around. "Stop. They want me. That's what this is all about. They're using her to get to me."

Colton's chest turned to stone as he studied the young man he thought he knew. "You'd better explain."

"I owe some money. They threatened Reagan. I created the stalker in St. Louis to get her to leave."

"You killed her cat?" Colton struggled to keep from strangling Garrett.

"I had to get her out of town! They told me they would kidnap her unless I paid, and I couldn't. No matter how much

I played, I kept losing. My debt mushroomed. But I had to get the money back plus enough for law school."

"That's messed-up thinking."

"I know. But they kept pushing. Started threatening her." Garrett ran his hands over his head again and again. "I had to get her out of St. Louis. This seemed like the perfect excuse and hideaway. But they still found us."

"The note on your car. . ."

"Not me. I swear."

"So they followed you. Now they have Reagan."

Garrett nodded, a miserable expression on his face.

"First, we call 911 and get the police involved. We get Reagan back, and they can straighten this out."

Garrett seemed to crumple into himself as Colton watched, but he couldn't focus on him. He had to find Reagan. The thought of her in the hands of some gambling enforcer made him want to move faster, rush in to save her. Instead, he forced himself to slow down, take a couple of breaths. Getting Reagan hurt wouldn't help.

After he pulled his phone out, Colton checked for a signal. Moved a few feet and checked again. Nothing. Should they split up? Should he send Garrett to get help? Pressure built inside him at the thought of what the enforcer could do to Reagan as they raced around. Could he even find the right cavern again? There was nothing that marked the one the man had pulled her into. He'd give it a few minutes. Try to find Reagan. "All right. We're going to follow them. This time we'll be the ones using the shadows."

Garrett nodded, but Colton got the sense he wasn't listening.

"Hey, if you're not with me, go find help. I won't let you get Reagan hurt." Any more than Garrett already had when he set this mess in motion.

Garrett's gaze darted around as if he expected to find a gangster with a gun waiting. "I'm coming with you."

"Fine, but focus on Reagan. She's all that matters right now." Garrett had no idea how much she mattered. The idea of her scared out of her mind about broke Colton. He had to get to her before something happened.

Once she was safe, he'd wring Garrett's neck.

He shook off his anger and focused on the slit Reagan had disappeared into. Time to move.

Reagan listened. Each scruff of a shoe on stone sliced the silence.

Her lungs demanded that she gulp air, but she resisted. The man was too close. At the smallest sound, he might find her.

She had to stay hidden. Her mind reeled with this man's allegations about Garrett. If any of his accusations held truth, then Garrett needed help. Gambling was a serious problem, with life-altering consequences.

Another scrape of a shoe against rock had her pushing deeper into the shadows. He couldn't find her, not when she had no way to defend herself. She brushed her fingers along the cave's face. Somewhere she could at least grab a rock. That would provide some protection, better than a scream and prayer.

"Come here, little girl. There's no way out except past me."

She bit her lip and slid another step back. Her heart raced until she thought it might explode. She gasped for air.

Another step, then a slice of light pierced the darkness. He must have heard her inhale, because he laughed. "Didn't think I'd come down here without a way to find you, did you?" The light switched to the other wall. "Will I find you here? How about here?" The light danced in rapid motions.

Reagan pressed farther back. She needed a plan. Her hand grasped at a rock. Her fingers barely wrapped around it. Not as comforting as a lethal weapon, but at least she had something.

"You want to make this hard? Fine." The man laughed, a sound that forced a shiver through Reagan. "No problem. I've got hours. I've got a jacket. I can wait. Eventually, the cave closes, and I have all night to find you. In the morning, the staff will find a surprise. I don't think it will affect them the way it will Garrett."

She clamped her lips together to keep from answering. She pulled the rock in front of her then groped along the wall with her other hand. How far back did the crevice go? She slid away from the opening a step, keeping an eye on the waving beam of light. It slid across the wall toward her, and she ducked farther back. *Please don't let him find me.*

Another press into the darkness. The crevice never expanded, yet she hadn't found the end.

The light winked closer.

The crevice narrowed.

Please don't let it close now.

She pushed back and fell into emptiness.

A woman's scream pierced the air. Colton broke into a run and headed in the direction of the shriek. "Reagan."

Garrett caught him and yanked his arm so hard Colton spun.

"We've got to get her."

"If we race in there, whoever's with her will just kill us." Garrett hissed.

"Better me than her."

Garrett rolled his eyes. "If you die, what's to keep him from killing her, too?"

Colton yanked free and stared at Garrett, disgust curling through him. "Man up. You got her into this. Now we have to save her."

"Sure, but not by rushing in blindly."

A laugh reverberated toward them. Colton picked up his pace again and headed that direction.

He turned back when silence surrounded him. "Go call the police now. We need help."

Garrett took a step toward the Bride's Veil then turned back. "I'll go till I find cell coverage. Then I'll be back."

Colton nodded. There was a fire in the younger man's eyes Colton wanted to believe, but Garrett had to prove himself.

The scream had come from in front of him to the right. No rushing in there, or he'd get both of them killed. Garrett had that much right. But sitting back waiting for the cavalry wasn't an option. The light was dimmer off the regular path that was laid out for the tourists who came through the caves. He'd have to go by gut instinct.

In his years since Boy Scouts, he hadn't spent much time in caves. As his eyes adjusted to the darkness, he shot up a prayer for direction.

He leaned forward, straining to hear anything in front of him. There. To the right. Were those footsteps? He crept forward a few steps then paused. There it was again. Ah, a small tunnel opened up, one he hadn't seen from a few paces back.

After waiting another moment to see if Garrett would return, Colton stepped into the tunnel and then down into another cavern. A narrow band of light zipped back and forth.

A flashlight? Maybe the man had lost Reagan.

Colton stepped into the cavern, sticking to the wall like a spider. Too bad he couldn't web his way up the wall and over the top of the enforcer. Then he'd disable him and find Reagan.

A muffled cry reached him, and he picked up his pace. His foot collided with a rock, sending it skittering across the cavern's floor. The sound ricocheted like a boulder crashing down a mountain. Colton froze as the beam of light pivoted in his direction. It teased across the front of his dark T-shirt, and Colton sucked in, as if that would make him disappear.

"Ah, someone comes to rescue the damsel in distress." The deep voice held an ominous tone and was followed by a snicker that was anything but funny. "Too bad you can't have her."

The light drew closer, and Colton felt pinned in place by its brightness like a mounted moth on display. He had to break free, get to Reagan.

The beam flashed to his face, and Colton squinted against the glare.

"You're not Garrett."

"You have a gift for the obvious."

"A smart one, huh." The man stepped closer still. Another step. Colton had to break free from the beam of light.

"That's what my mom said."

"Too bad, this will end badly for you." A glint of metal. Then the metallic sound of a gun hammer cocking. "Any last words?"

Chapter 11

Last words?

Pain throbbed through Reagan's ankle with each heartbeat. She muffled her whimpers as tears slid down her cheeks. She'd fallen into another chamber and crawled into a crevice fighting pain. Now she tried to push to her feet.

She had to help whoever the thug threatened. Colton or Garrett. She cared about both.

The realization of how much she cared for Colton swept over her.

As she tried to stand, her ankle collapsed. She couldn't reach them. Not now. She slid her cell phone from her pocket and tried to find a signal. Nothing. Any hope she'd held threatened to evaporate.

"Nothing for you." Colton!

She screamed long and loud. She had to distract the man, turn his attention away from Colton. She screamed again, wincing as the shrill noise ricocheted off the rocks, bouncing back.

The light swiveled away with Reagan's scream. Colton launched out of position, unpinned and desperate.

"Going somewhere?" The man pointed the gun at him and fired. Colton spun away from the man, feeling the brush of the bullet along his arm. He grunted, but kept moving away from the direction of Reagan's scream.

He had to keep the man moving. Get him as far away and occupied as possible.

The man laughed. "You can't escape. I've got lots of time. Nothing else to do."

Colton moved again, ignoring the fire flaring across his arm. Just a few more steps. He could see the entrance to the next cavern. If he could get near there, maybe someone would be there. Would see and understand what was going on. Maybe a tourist had heard the gunshot and was already getting help. Or maybe Garrett would show up. All that mattered was that every step drew the man from Reagan. He had to lead him away from her without taking him and his gun straight toward tourists.

"Colton." Garrett's voice sounded from off to Colton's right.

"Stay back." Colton flinched as the man laughed, a bone-chilling sound.

"You drew him here." The light swiveled like a firefly, darting around until it landed on Garrett's white face. "Welcome back, Mr. Graham. Have the forty thousand with you?"

"Not yet. I'll get it."

"Empty promises, kid. My employer is out of patience. Time to pay."

Garrett's eyes grew wide. Colton took advantage of the man's distraction to slide to the side. Then he took slow steps around. A couple more and he could jump the man. Between himself and Garrett, they could surely contain the guy until reinforcements arrived. They had to.

The light bobbed as if the man had remembered him.

One.

Two.

Colton lunged.

The gun fired again, and Reagan screamed again. Where was Colton? What had happened to Garrett? Horrible images flashed through her mind.

She had to get help.

No matter the cost to her, she couldn't let them get hurt without doing something. She reached for her hiking boot and tightened the laces to the point she almost couldn't bear it. If she escaped, she'd need all the stabilization she could get.

Reagan pulled to her feet, her weight balanced on her good leg. A wave of pain coursed over her, but she closed her eyes and gritted her teeth until it passed. She could do this.

She leaned against the rock. The fall didn't mean she couldn't find a way to crawl out.

Fifteen minutes later, as sounds of activity carried toward her, she had to admit defeat. There wasn't a way out she could manage with two arms and one leg.

Should she yell for help?

What if it wasn't help that had come but instead reinforcements for the man who'd haunted her nightmares?

Could she risk it?

She closed her eyes, the darkness not any different from what pressed against her when her eyes were open. Then she shouted, "Colton. Garrett. I'm here."

Over and over she yelled. The words bounced off the walls, echoing in her ears.

"I hear her." A strange voice carried to her. She shrank into the shadows. Had she called the enemy to her?

"Bring the gurney. If she's calling for help, she'll probably need it."

At the word *gurney*, she relaxed and started shouting again. A few minutes later an officer was lowered over the side. "Are you hurt, ma'am?"

"I think I broke my ankle when I fell."

"We'll get you out and checked over."

"How are the guys?" Her heart squeezed as she waited for an answer.

The light on his miner's hat blinked, and she wished she could read his face. "The paramedics are working on one. The other'll be fine."

She swayed, and he caught her before saying, "A little help."

In a minute, several rescuers had her out of the sunken cavern and on the gurney. But all she wanted was to see for herself, verify that Garrett and Colton were okay.

What was taking them so long?

The paramedics had descended before Colton could get to Reagan and refused to let him go. He knew he had a scratch—one that hurt like the dickens—but all the same, just a scratch. What they didn't understand was he wouldn't relax until he knew Reagan was okay.

She wouldn't shout for help if she didn't need it.

A screeching like wheels bouncing across gravel finally reached him.

"Relax."

"I can't."

The paramedic shrugged as he prepped the needle. "Have it your way. But this injection will smart." The man stabbed the needle in Colton's arm. "Told ya."

Colton ignored him as he tried to get a glimpse of Reagan. He needed to see her. How was he going to tell her Garrett had been shot? That he'd manhandled the man, fighting him until the police arrived? That the police had her stalker in custody and Colton had a split lip and sore ribs and an injured arm? But the reason behind the man's chase? How could he explain that Garrett had pretended to stalk her? God would have to give him the words. Otherwise, Reagan would hate him as the bearer of the news.

The gurney finally pulled into view. Reagan flinched with each jolt.

"Can't you guys take it easy on her?"

One of the paramedics grunted as the gurney skidded to a halt on a rock. "There aren't smooth surfaces down here. Want us to carry it?"

Colton focused on Reagan, trying to gauge her status. The paramedics wheeled to a stop next to him.

"Colton." The word whispered from her like a caress. Then her gaze darted around. "Where's Garrett?"

"On the way to the hospital." There was no way to sugar-coat it.

"How bad?" Even in the dim light, he could see her tremble.

"I don't know."

"Is the. . .where's the. . ."

Colton didn't know what to call the man either. Thug? Enforcer? Criminal? "The police have him."

A uniformed man stepped into view. "I'll follow you to the hospital. We'll need your statement as soon as you can give it."

The next hours were a whirlwind. Answering questions. Piecing together what had happened. Waiting to see if Garrett would pull through surgery. Through it all, Colton stuck close to Reagan.

He held her hand in the ambulance, assuring himself she was all right. He sat next to her as the doctor examined her ankle then sent her to get it x-rayed. He felt relief when the diagnosis came back as a massive sprain, not a break. She'd have to stay off it for a while but would recover.

Finally, the police left, the waiting room quieted, and she curled against him.

"You okay?" The question seemed inane, but he couldn't read her quiet reserve.

"I'll be okay."

He waited a minute, but she didn't elaborate. "Can you believe Garrett got involved in gambling?"

She shuddered against him, and he eased her closer. "I don't like it. He knows better. But it does explain some of his disappearances and tension. To think the man from the boat was the one in the cave. All because Garrett acquired gambling debts."

"I'm sorry."

She sighed. "Me, too. I don't know what to say to him."

"That makes two of us." Colton would never understand how Garrett had hatched a plan to "stalk" his sister. How could he think that was okay? Maybe he thought he'd protected her, but Colton didn't buy it. An awful lot of fear and worry had resulted from those selfish actions.

The doors opened, and the surgeon came out. "You folks waiting on Garrett Graham, right?"

Reagan straightened as much as her extended leg allowed. "Yes."

"Good news. Garrett's out of surgery and doing as well as we could hope. The bullet missed his organs, so he'll be sore, but as long as he avoids an infection, he should heal."

Reagan relaxed. "Can I see him?"

"You can, but don't expect much. He'll be under anesthesia awhile longer. It'll be tomorrow before he's aware of much."

Colton helped Reagan to Garrett's room. The young man matched the white sheets. Colton was glad the surgeon had told them everything went well because, based on what he could see, Garrett looked terrible.

After holding Garrett's hand for a minute and praying softly, Reagan turned back to Colton. "Can you take me home?"

She had no idea how much he wanted to do just that. As he helped her to a wheelchair and then wheeled her to a waiting taxi, he knew what mattered now.

It wasn't winning some contest.

It wasn't even figuring out everything with Garrett.

No, where he wanted to focus the last couple of weeks of summer was on the beautiful woman seated next to him. If he did nothing else, he vowed to remove the weight from her shoulders and show her how very special she was.

Chapter 12

The next days passed in a fog. Reagan and Garrett's mom arrived within twenty-four hours, and Colton slipped into the background. Colton stayed helpful but distant. She'd wanted to protest the change—missing the comfort of his presence and arm around her shoulders—but didn't. Reagan wouldn't be able to take care of Garrett when his doctor finally discharged him, not while every hobble sent shocks of pain racing up her leg. So Mom spent her days at the hospital while Reagan grew tired of the condo's four walls. What had seemed more than adequate before had shrunk now that she felt trapped and alone.

Colton must be busy finding more caches.

But when he came over the next afternoon, he denied it.

Reagan crossed her arms over her chest and stared at him. The feeling that he'd abandoned her left her empty. "Then where have you been?"

"Thinking." His thinking must have involved the outdoors, because a layer of pink was showing through the tan he'd built over the summer. When he walked on campus after a summer of hiking, he'd turn the head of every unattached female student. The thought made Reagan want to either fight or crawl under her covers and not come out until she was suddenly transported back to her life in St. Louis. Orderly rows of numbers marching in boring rows across reams of paper.

The realization that that wasn't enough anymore left her cold.

What more did she want?

The answer smacked her so hard she sank onto the couch. She wanted an adventure. An adventure with the man seated at the island. An adventure like the one she'd had this summer.

They watched a movie, a classic black-and-white with Cary Grant and Katherine Hepburn. But instead of laughing at their antics, she could barely hold back the tears.

Her fairytale summer had reached an end. The least she could do was send Colton off as the champ. Even that was impossible, if he didn't seek more caches. As soon as the ending credits scrolled across the TV, she turned to him.

"What cache are you hitting tomorrow?"

"Don't have any plans."

"Why not?" She studied his face, hunting for the answer. "You haven't given up?"

He shook his head with a serious turn to his mouth. "Can't go out without my best girl. It doesn't seem right."

She rolled her eyes. "All I've done is take photos."

"And found a few caches. Don't forget that. Maybe I'm content with second."

"Since when?" She reached over to touch his forehead, and he jerked back.

"What are you doing?"

"Making sure you haven't got a fever."

"Do you want to get out of here? Go get a custard or drive around the lake?"

Reagan considered him then nodded. "I'll need a minute to get ready."

"No way. You look great, so let's leave now. There's nothing to hide from. Not now that the police have taken care of the stalker."

"Sorry. This girl isn't going anywhere without makeup." She went to her room and freshened up. Even though he made her feel like a million bucks, she hadn't put makeup on in days and didn't want to scare everyone else. When she came out, Colton had pulled his car to the door.

She hobbled outside into an afternoon alive with sunshine and the cloved aroma of the tea roses beside the door. The humidity smacked her after the air conditioning, but she rolled down the window and enjoyed the drive along Osage Beach. She smiled as he pulled into the parking lot of Randy's Custard. "You read my mind."

"I figure it's time for another turtle."

"Absolutely."

Colton helped her to the bench then ordered the sundaes. A few minutes later, he returned with the treats.

As they sat shoulder to shoulder on the bench, she could almost ignore the heat and humidity. Instead, she enjoyed the moment and the company.

"You ready to head back to St. Louis?"

His question snapped her back to the reality pressing down on her. The hunt would end, and they would go their different directions. "I guess it's coming."

"Yep." He kept looking at the passing cars. She twisted to try to read his eyes but couldn't.

"Ready for law school?" She didn't want to think about what that meant. He'd be too busy for her. After all, he'd made it clear from the beginning that he wouldn't start the school year with anyone special in his life. She couldn't really blame him, could she?

The next morning Garrett's parents moved him back to St. Louis. Colton considered the mess that awaited Garrett. Reagan insisted she wouldn't press charges, but that wouldn't be enough to keep Garrett from facing the consequences of what he had done. At the minimum the district attorney would be interested in all his efforts to keep the police hunting for a nonexistent stalker. Then there was his outstanding debt. Colton doubted Garrett would make it to law school—as soon as all this broke publicly, his acceptance would probably be revoked.

His phone rang, and he smiled when he saw Reagan's number. "Yes ma'am?"

"I'm sick of this condo. Find a cache that doesn't require hours of hiking. I'm ready to get more points."

He laughed. "Your ankle must feel better."

"Almost good as new. All this time off it helped. We only have a few days to close the gap."

"I'll be there in fifteen minutes." The gap created between first place and where he rested was daunting. Still, he scanned the list of caches they hadn't hit and grinned. How had he missed this one? It would be the perfect hunt for Hopalong Reagan.

In no time, he had her in downtown Osage Beach. When he stopped in front of the custard shop, she frowned. "I don't want another sundae, Colton. That won't get you points."

"Us points. And yes, it might. Listen to this:
Where the turtles cross the window
And the sweet treats flow,
Look high, but focus low,
To find it take a bow."

Reagan groaned. "These clues aren't getting better."

"But it paints a picture."

"I'll give you that. What if the cache is at our bench?" Color blushed her cheeks in a way that made him want to lean close and kiss them.

"I like that. And why not? Let's start there." It didn't take long to look around and find the box. This cache was practically tucked in plain view underneath the bench. "You were right."

Her smile reached her eyes and made them shine. He leaned close then hesitated. A question appeared in her eyes, but she didn't pull away, so he closed the distance. The kiss tasted sweet, everything he'd imagined and more. She sighed, and he eased back.

A dreamy expression coated her face. "If that's what happens every time we find a cache, we should find more."

Her words surprised a laugh from him. "Let's get our names in the logbook and find another one."

Over the next couple of days he tried not to second guess the kiss. And he resisted the urge to sweep Reagan into his arms every other moment. Instead, Colton spent the early morning hours hiking and asking God for direction and wisdom.

He'd always planned that law school would be his sole focus over the coming three years. Yet the more he evaluated, the more he realized it was simply that: his plan. Had God brought Reagan into his life at this moment for a reason?

What if God had?

The answer to that question could change everything. Suddenly, law school didn't have to be the consuming focus of his life. Maybe it could fill a large part of it, but time would remain for other things, like learning if he and Reagan had a future.

The morning of the final rally for the Rainbow's End hunt,

Colton prayed for direction. Tomorrow, they'd each drive back to St. Louis.

The summer had ended.

Now he had to decide if he'd also let it signal the end of their friendship—and the hope of so much more.

Reagan dressed in a new pair of denim capris and a frilly blouse she'd found at the outlets. She added makeup and left her hair down, knowing she looked overdressed for the final hunt rally. But she couldn't shake the feeling this was also her last night to spend time with Colton.

When the summer had started, all she'd wanted was a place to escape the fear of the spring. She never imagined that her stalker would turn out to be a fabrication that was replaced with the real thing. She never dreamed Garrett's demon would be exposed or the cost it would carry. Or that her heart would fall for the strong, godly man Garrett had brought along. Instead of annoying her like he once did, she now feared her heart would shatter when they climbed into their separate cars and headed for their separate worlds in St. Louis.

Taking a final glance in the mirror, Reagan practiced a smile until her lips didn't tremble at the edges. Time to end this.

Colton stood at her door, fist raised, when she opened it. "Ready?"

"Um-hmm."

The short drive passed in silence. She couldn't think of anything to say worth pushing past the lump in her throat. The quiet felt heavy and oppressive rather than easygoing like it had in the past. Colton dropped her off at the park's entrance. "I'll go find a parking place and come meet you."

"All right." The park overflowed with a smaller group than at the opening rally. The same stage stood at the far end, and a celebratory air filled the area. Balloons weighted to each picnic table danced in the cooling breeze. She turned her face into the gentle wind and imagined it wiping away her disappointment.

"You okay?" Colton's voice and the way he touched her shoulder made her want to cry. Instead, she forced a smile and turned to him.

"Ready to see who won?"

"You can't answer my question with a question."

She started to respond but shut her mouth when the pastor approached the microphone.

He took her hand and led her away from the crowd. He seemed relaxed, but she slowed, surprised he'd walk away from the results. "Colton?"

His steps slowed when they neared his car. He leaned against the side then wrapped his arms around her. She snuggled into the safety he offered.

"The results will be announced back in the park."

He shrugged. "I'd rather be here with you."

Reagan reached up to touch his face. "Colton. . .what's going on?"

"Nothing." His hold tightened, but not in a way that made her feel trapped.

"You wanted to win."

"Sure. Who wouldn't?" He tipped her chin up, and she fell into the light in his eyes. "But I learned there was something else I needed more. A prize that is greater."

She wrinkled her nose as she tried to make sense of his words. "What do you mean?"

"I found you. If you'll have me, I've won far more than they offered. You."

Her mind couldn't quite keep up with his words. "What about your plans and law school?"

"I've been thinking and praying. I'm still going to school, but I don't have to do it alone. I want you by my side. If you're willing."

His words hung in the air as she tried to inhale. Were her dreams coming true? "Colton, I want nothing more."

"Then I have a bigger prize than this contest could ever give me."

As he leaned down to kiss her, she melted against him, thanking God for bringing this amazing man into her life.

Love had found her, when she least wanted it or expected it...the greatest prize of all.

Cara C. Putman lives in Indiana with her husband and four children. She's an attorney and a ministry leader and teacher at her church. She has loved reading and writing from a young age and now realizes it was all training for writing books. An honors graduate of the University of Nebraska and George Mason University School of Law, Cara loves bringing history to life. Learn more about Cara and her books at her website, http://www.caraputman.com, and her Facebook page, http://www.facebook.com/caraputman. Cara loves interacting with her readers.

WELCOME HOME, LOVE

by Nicole O'Dell

Dedication

This story is dedicated to all of the women—old, young, and in between—who struggle with low self-esteem and a poor body image. Having camped there most of my life, I know the stronghold well.

May you rise up with wings of beauty and take flight with your Savior as He gazes upon one of His most beautiful creations—you.

Chapter 1

The rented SUV glided up the cobblestone driveway toward the quaint cottage. It stood like a scene right out of a Thomas Kinkade painting, complete with window boxes and lanterns, exactly as Hadley Parker remembered it from her childhood summers when the house belonged to her grandmother. Flowers burst from every corner of the yard and dripped from every inch of the wraparound porch. The lawn was plush and expertly preened—not a weed or errant dandelion in sight. The porch beckoned with its two swings and four rocking chairs. This was a house accustomed to visitors, just as it was when Grandma was alive.

As though anticipating a friend, a tray with a pitcher of iced tea and two water goblets sat waiting on a side table. Hadley could get used to staying here again—two months hardly seemed long enough after thirteen years.

She climbed the white wooden steps toward the front door—open to let the summer breeze into the parlor. Parlor? Hadley hadn't thought that word, let alone used it, over the past decade. But it seemed so natural there. She stepped around the wind chimes tinkling their airy song and reached for the buzzer. Before she could press it, a plump—oh, how

Hadley hated that word—woman appeared at the door, wiping her hands on her apron.

"Hadley Parker?" The screen door burst open, and a pair of kind eyes searched Hadley's soul. "Oh, you poor dear. Come in, come in. You're home now."

What on earth? Poor dear? "You're Norma?"

"Why of course, dear." She pulled Hadley into a tight, yet fluffy, embrace. Norma held on longer than one would expect, but not quite long enough for Hadley.

Norma seemed to know Hadley already, but what could she know from nothing more than a phone call? Maybe the rental lady had blabbed. "Should I get my things from my car?"

"Oh, pish." Norma waved her hand. "There will be plenty of time for that, dear. Let's sit for a glass of tea. I'm parched." She settled into a creaky chair and began to rock. If the dents on the wooden planks were any indication, that was her favorite pastime. "Pour me a glass, will you, dear?"

"Of course." Hadley let her shoulder bag slide to the floor and reached for a goblet. The clinking ice gave away her shaky hands.

"Now you tell me what's wrong, dear." Norma took a swig of her tea, slurping around the cubes.

What made her think something was wrong? "Oh, nothing really. I'm just nervous. New place, new adventure. You know how it goes." Did she know? Had Norma ever lived outside of Osage Beach? Hadley didn't remember ever seeing her, but visiting over the summers during her childhood hadn't made Hadley a local expert.

"I'm sure that's part of it. But honey, there's no mistaking the pain in those sad green eyes of yours." Norma waved her hands. "Now don't you worry. I'm sure no one else can see it—except maybe my grandbaby boy—young'un has an inno-cent way about him that can peer into people, too. But most people wouldn't be able to look beyond your beauty to the soul inside there. That's one hurting soul." Norma squinted at Hadley as though sizing her up.

Was there a rock nearby Hadley could crawl under?

"Where's your mama and daddy, dear?"

Hadley gasped. How had she known? "They. . .um. . .died several years ago in a car accident."

"Mm hmm." Norma nodded. "How about a husband?"

"Not married."

Norma clucked her tongue. "Brothers and sisters?"

"None."

"Oh my sweet baby. You're all alone. That's why Jesus brought you here to Norma. You need a family."

Hadley's eyes stung as she forced the tears down. How could a stranger affect her so deeply? Was Norma an angel or a psycho? She *seemed* crazy, but Hadley didn't *feel* like Norma was crazy.

"Well, now that we have that figured out, I'll show you to your room." Norma jumped from her chair and motioned for Hadley to retrieve her bags from the car, the rocker banging back and forth in protest of her rapid desertion.

Hadley scurried down the steps and gathered as much as she could carry then followed Norma into the house, straight up the stairs, and down the hall toward Hadley's old room, not that Norma could have known.

Norma stopped at the second room on the right and gripped the antique glass doorknob. "Now I didn't mean to rush you past the rest of the house. Don't take my rudeness to mean you're not welcome to enjoy it. This is your home for as long as you're here, darlin'. All of it. I want you to feel at ease here." She opened the door and stepped back, allowing Hadley to move past her into the room.

A tiny gasp escaped Hadley's lips. No more yellowed wallpaper. No more antique quilts. If Hadley designed a summery, country-cottage bedroom, this would have been it. It looked like an award-winner right off a *Southern Living* centerfold. Flowers everywhere—on the wall, the curtains, the upholstery, the bedspread, the area rugs. The hardwood floor gleamed. Even the throw pillows were plush and inviting. She was home. It would be hard to leave this room every day—but oh, so nice to return.

Time to shop. Armed with directions from Norma, Hadley peered up and down the row of shops until she spotted the shoe store and pulled into a spot in front of it. Hah. She'd found it easily without the GPS.

The door chimed as she strained to pull it open against the Ozark breeze.

"Welcome to Road Runner. What can I help you with today?" A boy of about nineteen grinned as he looked up from the cash register.

Yeah, I'll bet he's happy. Hadley eyed the back of the customer in front of him—a rather scruffy-looking man about her own age. He had to be a marathoner, with those sinewy legs. Though only a few inches of them actually showed beneath his cut-off shorts and above his black socks. Was he serious? He ran a hand through his sandy waves and nodded at Hadley then handed over a credit card to pay for three of the same pair of shoes. Maybe he should throw some white socks in there while he was at it.

She forced her gaze back to the clerk. "I–I'm not sure. I think I'm just looking?" Great. Way to sound confident.

"Okay. Take your time. My name is Stewart; let me know if I can be of service in any way." He let his dark eyes rove Hadley's body from head to toe. Right. Bet he just couldn't wait to finish with his professional athlete and move on to Hadley, who couldn't possibly be a runner.

Hadley knew she didn't look like someone in need of anything athletic, in her baggy jeans and gray flannel shirt. What could she do? Nothing fit anymore. Her wallet hadn't quite caught up to her weight loss until recently, and all she'd been able to buy had been dress clothes for work since moving into her expensive lakefront apartment. But now. . .thank heaven for bonus checks and big commission checks. The tide had changed just in time for her thirtieth birthday. Three days away.

Would the world feel different when she poured herself into a new decade? If her birthday song were a geocache clue:

Happy Birthday to me.
Happy Birthday to me.
I once was a fat girl,
But now I'm skin–nee.

Hah. People had called her skinny lately. Were they crazy? Couldn't they see she was the same "Chub Monster" Jimmy Moskel had teased all through middle school? She was still that same fat girl posed as a slimmed-down version. If people could see her without clothes on, they'd agree.

Argh. Constantly with the negative thoughts. Why did she do that to herself? No. It was just as her roommate, Ava, had said before Hadley left: it was time to let go of the outdated image Hadley had of herself. That's what this trip was all about, after all. Could she do it? Could Hadley let herself transition to thirty and, at the same time, to a slim, fit woman? She had two months to give it an honest effort. If that didn't work, she'd try therapy.

She turned away from the clerk and his customer and scanned the aisles and aisles of athletic shoes. How would she ever figure out what she needed without making a complete idiot of herself? Cross-training. Running. Walking. Aerobics. Were they kidding? How could she pick from all these shoes? Now, if the rows had been filled with wedges, stilettos, sandals, and the like, Hadley would have been in her element. She rubbed the beginnings of a headache from her temples.

"You look confused—trust me, everyone does when they come here the first time."

Hadley whirled around to find the salesclerk staring at her again. Was it that obvious she'd never been in there before? "Yeah. Um. I think I'm going to just go."

The boy shook his dark curls. "No way. You're not leaving until you try on some shoes. You came in here for a reason. People don't just browse in a store that smells like feet and Ben-Gay." His eyes narrowed like he was trying to figure her out. "What are you looking for, really?"

What was she looking for? Acceptance. Peace. Ease in her own skin. Not that he could help with that. "Shoes, I guess."

"Well then you *are* in the right store." He chuckled, eyes twinkling. "Let's see if we can narrow that down a bit. What do you plan to be doing while wearing said shoes?"

"I'm going on a vacation. Hiking, walking a lot, maybe some climbing—but not too much of that, I hope." Hadley bit her lip until she tasted blood.

"Sounds like my kind of trip. Let's start in the hiking section, and we'll figure out which shoes are best for you." Stewart pointed across the store then hung back as Hadley plodded over to the appointed aisle.

She felt his eyes burning holes in her back—she'd had enough practice in her life to know when she was being watched—and whipped around to catch him in the act. What was he staring at? Why didn't he say something? He probably couldn't believe she planned to do something physical. That had to be it. Fine. She'd leave before he said anything. Now, how to make her escape without being too obvious.

"Okay. I watched you walk—that's how we can tell what your feet need. Your arches are a little flat, which is totally normal."

Yeah, for fat people.

"Most people need some kind of adjustment, so we'll find a shoe that compensates for that—you'll be much more comfortable. Now. Hiking boot or shoe?"

Hadley shrugged. How would she know?

"How many miles a day do you plan to hike, and on what kind of terrain?"

Ugh. This got more personal with each question. Just spit it out so the questions stop. "I'm doing the Rainbow's End geocaching hunt. It'll be a lot of walking. I don't know how much, but it's a two-month event."

Stewart's eyes widened. "Oh man! I wanted to do it but couldn't get enough vacation time to make it worthwhile. You're going to have a blast." He turned toward the wall of shoes. "Okay, well you'll log lots of miles, probably on varied terrain. I recommend a hiking boot with a lot of breathability, because it's really hot here this time of year. With that in mind, and considering your pronation, how about this pair?" He held up the boot under the sign Asolo Drifter GV.

"They're pink." Cute shoe, but there was no way she could pull off something like that.

Stewart laughed. "The color is actually called grape-ade. This particular shoe is the best for comfort, durability, and breathability. There's also a removable insert that will help with your overpronation. Try 'em on. I think you'll love them."

Hadley wrestled to pull on the boots. Once in place, they felt amazing. She walked around a bit. Her feet really did feel different when they weren't turning inward. "These are the ones. You're really good at your job, Stewart."

He talked her into a few pairs of socks that would keep her feet dry and some sealant for her boots then rang her up. "That'll be two hundred ninety-three, eighty-six."

Hadley handed over her credit card then signed for the purchase.

"Here you go." Stewart cinched the bag. "I hope you enjoy them—and your hunt. Just be careful—skinny girls like you can overheat pretty easily."

There was that word again. *Skinny*. Hadley glanced down at her body. Just because people said it, it didn't mean it was true—obviously.

She stepped up to the door as it chimed, and waited for someone to step through. No one appeared, so she made a move toward the threshold, running right into the scruffy customer digging in his wallet.

She wobbled and dropped her bag.

His hand reached out to steady her as she bent to pick it up.

"You okay?" the salesclerk called from behind the counter.

"I'm fine—no harm done." Hadley shot him a smile.

She pulled her sleeve from the stranger's grip and looked up to meet his eyes. "I'm sorry. I didn't—"

Noah Spencer? Oh great. The last thing she needed.

Chapter 2

Noah Spencer stood on the sidewalk outside Road Runner and balked at the total on the receipt. Three pairs of hiking shoes cost more than his monthly mortgage payment. How could that be? One for him, two for the boys he big-brothered. Maybe he should at least return his.

He dug in his wallet for his credit card as he pushed the door open with his foot. Surely they'd let him return shoes he'd only walked out with ten minutes ago. There was the card, in the back.

Noah stepped through the door and ran right into a woman. He reached a hand to steady her as she teetered in the doorway.

He locked eyes with a pair of familiar hazels, gold flecks reflecting the rays of the sun as their owner stepped over the threshold. Engulfed by a huge flannel shirt, the body was almost unidentifiable, but her squared jaw and long, slim neck were unmistakable. Hadley Parker.

Oh, no. After all this time and this was what he was wearing the moment he saw her again? It wasn't his fault his pant leg had gotten caught in his bicycle chain and he'd had to cut it off and make shorts. Too bad he'd had black socks on, but there was no spare pair in his bike bag. Besides, she didn't look like a fashion critic in that getup. Yet his heart raced. What was he, seventeen again?

His ears buzzed as her lips parted to respond to something the salesclerk had said. The reward? Dimples so deep they reminded him of long-ago summers of pure joy. What Noah wouldn't give to see them shot his way in response to a funny joke or sweet comment he'd made. Poof. The dimples disappeared just as suddenly as they'd flashed, and sadness took over her gaze. She nodded as she stepped around him and walked out the door.

Again.

With only a few hours before the hunt started, it was probably time to figure out how to use the GPS thingy before she dropped off the rental car and made her way to the park for the kickoff. Hadley tied her new shoes then reached into her carry-on and pulled out her Garmin—still in its package. Ava thought it crazy to drop four hundred dollars on a unit when she could rent one in the Ozarks. If Ava only knew that the four hundred had barely scratched the surface of her expenses. Add another eighty for the North American Navigator microSD card, forty for the carry case, two hundred ninety for the shoes and socks, three hundred for the flight, and a thousand to rent a room for the two months. Not to mention the four hundred she'd dropped at REI for moisture-wicking hiking attire like tank tops, T-shirts, and shorts, and another hundred for the hydration pack the salesgirl had talked her into. Plus the mountain bike.

Hadley could have hiked near home and saved a fortune, but if she was going to do this, she intended to do it right down to the tiniest detail. If she stayed home in Chicago, there were too many diversions and opportunities to make excuses. Plus, returning to Osage Beach was like coming home.

Guided solely by the GPS clues and the voices in her head, Hadley found Hertz with little trouble, once she figured out which way was north. She parked and went in. The keys to the rental car jingled as Hadley dropped them onto the counter at the return desk. She wouldn't need those anymore. Just outside the window, a boy lifted the brand-new, top-of-the-line mountain bike she'd just purchased from OZ Cycles from the back of the SUV and settled it against the Hertz store.

The old man behind the counter chewed on a half-digested pencil then slid it behind his ear, eyes never leaving the bike outside, as though it were an alien spaceship. "You planning to ride that all the way back to Osage Beach?"

"Sure. Why not? Should only take an hour or so." Hadley had checked her GPS and mapped her route before she left Norma's. Hopefully her first attempt at using her coordinates wasn't a bust.

The old man lifted his cap and wiped a handkerchief across his sweaty, bald head. "Crazy health nuts." He shook his head. "We get fitness folks like you every summer." He chuckled and handed Hadley her receipt. "Best o' luck to you. Drink lots of water. If you're not used to this heat, it'll get to you."

No one had ever mistaken Hadley for a health-crazed fitness aficionado before. Maybe she could store up every comment like that and let them erase at least the jeers and taunts of childhood. One down, a million and a half to go. It was a start.

No more putting it off. Hadley searched her mind for any

last-minute preparation she could—which was far easier than stepping out into the real world. Why was she making this so difficult? People did this sort of thing every day. "Yeah, normal people," she whispered. "People with normal bodies. People who don't talk to themselves. . ."

Her bicycle turned as though propelled by GPS coordinates of its own, down the easement between the Osage Beach Community Church and the wooded park beside it for the kick-off rally. The bike seemed to want to be there, and Hadley felt powerless to stop the wheels from turning. Within moments, she stood amid a group of several hundred geocache hunters—acting, if not looking, like she belonged there. *Fake it till you make it, Hadley.*

She chained her bike to a tree and whirled around to face the crowd again, but instead, she got a face full of someone's backpack as he swung around, knocking her off balance.

A strong hand grabbed Hadley's elbow to steady her before she fell. Twice in two days?

"Careful, sweetheart. Looks like a wisp of wind could knock you off your feet."

Hadley wilted under the scrutiny of the handsome stranger's dark eyes. The invisible superpower she'd wished for as a child would sure come in handy right about then.

"Or you can let me sweep you off your feet."

Oh, great, a sympathy flirt. "Um. Yeah. Right. Nice line."

"You like that one? I've got more where that came from." He ran his hand through his thick black hair, the silver above his ears glinting in the sunlight.

Hadley laughed for the first time since she'd arrived back in Osage Beach. "I'll pass. But thanks."

"Whoa! If I'd known getting you to laugh would reward me

with those dimples, I'd have opened with a joke. I tell you what, let's talk hunts and haircuts over lunch this afternoon. What do you say? There's a neat little bakery/bistro called On the Rise. They have a lobster pot pie that's to die for."

Yeah, put all ninety-six pounds back on in one day? "I don't think so—I'm allergic. Thanks, though." Hadley turned her attention away from the tan, muscled beach god and toward. . .

Noah? With a microphone?

Her first love stood at the front of the crowd and introduced himself as Pastor Noah Spencer. She should have known. He looked much more comfortable behind the mike than he had in front of the cash register. And no more black socks. Phew.

". . .let's kick off this hunt with a prayer—"

"Well you can order anything. Come on. I won't take no for an answer."

"Shh. I want to listen." Hadley held a finger up to her mouth and nodded her head toward her old friend. "Besides I don't have out-to-lunch clothes with me, and I don't have a car," she whispered.

"No sweat. Come as you are, and I'll pick you up."

Hadley squinted against the sun. He sure was handsome. It had been years—thirteen, actually—since she'd been on a date. Might as well give it a try. "Okay. But I'll meet you there at noon." Before he could argue about picking her up, Hadley turned her attention to the front. She wanted the information, even if salt-n-pepper guy didn't.

While Noah spoke, Hadley searched the crowd. A couple of chubby girls, but no one seriously obese. Lots of twenty-something enthusiasts, by the looks of their equipment. After all, they couldn't all be posers like her. *Fake it till you make it, Hadley.*

She pulled a wisp of blond hair from her mouth and tucked it into her ponytail. She was used to Chicago winds, so this light breeze was refreshing through the mugginess of the June Missouri morning. Hadley pulled on her sun visor and peered around the little park, cordoned off for the event. Across the yard she spotted the registration table. Time to commit.

As she approached the picnic table, a pretty, dark-haired girl grinned at her. Bet she'd never had to diet. "Hi, I'm Lyssa. Welcome to the Rainbow's End Treasure Hunt. I just need you to fill out an information sheet and sign a waiver of liability. You know, in case of an accident or heat stroke." Lyssa laughed and handed over a clipboard.

"Thanks." Hadley ignored the picnic tables with the pens strewn across the tops, likely designated for filling out papers, and walked away from the crowd, up a slight hill to a weeping willow, where she settled beneath its enveloping boughs. She could just stay there, nestled safely in the background, like always.

No!

Hadley gripped her pen and scratched her name and pertinent info onto the forms. Enough was enough. She was there to complete the change she'd been making all year. She strode to the table and thrust the pack of papers at Lyssa. "Here you go."

"Great"—Lyssa peered at the papers—"Hadley. You can join the others over there. Pastor Noah hasn't begun the instructions yet, so you're just in time."

Hadley made her way to a huge boulder at the back of the crowd and scrambled to the top, where she huddled like a mountain goat. She could see everything and everyone from atop her perch—and, better yet, no one was looking at her.

Chapter 3

Focus, Noah. Why did she have to sit right in his line of sight, like a gazelle, delicately perched on that boulder? He'd noticed her blond hair and dimples the minute she'd arrived on the scene. He'd barely been able to peel his eyes from her since. Good thing he wore sunglasses, or the rays glinting off the gold in her hair might blind him. She'd hardly aged a bit.

Just then, the tree sheltering the rock parted in the wind, and the sun shone directly behind her like a beacon from heaven. Oh, come on! That only happened in movies and stupid romance books. This was real life. Trees didn't part. God didn't send a beam from heaven. Did He? Noah shook his waves from his shoulders and fanned himself with his clipboard. His heart raced. He'd never experienced such an immediate attraction to someone—but Hadley was no stranger to him, and neither were the feelings stirring in his heart.

She lifted a bottle of water to her lips. No wedding ring. Then there was hope.

But why had she been talking to Brad? Brad Hopper was up to no good—if history offered any indication, anyway. If she liked that type of guy now, no way she'd be interested in Noah.

Then again, after the way she'd left him years ago—well, she had some serious explaining to do.

Lyssa caught his eye from the registration table. She nodded at the crowd and gestured for him to talk. How long had he been standing there like an ogling fool? Had anyone noticed?

"Okay, folks." He took a deep breath to keep his voice from shaking. So this was what nervous felt like? "You've all got your registration packets—hopefully you've obtained a GPS unit from Communication Location—but if not, they're ready and willing to outfit you with whatever you need and are offering hunters a great discount. Directions to the store are included in your packet." He held his plastic cup between his teeth while he turned to a new page of notes. He reclaimed the cup and held it up. "One other thing I want to mention before I kick off the hunt is that Common Grounds, a local favorite, is offering all registered hunters free coffee beverages with the purchase of a sandwich or a bakery item between five and six o'clock on Tuesday evenings. This is a great way for y'all to mingle and catch up on hunt stories."

Noah grinned as many in the crowd lifted their Common Grounds coffee cups in salute.

"I should tell you guys, this is special coffee—it's the best you'll find in all of Osage Beach. It's"—Noah looked at his notes—"estate-grown, unfiltered Arabica, custom blended and microroasted. I used to think coffee came from a metal can with a plastic lid—start to finish—until I found Common Grounds. Now I don't settle for anything less than the finest." He took a well-timed sip from his steaming cup.

Hadley smirked. Was his shameless plug that obvious? A sponsor was a sponsor. What could he do?

Come on, Noah. Focus.

"The hunt itself will last two months, ending with the final ceremony right here when we announce the winner, which will be decided by the accumulation of points. You'll find the point sheet in your registration packet, and you can refer to that whenever you have questions.

"I want to point out that everything is worth one point except for the official Rainbow's End geocoin." Noah held up a coin the size of a silver dollar. "It'll be planted in a secret cache—no one will know which one contains the coin—and it's worth five points. The finder can choose to keep it, preventing other hunters from finding it and receiving five points. Or he or she may return it to the church office so it can be rehidden and so that someone else might earn five more points, too.

"Please, folks, we're human beings, and we'll do our very best to keep track of points and award what is due. But don't rely on us. Keep good records and be diligent about your details so there's no confusion at the end.

"Now, other than the unofficial meetings at Common Grounds on Tuesday nights, we won't meet up again until our midpoint rally, at which time the big prize package will be unveiled. Donations and prizes are still coming in, so all I can say is—it's going to be a whopper!"

He shielded his eyes from the sun and scanned the crowded audience. "Okay. Here we go folks. If you have any questions about the hunt, the caches, the use of your GPS units, hit up any of these folks up front wearing yellow Rainbow's End T-shirts."

Noah closed in prayer then climbed down from the picnic bench and searched the crowd for *her*. He just had to see her. He'd made it the entire thirteen years since Hadley took off with no warning without getting sucked into romance or rushing in and out of relationships like all his friends had. Who knew? Maybe now was the time for them. Noah shook his head. He'd better settle down and remember how much she'd hurt him.

There she was. Noah gasped as his heart fluttered to the ground. She flipped her gorgeous ponytail over her shoulder, and it hung down her back between her tan shoulder blades. He had to talk to her. She laughed at—Brad? Noah's stomach churned. If her eyes were going to turn from the flashy Brad, who always got the girls, and onto Noah, who never did, it would take a miracle.

Hadley settled into a seat at a table for two, waiting for. . . what was his name? How could she have agreed to go on a date with someone whose name she didn't even know?

The door jangled as it opened, and a handsome figure filled the frame.

Oh, that was how. Hadley chuckled quietly. She'd fallen for the first gorgeous guy who'd hit on her. Why not—he would be a diversion and a good experience for her. He seemed nice enough, after all.

Flashing a full set of veneers, what's-his-name turned the wooden chair backward and straddled the seat. He reached forward and engulfed Hadley's left hand in his huge paw and dusted the back of it with a light kiss. Hadley watched the scene unfold as though it were happening to someone else—but the tingles up her spine and on the back of her hand brought her down to reality.

She pulled from his grip. "I don't even know your name."

"Yeah. That's how true love works, baby. Names are nothing but a formality."

"Not to me. I'm Hadley Parker." She reached out her right hand to shake his.

He wiggled his eyebrows as he kissed the back of it, electrifying yet another part of her body. "I'm Brad Hopper. Nice to meet you, um, Hadley Parker. That's an interesting name."

Wait until he heard the middle name. "Yeah. Hadley Emmerson Parker. Sounds like a law firm."

"Sounds sexy when you say it."

Hadley picked up her menu and tried to hide her reddening cheeks. Brad was hot, and her blood pressure was on the rise. He might be more than she could handle. But it sure was fun trying.

Alone in the dark church after planting the special cache with the Rainbow's End coin under the night sky, Noah leaned his shovel against the wall then picked up the stack of registration forms and rifled through them.

Where was hers? *Hadley Parker.* Age: twenty-nine. Birthday in a few days. Employment: drug company sales rep. That was her.

Noah felt for his desk chair across the room without taking his eyes off the paper in his hands. He spun the chair around and rolled it over to his laptop and touched the mouse pad. Feet bouncing, Noah waited for it to spring to life.

Going straight to Facebook, Noah entered "Hadley Parker" into the search bar on the top of the page. It brought several Hadley Parkers up right away, but he found her easily by the picture of herself as a little girl that she used as her profile image.

Noah scanned her info page. A graduate of Loyola

University in Chicago. A sales rep for a major drug company based in Chicago. Not married, no kids. She had no pictures posted, no other personal information at all. Why, with all of her many Facebook friends, wasn't she tagged in any photos? She'd left her profile public, so they'd show up there if they existed—but hadn't anyone ever taken her picture? If he were her friend again. . .or more, Noah would take a new picture of that face every single day of his life.

Religious views: Christian. Well that was an absolute plus. Wonder if that meant American Christian—like by association—or a follower-of-Christ type of Christian. Time would tell.

Political views: Conservative. Hmm. Reagan Republican? Or Colin Powell conservative? Big difference.

Favorite Quote: The one thing that matters is the effort. It continues, whereas the end to be attained is but an illusion of the climber, as he fares on and on from crest to crest; and once the goal is reached it has no meaning. ~Antoine de Saint-Exupéry

Music: Carrie Underwood. Blake Shelton, Miranda Lambert, Third Day, Maroon Five, Casting Crowns, Sugarland, Chris Daughtry, Kelly Clarkson, Stephen Tyler, Aerosmith, Bon Jovi.

Movies: Steel Magnolias, The Devil Wears Prada

Television: American Idol

Interesting information, but too basic. Noah wanted more. There was a big piece to the Hadley Parker puzzle missing. Time for good ol' Google.

Hadley Parker.

Search.

Did this make him a stalker? He didn't feel like he was doing anything wrong. Just checking things out. That was okay, right? It was all public information. It wasn't like he paid for one of those background checks. Should he do that? No! That was pushing things a little too far. The search results popped up. Noah glanced over his shoulder to make sure no one had come in the office then scrolled through the Hadley Parker entries. Some celebrity stuff came up, lots of businesses, and other types of pages. Nothing that appeared to point to her until the third page.

Noah clicked on the link for Impressa Drugs. Ah-ha! A page for sales representatives. He scrolled through the two pages of images; none were her. Then he looked to the left where the names were listed in alphabetical order. Parker, Hadley. How had he missed her photo? He'd recognize those dimples anywhere. He clicked her name.

The page opened slowly to the image of a Hadley look-alike. . .if you added about a hundred pounds.

Chapter 4

One foot in front of the other. Hadley plodded along the lakefront trail, following the coordinates for the first cache, which she'd downloaded from the website that morning. Walking on the uneven terrain in the muggy Missouri heat hit her body a lot harder than the hours and hours she'd logged on her treadmill over the past year. Her body wasn't used to regulating itself against natural elements—it liked air conditioning and fans, lots of fans.

She lifted the tube extending from her hydration pack and took a long drink of water. She'd have to make the hundred ounces last several hours, judging by the location of this first cache. Why had she started with one so far away instead of the easy ones like most of the others probably had? Because she wanted to avoid the crowds. Because she had something to prove—at least to herself. And because she liked the clue poem:

Only the strong survive
Get ready like you're going to dive
Perch atop the stone
Make sure you're all alone

No idea what it meant, but the first line had intrigued

Hadley. She figured the rest would make sense when she arrived at the location—at least that's what her information packet had promised. She glanced at her GPS unit, at least an hour to go. After seeing the poem, Hadley was even more glad she'd declined Brad's company on the hike. It was something she needed to do alone, at least for a while. Who knew how she'd feel as the summer drew on? But for now, she needed to rely on herself and not get distracted by Brad's charm and good looks.

Yet here she was, distracted.

Hadley adjusted her pack and picked up the pace.

The trail was noisier than she'd expected. Not background, filler noise like her MP3 player—more like the sounds of life. Rustling of leaves in the wind. Fluttering of wings as birds startled from their hiding spots. Chipmunks, squirrels, and rabbits foraging in the underbrush. Birds and crickets chirping in harmony. Fish jumping in the lake that ran beside her path. Hadley filled her lungs with the fresh air. She felt invigorated— much more than after a five-mile trudge on her treadmill.

So this was why people teemed the Chicago lakeshore bike path every day? Hadley had wanted to try a run over there since her birthday last June when she embarked on this personal journey toward health and fitness as a gift to herself. Her apartment overlooked the mayhem of people running and biking while Rollerbladers weaved between them all, and there was no mistaking the freedom they felt. But she just couldn't bring herself to put on her shoes and join them; she was too afraid of running into someone she knew. She didn't want to see the judgment in their eyes. Whenever she happened on someone who hadn't seen her in a while, she could read their thoughts, which always seemed to go one of two ways. Either they gazed at her with pity at how much she'd had to work to take the weight off, assuming she'd put it right back on before year's end, or they eyed her in wonderment that she'd ever let herself get to the point where she had to work so hard. It was much easier to exercise at home than to endure that scrutiny.

Ava said Hadley was crazy, that she wouldn't accept a compliment if it was handed to her on a silver platter with a big red bow. She tried. It was hard, though.

At least here Hadley was a stranger. Brad had no idea who she really was. If he saw the driver's license picture in her wallet, he'd probably run away out of fear she'd look like that again, and Hadley wouldn't blame him. Maybe that would be for the best anyway. Would she ever escape the demons that chased her?

The time passed quickly, and Hadley realized she must be near her target. She checked her GPS, examined her latitude and longitude coordinates, and grinned. She broke into a slow jog up the hill to her destination—the approximate location of the first cache. Now to pinpoint the exact spot with the clue poem.

Only the strong survive. Did that mean only the strong could make it that far? Maybe. She could go with that for a minute.

Get ready like you're going to dive. A swimming pool? No there wouldn't be a pool out here. Hadley scanned the horizon but saw no water access. She could hear it, though. A dive. . .a dive? Where was the lake? It had been at Hadley's right during the hike up, so it had to be over the rise in front of her. She trudged up yet another hill and peeked over a huge rock.

She gasped at the sight. The boulder led to a steep drop-off overlooking the lake. Did people dive from the rock? How could she know if the water below was deep enough? She looked for evidence of that but found none. She scrambled up and stood atop the stone, searching the water below for assurance. Surely the hunt people wouldn't ask her to take a blind dive into uncertain waters if it wasn't safe. Was she supposed to trust they knew what they were talking about? What if she dove in but that wasn't what the clue meant at all? What if she came this far only to break her neck on day one?

Perch atop the stone. Wait. What? That's exactly what she was doing. How did the cache's creator know she'd do that? She stared at the rugged rock beneath her feet as though it had magical properties.

Make sure you're all alone. She glanced in every direction. Alone.

Okay. Here goes nothing.

Noah couldn't believe his luck. Hadley had chosen this cache as her first hunt. The one he'd written and added just minutes ago. He watched her eyes dance in the sunlight as she reasoned the clues until her face shone with excitement at having figured it out.

Her strong, lithe body looked so perfect as she climbed atop the rock aptly named Love's Reward.

But, wait! What was she doing? Was she about to dive? She'd never survive a dive from that spot. The lake below was deep enough for a canoe this time of year, but she had to be two stories high. He had to stop her. Somehow. If only he could do it without giving away his presence. Noah glanced in every direction. Frantic. He was running out of time.

She dropped her backpack beside the rock, kicked off her shoes, and inched her toes forward.

"Stop!" Noah bolted from his hiding place. "Stop!" He

reached Hadley and grabbed the hem of her shorts before she could carry out her plans. "Are you trying to kill yourself?"

She turned on him with fire in her eyes. "Excuse me? Get your hands off me." She jumped from her perch in a fluid motion, like the gazelle he'd known she was.

"Hadley, I—"

She searched the area around her, fear mingling with the anger that already clouded her face.

"Why did you stop me? I was about to jump in for the cache." Hadley held up her waterproof GPS unit.

"Why on earth would you jump in the water from here? The clue never told you to do that. You'd have killed yourself." Simmer down, Noah. "I meant. . .you're only supposed to get ready to dive so you can find the cache from the viewpoint on top of the rock. Can't you see that right here?" He leaned over her shoulder to point at the geocaching site on her web display. Why had he written such a stupid clue?

"Yes. I see it," Hadley sputtered. "I just thought. . .oh, I don't know what I was thinking. But thanks for ruining it for me. Now if I uncover the cache because you helped me—it wouldn't be fair. There goes a wasted day."

Not for me. "Oh, don't worry about that. You can still find the cache. I didn't tell you its location."

"No thank you." Hadley pointed her nose at the sky and turned away. "I'm finished here."

Of all the nerve! First he had to write an ambiguous clue. Then he intruded on Hadley's privacy—although he did save her life. . .but that was secondary to her humiliation. What had he been doing hiding in the bushes anyway? Come to think of it, had he been following her? The horror of being a spectacle while exercising flooded into her brain, and Hadley hated the young youth pastor for ruining her day. . .maybe even the whole hunt. How could she go out again tomorrow? And now she was behind, since it was likely everyone else had already retrieved their first caches of the hunt.

If a bike could stomp, hers acted like a petulant child all the way back to Norma's. Hadley paced alone in Norma's living room. If only she could avoid *him* the rest of her time, she'd be fine. Maybe, if she gathered the nerve to go out tomorrow, she should follow the crowd and hope he wasn't among them.

A light knock sounded at the front door. Who could that be? It better not be Noah there to apologize. Hadley wanted nothing to do with him. She jerked the door open. "What do you wa— Oh." Her tone fell, and her anger washed away as she saw Brad grinning on the other side of the door.

"Hey, gorgeous. I'm here to take you to dinner. Let's go."

Why was he whispering? "Um. . .I don't remember setting up a date for tonight."

"No, it's a surprise. Come on, let's go."

"Can I at least change my clothes?" Hadley plucked her damp shirt away from her sticky, grimy body. "Come on in."

Brad glanced at the stairs. "Nope. You won't care in a minute. I promise." He held the door open for Hadley to walk through.

At least *someone* was a gentleman. Brad steered his beemer through the streets of Osage Beach and turned on a dark road— almost a path—into a wooded area. The trees cleared almost immediately, and they were in a clearing that housed a modern two-story house.

"This is a great location, Brad. Do you live here?"

"Yep. Wait until you see the back." They walked around the

house, climbed the stairs to the deck, and stepped into another world. The deck was actually a dock where several boats were moored. The private lot shielded them from everything but an expanse of water and the stars in the sky.

Hadley could get used to this.

Brad stepped onto a small yacht and steadied himself as the water level ebbed in the wake of passing boats. He held out a hand to Hadley. "Come onboard. You'll love it."

She placed her hand in his and climbed into the most luxurious private boat she'd ever been on. Luxury boat, handsome man. Yep. She could get used to this.

Brad's eyes twinkled, and the moonlight glinted off the silver hair around his ears. His gaze held intent. . .intent to. . .

He leaned his face close enough that she could smell the musky scent of his cologne mingled with the salty sweat of the day and feel his hot breath on her face. Realization smacked her: she was about to receive her first kiss in thirteen years.

No! Hadley needed time to think about this. It was happening way too fast. She wasn't prepared. She stepped back and put her hands on Brad's shoulders. "Sorry, I'm—I don't think I'm ready for all this. Can we just slow down a little?"

Brad's eyes darkened momentarily, but the corners of his mouth raised. "Of course, doll. I'm sorry. We'll slow down for a while. We can take a quick buzz around the lake and enjoy the night sky. Sound okay?"

Hadley nodded. She'd heard the "for a while." What did that mean? How long was a while? She'd hurt his feelings, obviously. Brad wasn't the kind of guy who was used to being turned down. She was out of her league with him. But maybe he was exactly what was needed to pull her from her shell.

Chapter 5

More determined than ever after the debacle of yesterday's hunt, Hadley woke at 5:00 a.m. She had some lost ground to make up. From conversations she'd overheard on opening day, it seemed that most people planned to find at least one cache each day. So three would make up for her lost day and put her ahead a bit. And she still didn't want to shoot for the ones closest to her. Those were too easy, and taking the easy road was not why she'd come.

Why had she come? To stretch herself. Push her body. Test her limits. Do something she'd have never done as the old Hadley. Maybe she could even bury that old Hadley once and for all before it was all over. In the meantime, she'd fake it until she made it.

Hadley plodded over to her laptop, rubbing the sleep from her eyes, and typed in *www.geocache.com*. Without too much trouble, she plotted a trip to the first cache of the day—fifteen miles away, toward the east side of the lake and around the tip. The second trip would veer off from there, headed southeast, six miles down and somewhat away from the lake and deep into the woods.

The third one appeared a bit more daunting. It would bring

her toward home, but via a different route. Uphill most of the way, biking through miles and miles of uncharted territory. Sounded fun. Hadley chuckled. A year ago she would have read about this sort of thing in a novel while she snacked on tortilla chips and soft drinks, thinking the cache-hunter was out of her mind.

To have any hope of getting through the day she had planned, Hadley would have to use her bike and would need to refill her water at least once. Where could she do that? She scoured the map until she spotted a public bathhouse in a wooded area. And several rest areas along the lake. Hadley felt as ready as she'd ever be.

By the afternoon, with the first two caches out of the way, Hadley pressed on to the third. Hill after hill loomed in front of her. The lake was far away—no hope for a dip in its cool water—and it had been a couple of hours since she'd happened upon a water source. Her pack was still full at that point, even though she should have drained it by then. But now she was going through it too fast. Time to tighten up the rationing to make sure there was some left for the way home.

Finally arriving at her coordinates, Hadley's knees shook as she climbed down from her bike and laid it on the ground. She stretched her legs and allowed herself a small drink while she considered her clue.

Who? Who? Says the owl.
The hiding place is hollow.

What? That didn't even rhyme. But Hadley easily found a hollow opening in a tree—right where you'd expect an owl to hide. And, just as expected, a cache was nestled right inside.

Okay. Three down, and all that was left was the ride home. It would be as tough as the ride there. What if she couldn't make it? What if she collapsed out there in the hundred-degree heat and humidity with no water supply? No one knew where she was. She could die. All she could do was press on. One hill at a time.

Finally, Hadley spied the cedar shakes of Norma's roof in the distance. It was a soothing beacon to her shaking legs and raspy lungs. She could make it to something she could see, no matter how far away it was, right? She pushed aside her fears of dying alone on the side of the road. As long as she could keep her eyes locked on home.

Rounding a mountainous bend, Hadley lost the comforting sight of the structure that housed her soft bed and promised her aching body a cool bath. She lost her grip on the hope of soothing hot tea and hearty soup. Suddenly, all she could see was the mountain that loomed before her. It was probably more like a hill, but it might as well have been Mt. Everest. Her legs couldn't coax another revolution from the pedals, no matter how much she willed them to push on. Her bike came to a wobbly standstill as her knees locked. She tried to put her feet on the ground, but it was too late. She was going down.

She crashed to the pavement, and a hot poker shot through her elbow and upper thigh. Her face took a beating from the handlebar, and her head rapped the cement. Pain filled her body, but it was the realization that she couldn't be seen by a motorist coming around the corner until it was too late that sent a chill through her bones. It would only be a matter of time before she got run over. She had to move. Forcing herself to a sitting position, Hadley could almost see the stars circling her head like they did in cartoons. She reached around with spaghetti arms to grasp her legs and swing them to the side, but it was no use trying to lift lead with a wet noodle. She collapsed back to the ground and began to cry.

What had she been thinking, coming out here alone like this? She was nothing but a fat girl in a weak, skinny girl's body. She wasn't fit. She wasn't powerful. A lifetime on a treadmill couldn't prepare her for the real world, and there she lay, about to be roadkill.

Panic coursed through Hadley's body as she heard the sound of a car cresting the hill just beyond where she lay. She gave a renewed effort to shove herself out of the way—if only to will herself to the shoulder of the road. The car began its descent. Hadley had moved but an inch or two. *God, make it stop in time.* She squeezed her eyes shut against the coming darkness.

The brakes squealed. The squealing grew closer. And closer. The car wouldn't be able to stop in time, not with its downhill momentum.

The screaming tires finally stopped beside her right ear. Was she dead? Hadley peeked through the slit of one eye.

The driver jumped from the car, ignoring the beeping of the keys in the ignition. "Are you okay?" The familiar male voice rushed to her side.

Hadley felt like passing out, but she held on long enough to make eye contact with this. . .angel. . .*Noah?*

Blackness descended.

He could do mouth-to-mouth. Noah glanced at Hadley's chest to see it rise and fall with steady breaths. Was he actually disappointed that he couldn't touch those lips with his own?

He pressed 911 on his cell phone as he lumbered back to his

car and threw open the back door. He leaned in and rummaged for a bottle of water. His hands grasped two that had rolled under the driver's seat. One still had a cylinder of ice through the center; the other had melted completely. Best to go with room-temp so she didn't have brain freeze on top of heatstroke.

After giving his location to the dispatch officer, Noah glanced at Hadley's crumpled, lifeless form, and his gut wrenched. She was probably dehydrated. If he could get some water into her, she'd probably be okay. She'd have a killer headache, but she'd make it. But he probably shouldn't move her until the ambulance arrived.

Hadley stirred, and a low moan escaped her cracked lips.

Noah hunched down beside her head and lifted it gently to place a rolled-up fleece jacket beneath her. He smoothed the dripping blond tendrils away from her face and held the water to her lips. "Come on, Hadley. Take a few sips. Just a little at a time." Noah poured some into her mouth.

Barely coherent, Hadley gulped at the fresh water.

"Not too much now. You don't want to shock your system." Noah patted her forehead with a towel then offered her another sip.

After a few more draws at the bottle's neck, Hadley looked up at Noah with those gold-glinted eyes. She'd have to appreciate his help this time.

The glints turned to fire. "You?" She sputtered. "Why is it always you?"

What? He'd only been trying to help. "Um, you might have died here on the roadside. It's a miracle I came along when I did. I guess you can ask God why He keeps sending me to you."

Hadley's head rolled back to the makeshift pillow, and her eyes closed. As the sirens wailed in the distance.

That woman is crazy. Straight nuts. A complete cuckoo. Out of her ever-loving mind.

Noah would be really smart if he took his hands off the whole thing and forgot she even existed. What did he want anyway? It was clear she wanted nothing to do with him. Why couldn't she forgive him? It happened so long ago. Noah shook his head to clear his thoughts. He had no interest in reliving the moment when Hadley walked in on him kissing her best friend.

There was no hope that things could happen between them. Too much history. Too much distance. Too much hate.

Then why couldn't he get her off his mind?

Lord, what are You trying to do to me here? Is there some reason this crazy girl is on my heart and mind so much? Are You trying to do something for her through me?

"No, I'm doing something for you through her."

Noah slammed on the brakes. It wasn't very often that he felt a direct answer to a prayer. At least not one so obvious. Was that his imagination? Was Noah imposing that thought on God because he wanted it to be so? Besides, if Hadley Parker had a mission to do something special in Noah Spencer's life, she sure hadn't gotten the memo.

Noah pulled his lanky legs from the driver's seat and hurried into the church. He didn't even bother to unlock the office door, just slid his new cache coordinates underneath it. Shoulders slumping, he returned to his car. Dinner, a shower, and then he could answer the call of his bed and try to forget this day ever happened.

Tossing and turning for hours, Noah couldn't get the

words out of his mind. His legs got tangled in the sheets as he wrestled to make some sense over what was happening and what he needed to do. He was attracted to Hadley, always had been. But anyone would be. She was so beautiful—but didn't seem to know it. Besides attraction though, he'd always loved her as his best friend. He thought they'd marry and live happily ever after. Until he messed it all up.

Would she ever get over the past?

Why had she fallen for Brad Hopper's charms?

What could he do to change things?

Would he ever find answers to the questions that haunted him?

Chapter 6

After the week she'd had, the last place Hadley wanted to go was Hunter's Happy Hour at Common Grounds, but she might as well size up the competition. Plus, maybe Brad would be there. Then again, maybe Noah would be there—she'd have to steer clear of him.

Hadley stepped from the bright sun into the shop, squinting as her eyes adjusted to the fluorescent light. She recognized some people from the kickoff rally in the corner sharing a table. A coffeepot was set up with all the fixings next to it just for the hunters. Hadley helped herself to a steaming mug and stirred in some fat-free vanilla cream and artificial sweetener while she listened to the buzz of conversations all around her.

One voice stood out from among the others. She peered around the group to find its owner. Ah, one of those guys. A middle-aged man with a tanning-bed tan and bike shorts. The kind of guy who wanted everyone to hear him and know what he was doing or saying at any moment.

"That's Chuck." Brad sidled up to Hadley, grinning. He nodded at the boorish man in the purple polo then turned his attention to Hadley. "But enough about him. How are you? I heard you took a spill?" He touched the bruise on her cheek.

Hadley shrugged. No sense letting him see her annoyance. "News travels fast around here." She pulled her sleeve down over her beat-up elbow.

"Eh. Small town. The pretty new girl is all people want to talk about. They know you're with me. . .so they bring me news." He smiled as the words rolled easily from his tongue.

Hadley didn't know which comment to process first—that she was the "pretty girl" in town or that she was "with" Brad. What did that even mean? Before she had a chance to ask him, his phone chimed.

"Oops. Have to take this." He flashed the screen at Hadley and ducked around the corner for privacy.

In the instant the phone faced her, Hadley read CRYSTAL'S CELL on the caller display. Who was Crystal? And why did he have to take her call in the middle of their discussion? Wouldn't Brad have been more discreet if it was someone Hadley shouldn't know about? Unless he didn't know she could see that far or read that fast. Or unless he wanted to make her jealous. Is that what she felt? Jealousy?

That was a first. Hadley had never been close enough to a man to have those pangs of fearful possession. Longing, sure. Loneliness, definitely. But jealousy implied some sort of ownership or claim. Did she even have a right to feel that about Brad?

Don't look again—it smacks of desperation. Noah tried to avert his eyes as he watched the pain cloud Hadley's eyes. She busied herself with her iced tea, but stole a glance at her watch every few seconds.

Finally, she covered the face of her watch with her hand.

Apparently, she no longer wanted the reminder of how late her date was. She held up a hand to signal the waitress.

Noah leaned close enough to hear.

"I'm going to order. If my. . .um. . .friend shows up, he can order then."

"Very good. What I can I get you, ma'am?"

"I'll take the roasted fig and goat cheese crispini and the caesar salad."

"Excellent choices. That'll be right out."

Taking his cue, Noah stepped to the table.

"Can I join you?"

Hadley flinched then recovered her surprise like a trained expert at hiding her feelings. "I'm expecting someone."

"Stood up on your birthday? Come on. You don't want to eat alone. Let me join you." Please. Noah wanted an invitation to take Brad's place at dinner.

Hadley raised her eyebrows in question marks. "You remembered it was my birthday?"

Should he lie and pretend the date had been locked in his mind forever? Nah. "Registration forms."

Brad bounded in and strode to Hadley, turning heads as he came. "So sorry I'm late, doll. I had an unexpected visitor." He bent down and lightly kissed her on the forehead.

Goose bumps appeared on her forearms.

Brad never glanced at Noah.

"Oh? The tooth fairy?" Hadley scowled, a hint of doubt creeping across her face.

Yes, Hadley, listen to the doubt. Listen to your gut. Noah cheered her on, begging her to see the real Brad for herself, knowing she'd never hear the truth from him.

"Very funny. Shall we order?"

"I already did."

Brad's eyes widened in surprise. Noah figured girls didn't do things like that to Brad.

"Can I have your cell phone for a sec?" When Brad handed it to her, Hadley punched some buttons. "Oh, I am in here. I guess I assumed I wasn't in your contact list, since you didn't call when you were late." She raised her eyebrows, and a slight grin spread across her face.

"Okay, okay. Enough. I said I was sorry." He gave Hadley a stern look.

As fun as this was for Noah, he knew when he'd worn out his welcome—especially since he'd never received one.

As he walked away, the waitress arrived with Hadley's food. "Would you like to order something, Brad?" She uttered Brad's name with awe, like a fan meeting a celebrity.

"No. I think we'll share. Thanks, doll."

Noah glanced back just in time to see Brad reach across Hadley to snatch one of the triangle crispinis and tip it toward her. "Let's eat."

The refrigerator trembled when Hadley slammed the door. She regretted the outburst instantly—a good Southern woman wouldn't do that, and it was sure to bring Norma scuffling in to see what was wrong.

And there it came, like clockwork, the flap, flap of Norma's bedroom shoes as she came down the hallway to the kitchen. "Something wrong, dear?"

"No. I'm sorry, Norma. I didn't mean to disturb you."

"Nonsense. Nothing interesting ever goes on in this house until you get home, so disturb away."

"Oh, it's really nothing. Just boy troubles." Was it a problem though? "Or not. I don't know."

"What don't you know?" Norma sank into a kitchen chair. "Seems to me like trouble is easy to feel when it rears its head."

"But I don't know if I'm expecting too much, too soon." Why couldn't Brad be more like. . .Noah?

"Ah. Well, there are certain things you should demand from the get-go. Respect is one of 'em. The other things, like diamonds and such—they come later."

"Okay, doll. Let's see what you've got." Brad grabbed Hadley's list. "You've found eight caches already? That's incredible. I've only found three."

Hadley shouldered her backpack. "Just be sure you're ready for this. I plan on three today. I have it all mapped out. We can do it on foot, but it will take about six hours if we stick to the trail."

"Okay. I'm not sure I'm as dedicated to this as you are, but I'm ready to go. Besides, six hours of following behind you. . . mmm hmmm. That sounds mighty fine to me."

Note to self: let Brad lead.

"So what have you found in your eight caches?"

"Oh, a couple of fishing lures, an Osage beach postcard, a charm, a Ram's magnet, and a flip-flop."

"A flip-flop?" Brad looked back in surprise. His dark eyes glinted in the sunlight.

"I know—weird, right?" Hadley shrugged. "Whatever."

"So you know right where they all are?"

"Well, sure. I know where I found them."

"How about if you just tell me then? You know, catch me up

to you so we can win together."

Hadley glared at Brad. "No way am I cheating. Don't be silly. You can still win. You just have to pick up the pace a bit. It's still early in the competition."

"Okay, okay." Brad laughed. "I was teasing, anyway."

Somehow, Hadley doubted that. Wiping the sweat from her forehead, she looked longingly at the lake. It stood so cool and refreshing to their left, just waiting to be called upon to heal their bodies from the heat. She had a bathing suit in her pack—if Brad weren't along, she'd have gone for a dip. But there was no way she'd wear a bathing suit in front of someone—especially him.

"How are you doing, Brad?"

"We're getting close to the first one, aren't we?"

"Yep, we're almost there. Right around this corner, I think." They rounded the bend to find a clearing for picnic tables and an area to grill food. Too bad they didn't have a nice steak with them. Or a salad. "Okay, here we are at the coordinates. Now we need to solve the clues."

Handle all your food with care
Hide it well from Yogi Bear
Eenie, meanie, miney mo
It's all about YOU, you know

"Seriously. Who wrote these?" Hadley laughed. "Well this one's pretty obvious. It has something to do with the garbage cans. In one of the cans, or buried beneath it." She gestured to the four rusty trash cans at the edge of the clearing.

"Are you saying we have to dig in those nasty things?"

"In or under—that's my guess anyway."

"What about the last line? Does it identify which can it is?" Brad whispered the lines.

"Ah! Miney is the third one, it's like you, mine—YOU. . . get it?"

"Good!" Brad jogged over to the can. "So assuming left to right, miney is the third can. Let's start under it. I can't imagine they'd hide it in the can. What if the forest service came to dump the trash?"

"True."

Brad pushed the can over on its side and rolled it out of the way, not even glancing at the trash that dumped out onto the path. In the circle of dirt beneath where it had stood, they saw a fresh mound. "That must be it."

Hadley pulled a spade from her pack and began to dig. Just a few trowels of dirt later, she hit metal. "There it is."

They stuck their fingers into the dirt and tried to pry the box from its spot. Hadley couldn't wait to see who had signed the logbook before them and when. Finally, the box made its entry into the sunlight, and Brad opened the lid.

Inside the box they found a stack of Bible tracts and a logbook to sign.

"Oh great. God stuff." Brad pushed the tracts aside and pulled out the logbook.

Well, that answered the question of whether or not Brad was religious. Hadley didn't mind that much if Brad wasn't, but it was definitely good to know.

"Cool." Brad flipped the pages in the logbook. "Looks like we're first to find this cache. We get to sign in, right?"

"Yep. But you have to make sure you log it in on the website if you want your points recorded."

Brad grabbed a nubby pencil from his back pocket and scrawled his name on the logbook then handed it to Hadley.

Would have been nice if he let her sign it first, since she

found it and led him right to it. Oh well. He must not realize the significance of being first. Not that there was any real meaning other than bragging rights. After all, they'd both get a point for the find. She reached into her backpack for a pen then signed her name and printed it beneath her signature. She added the date and a mention of the Rainbow's End Treasure Hunt.

"Oh, are we supposed to put all of that on there?"

"I just thought it would be nice to add the information. No one said we had to." Hadley shrugged and snapped a quick picture of the logbook.

"You're really into this stuff, aren't you?"

"I guess so. It's fun. I had no idea how much I'd love it." Hadley grinned and pulled out her GPS. "Let's pick up all that trash and then move on."

"Another one?" Brad groaned as he followed Hadley while she scooped up the remains of several picnics.

"Thanks for the help."

"Sure. No problem."

Men.

Chapter 7

Hadley's eyes popped open in the pitch-black room. Someone was in there—she could hear shallow breathing like someone was trying not to be heard. Norma? No. She wouldn't sneak around like that. Brad? Was he there watching her sleep? Some stranger? Noah?

What should she do? Hadley kept her breathing even, trying not to let on that she was awake, while she formulated a plan. She could freak out her attacker by jumping from the bed, flailing her arms, and screaming. Or she could just continue to feign sleep and see what happened. That seemed dumb. What if the person intended to harm her? No, her best bet was the element of surprise.

A few more deep, slumbering breaths—one, two, three. NOW.

Hadley jumped from her bed, flipped on the light, then squeezed her eyes shut against the sudden brightness. She spun in circles, kicking like Bruce Lee—kind of—throwing her arms around and up and down, trying to fend off an attack or at least confuse the assailant. But she felt no blows. No contact whatsoever.

She pried open her eyes in the bright room. No one was

there. She put her karate foot down. What was that sound? Giggling? Hadley whirled around and found the culprit now lying across her bed.

"I've come to suck your blood!" Ava dissolved in laughter as she rolled on Hadley's sheets. "Oh my goodness, Had. You should've seen your face! Luckily I have it all on tape. This is so going on Facebook!"

"It better not! I'll kill you!"

"What? You want to withhold this priceless piece of footage from the world? Oh, that's gonna cost ya. Big time."

"What are you doing here?" Hadley tried to still the drumbeat in her heart. Deep breath. She checked the alarm clock: eleven. She'd only been asleep for thirty minutes.

Ava smiled the grin of a person who felt welcome anywhere, anytime. "I'm here to visit. Didn't you miss me?"

"Of course I did. And it's great to see you." Hadley put her arms around her friend and squeezed. Ava had no idea just how glad.

"You look magnificent, girl! This outdoorsy stuff is treating you right." She looked Hadley up and down then spun her around to take in the backside. "You look like the cover of *Shape* magazine."

"The cover? Not so much. Maybe one of the internal articles about weight loss. . ." Hadley stopped when she saw Ava's expression. "Sorry. Thank you. That's a very nice thing to say."

"Much better. Young student learn much." Ava grinned and popped the top of a cola.

"How'd you get in here, anyway?"

"Oh, that kooky lady, Norma? Is that her name? She let me in. Said I'd be good for your soul. Is she for real?"

"Norma's as real as they come—and she's not kooky, but I thought so at first, too." Hadley laughed at the not-so-distant memory. "How long can you stay?" The needy little girl in Hadley wanted Ava to say the rest of the summer, but the emerging woman wanted to protect her alone time.

"Oh, I only have a couple of days—have to leave Wednesday morning. But now that you have me here, what should we do? Want to go hunting for one of those cache thingies?"

"Well. . .it's the middle of the night."

"Unless there's some rule about finding your stuff during the day, let's go for it."

Hmm. "Now that you mention it, there is a cache I want to find, but don't want anyone to see me. I guess now's as good a time as any. Just give me five minutes to pull myself together." Hadley padded off to the bathroom, rubbing her stinging eyes.

"According to the coordinates, it's back here." Hadley led Ava around Osage Beach Community Church to the wooded park in back where they'd had their kickoff rally. "Here. It's in this general area."

"Okay, open up the clue. Read it again. What does it say?"

Hadley toggled the display to life and stared at the little poem for probably the hundredth time.

First day, sat on a gazelle's perch
Those dimples made his stomach lurch
Spotlight from God framed her face
How long would she make him chase?

What did that mean? Hadley had a lump in the pit of her stomach. Dimples? It was her, she knew it. Oh brother. It seemed so unlikely. But if the boulder where she'd sat that first day was where the cache was hidden, then Hadley would know for sure. "Come on, Ava." She led her friend across the clearing and stopped in front of the giant rock where she had sat for the kickoff rally.

It was obviously too big to move, so the cache couldn't be under it. Ava felt around behind the rock, nothing.

Hadley looked from the rock to the tree. If the sunlight. . . "Never mind. I know where it is." Hadley placed one of her boots on the lowest branch of the big oak tree and swung herself up into its boughs, heading toward the break in the tree from where she had felt the heat of the sun shine on her back. She continued her way up the tree until she spotted a gray metal box tucked in the nook of a branch right in front of her. She couldn't reach it unless she climbed sideways, but there didn't appear to be another branch strong enough to step on to.

Ava watched Hadley from below. "What are you going to do?" She pointed the flashlight beam at Hadley's feet.

Hadley gripped the branch then dropped her body down until it was dangling much too far above the ground to jump.

"Be careful, girl."

She eyed the branch she was aiming for a few feet away and began to swing her body towards it, gathering momentum. When she felt confident that she could swing and reach the other branch, Hadley let go with one hand and used the weight of her body to propel her to the distant bough and grabbed it as soon as she got close enough. Now what? Suspended between two secure spots, dangling over nothing, Hadley didn't know if she could let go with her right hand and complete the swing, or if she'd fall the minute she loosened her grip.

"Do you need me to go for help?" Ava shouted from below.

"No! Shh!" That was the last thing Hadley wanted. Okay.

Now or never. She shifted her body back and forth to gather as much momentum as she could. When the time felt right, she let go and easily sailed to her target and grabbed hold. She pulled her feet up and linked them around the branch like a lemur then shimmied toward the tree trunk.

"Ava, I'm going to drop a heavy metal box down. Make sure you're out of the way." Hadley heard scurrying.

"Okay. Go for it."

The box whooshed through the nighttime air then landed with a soft thud in the blanket of grass and leaves. Hadley climbed down the tree and hopped off the lowest branch, onto the ground beside the cache. She dusted off her hiking shorts and smiled at Ava. "Found it."

Ava stared, openmouthed. "I can't believe you just did that. That was amazing, Had."

"Thanks. Okay, now we need to open this and sign the logbook to prove we were here." Unlikely anyone but her would have had a chance at figuring out the clue, but there was no way Hadley wanted to risk someone else figuring out that poem was about her.

She popped open the lid, and there it was.

The Rainbow's End geocoin.

"What's that thing?" Ava peered over Hadley's shoulder.

"It's some special token-coin-thing. I get five points for finding it."

"That's awesome. How do we turn it in to collect your winnings?" Ava flipped it over and looked at the back.

The last thing Hadley wanted to do was show up at the church office with that token in her hand, admitting to Noah face-to-face that she'd found it. He'd know she figured out his poem. What did the poem say to her about him? What would the fact that she figured it out say to him about her?

"No. It's not worth five points to me to turn it in. I want to keep it for. . .um. . .a souvenir." Hadley hoped Ava would buy her explanation and not ask any more questions. She was thankful that clouds had moved in and it was too dark for Ava to see Hadley's face, which must be crimson with embarrassment. "Plus, I don't want to give my competition a chance to earn the five points."

Ava shrugged. "If you say so."

Chapter 8

Oh, quit with the mirror, Had. You look great. We're only going for a free coffee." Ava held the bedroom door open and tapped her foot.

They made the short ride to Common Grounds in Norma's little blue Prius. Hadley waited for a snarky comment from Ava. She sensed it was coming. . .

"I. . .uh. . .never had to. . .um, unplug a car before I drove it before." Ava giggled.

"Don't knock it. It saves on gas, and it's better for the environment, I guess. Norma thinks she's doing something good. So. . ."

"Uh huh." Ava laughed. A city girl through and through. She'd rather take the el or hop a cab than own a car any day.

"So do you, like, know any of these other gee-pers?"

"Gee-pers?"

"Oh, that's what I call these GPS hunters in my head. Gee-pers."

Hadley laughed. "Yes. I know some of them." Hopefully two of them wouldn't be at Common Grounds that night. Ava would come unglued with all the meddling she'd been missing out on. She'd be setting Hadley up with Brad in no time if

321

she didn't claim him for herself first.

They stepped into the red-brick restaurant and glanced around the crowd. Hadley saw some regulars gathered in the normal place and headed in that direction. Madison was at Hadley's favorite table—might as well join her. She at least seemed normal.

"Mind if we join you?" Hadley rested her hand on the back of a chair.

"I'd love it." Madison beamed.

Hadley snatched the chair facing the door so she could keep an eye on things and motioned for Ava to sit across.

"There's my doll." Brad stepped around the corner and planted a gentle kiss on Hadley's cheek, blocking their path.

Ava's mouth fell open.

"And who is this lovely lady you've got with you tonight?" He picked up Ava's hand and gently kissed the back of it. Hadley saw the goose bumps travel up Ava's arm. Looked like even she wasn't immune to the Hopper.

"Brad, this is my roommate from Chicago in for a visit. Ava, this is Brad, you know, that friend I've been telling you about." Hadley gave Ava a just-go-along-with-it, I'll-tell-you-later look.

In true best-friend form, Ava took the hint. "Oh, yes. It's wonderful to meet you, Brad. I've heard so many nice things about you."

Okay, don't lay it on too thick, Ava.

A waitress appeared. "What can I get you girls?"

"Mint mocha latte for me. How about you, Ava?"

"Perfect."

The waitress turned to her right. "Brad?"

"A Midnight Espresso and a smile." He grinned. "I'll be

back in a few minutes, ladies. I see some business associates I need to speak with for a moment."

Ava practically dove on Hadley the minute he walked away. "You're keeping things from me, young lady. That gorgeous man is smitten with you—and himself, but that's beside the point."

Leave it to Ava to nail it on the first try. "I don't know about all that. He's nice, though. I think I like him."

"Oh, honey. He's not the kind of guy you fall for. Has Mama Ava not taught you anything? He's the kind of guy you have fun with for a while. Let him take you fancy places, maybe have him around for a birthday or Christmas or two. But fall for? No. Nope. Never."

"Why? He's really nice."

"He's a player, Had. Nothing but a player. I think you know that, but you want to pretend differently. You'll see. Hopefully before you get hurt." Ava nodded at someone behind Hadley. "Now that's the kind of guy you should fall for. The real deal."

Hadley was afraid to look. "How can you tell without talking to him?"

Ava eyed her quizzically. "You know who I'm talking about?"

Gut feeling. "Oh, it's probably Noah. But who cares? You haven't even spoken to him."

"I don't have to, Had; he has kind eyes. And he's coming this way."

"Great," Hadley muttered and looked for an escape.

"I don't believe we've met." Noah extended an arm over Hadley's head and pumped Ava's hand.

"I'm Ava, Hadley's roommate, visiting from Chicago."

"Ah. Great! I hope you'll be around for our rally this weekend—it's going to be a blast."

"I'm going back tomorrow morning, but I'm sure it'll be fun."

Noah glanced down at Hadley. "Hi."

"Hi." She inspected her fingernails and picked an invisible piece of lint from her jeans.

"Anyway." Noah turned back to Ava and laughed nervously. "If you can put in a good word for me with your roommate, I'd really appreciate it."

As soon as he was out of earshot, Ava leaned close to Hadley. "What is the matter with you? That was plain rude."

"You have no idea what I've been through with him. I'll tell you all about it sometime. But not now."

Ava's eyes grew wide. "Wait a sec. Is that *the* Noah?" She craned her neck to catch Noah's retreat through the front door. "Huh. Who'd have figured he'd still be here after all this time?"

Hadley sighed. "Yeah. Who'd have figured?"

Ava nodded. "What's that old saying? Something about how you can only really know someone if you hate him before you love him?"

"Welcome to the Rainbow's End Midhunt Rally. Be sure to sign in with Lyssa at the registration table to have your attendance points recorded." Noah smiled down on the buzzing group. "There's a schedule of the day's events on the table, so grab one of those, and be sure to participate in everything you can."

Hadley let Noah's voice fade to a drone in the background. He was cute in a Woodstock sort of way—always had been. His voice had grown so much deeper over the years since she'd last seen him. That deep voice didn't really go with the long, lanky body. And the wavy hippie hair didn't seem to suit a pastor-type. Too many riddles about that man. Then there were the real riddles to consider, like the one he'd used to guide her to the cache. What was he trying to accomplish with that? What did he want her to do with that information? Did he even know she'd found it yet?

Shaking her head, Hadley wandered over to the registration table and signed in then grabbed a schedule printed on a half-sheet of blue paper. *Ugh.* They weren't going to announce the prize package until four o'clock? Nothing like keeping everyone in suspense. Relay races, food, a dunk tank—ooh, maybe Noah would get in there—more food, a water balloon fight. Who scheduled a water balloon fight? Weren't they supposed to just happen? A watermelon-eating contest. Hot dog lunch. An afternoon ice cream bar. Then the announcement. Then s'mores over a bonfire. Didn't these people do anything that didn't involve food? She could handle the wait until four for the news, but there was no way she was going to stand around and eat all day. She could go hunt for a cache or two while waiting. Maybe she could even hook up with Madison for some girl talk.

"Oh, folks, I forgot to mention—all cache hunting is canceled for today, and any found will not be credited to your name. We want you to stay and participate with the group, so no big ideas of sneaking off." Noah laughed when the crowd groaned. "You see—I knew what you guys were thinking."

Oh, goody for you.

Hands reached around from behind her and covered her eyes. Hadley squealed and grabbed the forearms of her assailant. She whipped around to face him. "Oh, Brad, thank goodness it's you."

"Who did you think it was? And how did you know it was

me and not some hot stranger?"

"I didn't think it was anyone in particular, but I knew it was you by your forearms."

"Oh? What is it about my forearms that gave me away?"

Hadley felt a blush creep up her neck and onto her ears. She couldn't tell him she'd studied his muscular arms. "Oh, you know." She giggled in nervousness, and Brad leaned in for a kiss.

Tongue like sandpaper on the roof of his mouth from watching Brad with his hands—and lips—on *her*, Noah reached for his water on the picnic table beside him and took a big gulp. The heat seared his throat, and the liquid spewed out across the table. He'd grabbed the scalding coffee instead. He barely noticed the pain in his throat over the searing of his heart as he watched Brad kiss Hadley a second time.

A few minutes later, the burning in his throat had risen to the surface of his consciousness, and he couldn't ignore it any longer. He shook his water cup until some ice fell into his mouth, and he let the cool water melt over his burns.

Why couldn't Hadley see through Brad's good looks? Was she stupid? Or did she find men like Brad attractive? If that were the case, Noah knew he had no chance with her. Not as though he'd want one if that was the kind of girl she'd turned into. But he wasn't buying it. Something kept niggling at him. . .pricking his soul with memories of her. There was something about Hadley. Otherwise, he was an idiot for keeping up with his hope in the face of her disdain. But no. Something rich, something real, lay beneath that protective barrier she kept in place. Noah could feel it.

She'd found his cache. It was gone, and there was no way anyone else could possibly have figured it out. She knew where she sat that day, and she knew he had feelings for her. So she could figure what he saw when he looked in her direction. . . and the cache was gone. Also, the coin hadn't been returned. Noah didn't expect Hadley to show up at the church with it. If she had, she'd risk him actually confronting her and addressing the poem and his feelings. Hadley wouldn't chance that for anything.

Should he let her know that he knew she knew? Why did he suddenly feel like he was back in junior high? Maybe he'd pass her a note after study hall. Do you like me? Circle yes or no.

It was time to lay it on the line. He'd mention the coin in a few minutes when he announced the prize package. If she didn't acknowledge it, then he'd take that as her final answer and let her go. Would he actually be able to do that? But did he have a choice?

"Can I get everyone's attention, please?" Noah hopped up on the picnic bench he used as a platform. "I hope you're all having a great day just relaxing and letting go of the competition for a few hours. I know that's difficult for some of you. . .cough. . . Chuck. . .cough."

The crowd laughed.

"I have a few announcements to make then we'll get to the big one." He searched the crowd to be sure that Hadley listened. It took a moment to find her, and then he wished he hadn't. She was leaning against Brad, who had his arms wrapped around her. "S–so, the thing is. . .well. . ." *Come on, Noah. It is what it is. Let it go. Say what you came to say, and move on.*

"Well, I'm pleased to announce the Rainbow's End

geocoin has been retrieved." He caught Hadley's gaze and held it. "But it hasn't been returned yet. This could be due to one of two things. Either we've got a real game player who has a plan. Or someone wants a five-point souvenir. My guess? We've got a game player in our midst."

The crowd booed.

Noah laughed. "Now, now. She, or he, has every right to hang on to the coin. It's strategy, folks. I just wanted you to know it's been retrieved. We'll see if it gets turned in at some point or not." He nodded at Hadley and then looked away.

"Now for the announcement you've been waiting for. The prize package."

Chapter 9

There she sat. Alone. Again. Stood up by Brad Hopper. When was Hadley going to demand better for herself? If only she could see what Noah had seen in her since they were best friends as little kids, and then later, when they were more. He saw deep green eyes that asked a million questions but wouldn't wait for an answer. Then there were her dimples. The good Lord must have given those to her because He knew the world couldn't take too much of them, and since she didn't smile all that much, it would be okay.

Ugh. Why was he doing this to himself? She was there for Brad. Speaking of Brad, where was he? Still not there. "This is ridiculous," Noah muttered as he stomped over to where Hadley sat by herself—stood up by Brad again from the looks of things. Noah refused to let it go. She didn't deserve to be treated like this. Even if she didn't like him, Hadley needed to know that at least Noah thought she deserved better than Brad Hopper.

"Stood up again, Hadley?" Noah gently touched her slender shoulder.

"Hey!" Hadley whirled around and toppled her water glass. Noah reached out to steady it, but not before some water spilled to the table.

"Hey! Do you have some sick obsession with making my life miserable? You leave destruction in your wake, and I'm tired of it."

"I don't see how—"

"Oh? You don't? The rock at the cache site, the bike accident." She ticked her fingers as she spat out her list. "This water…what else? Well, let's see, I could go back a few years…"

"You know what? You're a real piece of work. That rock at the cache site the first day—you were going to kill yourself if you dove. I saved your life. The bike accident—pretty sure you were about to get killed there, too. Another attempt at saving your life. This water? Um, sweetheart, you spilled that water because you're wound up so tight a light breeze would startle you. Look if you want me to stop saving your life, tell me. Better yet, let me do it one more time right now then I'll leave you alone."

Hadley closed her mouth.

Finally.

She crossed her arms and cocked her head. "I'm waiting. Go ahead, save my life again, and then leave me alone—make my day complete in more ways than one."

Should he say it? She'd never take it the way he meant it, but he couldn't just let her continue to walk into Brad's lair unwarned. "Dump Brad." There, he said it. Uh-oh, her mouth was open again. She shook her head, the ponytail whipping her cheeks.

"How dare you? How could you say that to me?"

Here we go again. If he wanted to make a point, he'd better get to it. "Listen, Hadley, I'll leave you alone, even though it's the last thing I want to do, but please don't make me leave you to him. Pick anyone else. How about that guy?" Noah pointed at Chuck, who let out a loud belch. Okay, bad example. "How about him. . .or him. . .?" Noah pointed out strangers. "Anyone is better for you than Brad Hopper." She almost seemed to be listening. "He's bad news, Hadley. You just can't see it." *Oh, Hadley, if you only knew.*

The fire lit up in her green eyes—flames licking her long eyelashes. "I can't see it, huh? Me, the big-city girl? The out-of-towner? Somehow I'm the one who doesn't get men? Maybe you don't understand women, Noah. Maybe Brad is exactly what I want. He would never, ever do to me what you did. But you're too shortsighted to see that. You in your little beachy bubble from your little pulpit world. People aren't always who you think they are—for better or worse. I learned that from you."

Was that true? Did Hadley know exactly what she was doing? No way. She wasn't that type. She was clearly inexperienced—but she just as clearly didn't want anyone to know it. She had issues. . .but what kind? She deserved to know the truth, but coming from Noah, she'd think it was nothing but sour grapes. She'd have to find out on her own. Noah prayed it wouldn't be too late.

"Noah, I think you're jealous. Green doesn't become you. Please just leave me alone." She dropped a twenty on the table and jumped to her feet, knocking the chair back into Noah's hands as she stormed from the restaurant.

He was growing weary of watching Hadley's ponytail bob as she fled his presence. This couldn't last forever, could it? He looked down at the table. Set for one. Oops. So she hadn't been stood up—so what? That didn't change who Brad was. He'd been exactly the same person since grade school. Nothing would ever change him in Noah's eyes.

Hadley jogged to Brad's car when he pulled in the drive at Norma's.

"Hi, doll." He leaned over and kissed her cheek when she climbed in. "Oh, that's not enough. C'mere." He pulled her over for an embrace and planted a kiss on her lips. "That's better. Yum."

Did he say *Yum*? Hadley giggled. "Have a good meeting?"

"Hmm? Meeting? Oh, yeah, it went fine."

Short-term memory. "It was a meeting, right? Who with?" Hadley glanced at him.

"No one special. Just some business associates. Boring talk." Brad grinned.

Was he lying? Or was Hadley too paranoid? Most likely the latter.

"How about you? Good dinner?" He glanced in the rearview mirror as he backed the car onto the road.

"Oh, yeah. I'm totally addicted to those fig crispinis. I'd better watch my calories." Hadley patted her stomach.

"I don't think that's a problem for you. In fact, you might want to have a double order next time. You're getting a little bony."

Hadley grinned. "Reeeeally?" Brad had no idea, but he had just paid her the best compliment of her life. She felt, for the first time, like she might have left her fat-girl image in Chicago, buried once and for all. She had no intention of bringing it back home again.

"You girls are so silly with the weight thing." Brad wiggled his eyebrows. "But I sure am glad."

She let the warmth settle over her, bathed in the compliments from Brad—truly the most gorgeous man she'd ever been near. He was older than her by about eight years, but that gave him the salt-n-pepper look to his hair she found so attractive. Men his age were getting ready to settle down. Ready for families. It could be just perfect between them. She'd even quit her job and move to Osage Beach if he asked her to marry him. A sigh escaped her lips.

"Hey, earth to Hadley." Brad snapped his fingers in front of her face. "Where are we going? You're the navigator."

"Oh! Right." Hadley scrambled to find her GPS and the notes she'd made. "We agree that the clue *Spring, Winter, Summer, Fall* means Village of Four Seasons, right?"

"Definitely."

"Okay, then take Horseshoe Bend out."

"Right. What's next?"

"*Shoulder pads, knee pads, helmet, and all.*
Just be careful you don't fall."

Hadley squeezed her eyes shut in thought. "Is there a roller rink or an ice skating rink there?"

"No. But there's a skateboard park."

"That's it!" Hadley leaned forward and flipped on the radio. They drove in silence until Brad pulled into the parking lot.

"Too bad we didn't hike or bike here. It wasn't that far."

Brad laughed. "Oh come on. Why do that when we can drive right to it?"

"Seriously? It's the spirit of the hunt. The adventure. The physical experience."

"Yeah—I'm not really feeling all that." Brad laughed as he pulled the car next to the curb along the skate park.

Oh well. So they didn't see eye to eye on one thing. That

was life. All relationships had that in one way or another. Right? Hadley could sense the nearness of her target. "The last line is,

Watch out for that big wall."

Brad surveyed the landscape. "Could it be as simple as that big wall over there? I mean, skateboarders would probably want to watch out for it if they didn't have a death wish."

"Maybe. Some of the clues have been that simple." Hadley hurried to the wall and felt along its rugged edges until she felt a loose rock. "I think I have something here." She pulled the rock out; behind it was a gray metal box. The cache! Her blood pressure rose as her heart beat faster.

She pulled out the spiral-bound logbook to sign their names. Hadley first, then Brad. Maybe chivalry hadn't died just yet.

Within minutes, they were back in the car, and Brad started it up again. "Do you mind if I take the time to use the restroom over there?" He gestured to a Porta Potty beyond the tree line.

"I don't know that I'd call it that, but do what you have to do." Hadley messed with the dial on the radio. Wonder what he'd do if she changed all his presets to country music. She jumped when the car door jerked open and Brad plopped hard onto his seat. "Wow, that was fast!"

Brad grimaced. "It's not like I wanted to read a newspaper in there."

"True, very true." Hadley settled back into her seat and closed her eyes. Things grew more and more familiar—natural—every day. Noah sure couldn't stand Brad, but Noah didn't have much room to point fingers. Maybe his opinion of Brad was a good thing. Could Brad be the one?

Noah paced outside the front door of On the Rise Bistro. How could he possibly go in there and accuse Hadley of cheating? It couldn't be true. There had to be a simple explanation. He would take anything that made sense at this point.

Deep breath. He entered the restaurant and approached Hadley at a table for two. Why couldn't she have been alone for this? He'd have waited until later, but he couldn't let it go on all day if it was true, and if it wasn't—he had to know.

Hadley's companion had her back to Noah, but judging by the dark braid and the cargoes with the GPS unit hooked on her belt, it was a hunter.

"I was hoping to you'd be here. I saw your bike outside." Noah couldn't believe what he had come to say. He wiped his sweaty palms on his khakis and checked out Hadley's breakfast partner. Madison. How to get her to leave so he could say what he'd come to say?

Hadley set her coffee cup down and turned a cold stare on Noah. "I was just enjoying breakfast with a friend. Emphasis on *was*. What did you want to find me for?"

Madison scooted her chair back. "I'm going to take this as a good time to excuse myself." She raised her eyebrows at Hadley. "I'll be right back."

Hadley stared at Noah, drumming her fingernails on the tablecloth.

How could he say this? "Hadley, I can't believe that I have to ask you this, but have you recorded any caches on the website that you didn't actually find?" She was the hardest-working hunter, but she'd recorded so many caches. Could she possibly have found that many?

She reared back as though she'd been slapped. "Excuse me? I've worked my tail off to find each and every cache I've recorded. Exactly what are you accusing me of?"

He shouldn't have said anything. But the logbooks. . .why hadn't she signed them all? "I don't know, Hadley. I'm sure there's a mistake somewhere. Just make sure you always sign the logbook, okay?"

"I always do. It's my favorite part." Her eyebrows knit together in concern. "Is there a problem?"

"No. Really. It's all fine. I think there was a mistake somewhere along the line. I'm sure it was mine." Noah closed his mouth then opened it again. No. He'd better quit while he was ahead.

"What were you going to say just then?" Hadley crossed her arms.

Nothing you want to hear. "Nothing. Really. Just be careful, Hadley." Noah turned and strode from the restaurant. How had he made such a mess of things?

Chapter 10

I think I'm going to quit and come home."

"What?" Ava shouted into the phone. "Are you crazy?"

"Look, I'm obviously not ready to be unleashed on the real world and should just dive back into my cave where I can't hurt anyone, including myself. Brad would get over it if I left. I'm sure he has a bevy of women at his beck and call to choose from."

"Oh, puhleeze. You know I love you, Had. But it's time I whop you over the head." Ava took a deep breath.

Uh-oh.

"Had. Get. Over. Yourself."

"What?" How could she say that? Hadley had been hurt. She'd had a rough life. She deserved sympathy, not accusations.

"Listen, girl. Let go. You're holding so tightly to the past and to what bad people have said or done to you, to losses in your life, that you're ignoring the words and love of the good people all around you. Hadley, we all have struggles in life. I had alcoholic and abusive parents. I've been teased and suffered bigotry for my race and family history. You've suffered, I've suffered. We've all suffered. You're nothing special for your pain."

Hadley crumbled in tears. How could her best friend say something so cruel to her?

"Let me finish. You're not special for the pain you've suffered; you're special for what you've done to overcome that pain. You've shown exactly how strong you are by how you've overcome your body image, your fears, and your lack of experience in matters of the heart. I admire you so much for how you've changed your life. Stop finding your identity in your pain, and find it in your strength."

Hadley sniffed. Was Ava right? Was that what had been going on? Was she missing the mark?

"It's time to let go, Had. Actually, way past time. The real you has been revealed. And she's pretty awesome."

"So what do I do now that I've messed everything up?" Brad. Noah. People thought she cheated. She should return to the safety of Chicago where things made sense.

"You stay put. You finish the race you set out to win. You make amends with that cute youth pastor who is obviously still head over heels for you—"

"Noah?" Hadley laughed. "Oh, come on, Ava. He hates me. I've been nothing but mean to him."

"Hate is just undercover love, Had."

"Brad. . .you home?" Hadley knocked on the front door. No answer, but the lights were on. Maybe he was around back. She walked through the dewy grass and climbed the steps to his deck. She smelled grilled food but didn't hear any sounds. They hadn't made any plans that night, but wouldn't it be cool if he'd sensed she was coming over?

It had been a rough day. Hadley had been fighting demons,

and she needed someone to talk to—a shoulder—well, not to cry on, but to lean on. Hopefully, Brad was home and would be her friend. She knew he wanted more than that. . .and they were definitely headed in that direction, but it would take Hadley time to catch up to where Brad wanted things to go. She'd have to share her reasons with him one of these days— maybe tonight if all went according to plan.

Brad's deep laugh boomed from the deck of his boat. Probably on his cell phone. He said a few words that Hadley couldn't hear as she took a few steps out onto the deck.

"Oooh, Brad. I like it when you touch me like that."

Hadley froze where she stood. Her world spun out of her reach, and her ears rang. What was happening? She couldn't even find clarity in the sounds around her anymore. She shook her head to clear the cacophony. She needed her senses clear because this was going to get ugly—she just knew it.

"I'll be right back, Crystal. Don't you go anywhere. We need more drinks." Brad bounded onto the deck like a man on a mission.

"Crystal, huh?"

Brad stepped into the moonlight and locked eyes with Hadley. He blanched and looked from her face back to the boat, then back to Hadley—still grinning stupidly. He dropped one side of the smile, then the other. He lowered his eyes. "Look, you have to understand, Hadley. Men like me. . .we—"

"Have needs? Don't tell me you were actually going to say that. How cliché. Silly me for thinking we had something special. For thinking *you* were special. You're selfish, immature, and a big, fat liar." Hadley looked him up and down. A disgusting shell of a man stood before her. "Look at you. Your clothes are all messed up. You've been drinking. You're a snake, and I'm so glad I came here tonight."

"Why couldn't you just call first?"

"What, call first and miss all this? Hah. Showing up here to surprise you was the best move I've ever made." Hadley turned on her heel. *Head high. Don't stumble. Don't trip. Don't fall.* She strode away in the moonlight, tossing her ponytail over her shoulder.

"Good-bye, Brad."

Hadley sailed her bike into the yard and let it fall to the ground. She climbed onto the porch. Numb. Norma's rocker looked the most inviting, so she sat on the edge. Unmoving.

A minute later, maybe thirty, Norma poked her head out the screen door. "Come on in, dear. Come to Norma."

Hadley rose and followed Norma into the kitchen.

"I can tell you've had a rough day, darlin'. Sit down right here and tell Norma all about it. I made you a mug of hot honey milk. If that doesn't soothe your soul, nothin' will."

Hadley took one look at the steaming mug and then back at the warm heart that had prepared it. A single tear escaped. She swiped at it, and three took its place. Then more and more appeared until her shoulders were shaking with sobs.

"Oh, sweet baby. Tell me. What is it?" Norma engulfed Hadley's body in her arms.

"It's just—wh–why—do—I—why—can't—I. . ." She sobbed and gulped. The words just wouldn't come.

Norma let her cry and rocked her back and forth. "Shh. Shh. It's okay. It's going to be okay."

"Why can't they just love me?"

"Who, baby?"

"Him. . . Them. . . Anyone." Hadley went limp on Norma's shoulder. It felt so warm and safe. Like home.

Norma clucked her tongue. "Sweet girl, I don't think the problem is that you need love from someone else. I think the problem is that you need to learn to love yourself. Look at ol' Norma, here. Shoot fire, honey, it's been decades upon decades since I've known the love of a man. But it hasn't made me think any less of myself. I love myself. You know why?"

Hadley raised her eyes and looked at the dear old woman. "No. Why?"

"Because I'm home. I'm safe in the arms of my Father, and I know how He feels about me."

"But mine is dead." Tears brimmed Hadley's eyes.

"No, sugar. Not that father. I'm talking about that one." She jabbed a meaty finger at the sky. "And He is very much alive. I sure would love to introduce you to Him. Want to meet my Daddy?"

Hadley nodded. "Yes. Please."

Chapter 11

A car door slammed, and someone bounded up the steps to the porch. Hadley looked at Norma with a question in her eyes. "Who. . . ?"

"I invited my grandbaby boy to come over. He knows Jesus, too. He'll want to celebrate with us."

Ugh. The last thing Hadley wanted to do was meet someone. But Norma looked so excited and proud. Proud of her grandson or proud of Hadley, she didn't know which. Either way, she'd never disappoint Norma. Not after tonight.

"Here he is, the man of my life."

A familiar form filled the doorway. Noah.

The tears sprang back to Hadley's eyes. If only. She shook her head at Noah. Would he ever forgive her for treating him like she had?

"Hi, Hadley."

Norma looked from Noah to Hadley then back again. "You two have met?"

"A few times, Mamaw."

Hadley wiped away her tears and nodded.

"Oh. . ." The light dawned on Norma's face. "You're. . . ?" She turned from Hadley to Noah. "This is. . . ?"

Noah nodded.

"Ah. I remember story after story about a precious young girl named Hadley. Then the stories stopped." Norma nodded and smiled. "Then Jesus brought you home." She heaved herself from the dining chair. "I think I'll leave you two alone for a bit. But I'll be back."

"And she won't go far." Noah winked.

Hadley giggled—then remembered.

Deep breath. "Noah, I. . .I'm so, so sorry." She hung her head. There is no way he could forgive her for being so mean—so unforgiving.

In one stride he was by her side. "I know. Shh." He wrapped his long arms around her and held on.

Hadley waited for accusations. Waited for her berating. But none came. She felt the love of Jesus in those arms. The tension in her back melted as her body relaxed and her soul healed. "There's so much to say, so much to talk about."

Noah put his finger over her lips. "Shh. There'll be plenty of time to cover everything. But right now. . ." He pulled away and grabbed her face in his hands. He looked deeply into her eyes. Imploring. "I just want to know if you're okay. Please, tell me you're okay." His hands squeezed.

There was an intensity to his question. He knew something. He feared something. What could it be? "Yes, Noah. My ego is bruised, and I'm embarrassed by my behavior. But I'm fine. I'm perfect. I'm loved."

"That's all I needed to hear."

The song said the sun'll come out tomorrow. So this is what tomorrow felt like? Noah stretched his long frame in his bed and yawned. The day held so much hope—so much promise. He sat up. But so much work! What was he thinking? It was the end of the hunt. He had to figure out the winner, prepare the announcement, and alert the media.

He jumped from his bed, knelt beside it for ten minutes giving thanks, spent five more in the shower, grabbed an orange and a banana, then flew to the church. Okay, drove. But he envisioned his car as a Delorian.

Piles of papers and logbooks spilled across his desk. Okay. He knew what to do. Time to match up the points with the logbooks and the website. He needed a winner, and he needed it to be accurate. There were going to be discrepancies along the way.

Oh no! He'd forgotten his coffee. He grabbed his cell phone and called Common Grounds. "Any chance one of your guys can run me over a cup of the strongest brew with a ton of sugar?" Oh, thank the Lord. "Thanks man, I owe you, big time!"

Noah dove in. An hour later, the beginnings of a migraine had set in, and his forehead started to perspire. Something was wrong. According to the website, Hadley was the clear winner—by a long shot. But the logbooks told a different story. According to them, Brad was the winner. Noah shook his head. He'd been watching the activity, and there was no way Brad worked as hard as Hadley. No way. He hadn't even worked as hard as Chuck, who barely held a candle to Hadley.

But what could Noah do to prove it? People would want to know why she'd only signed twenty logbooks. Twenty? Everyone knew she'd found way more than that. But why hadn't she signed in? Noah rubbed his temples. This wasn't right. He searched the ring binders of the spiral books, but they showed no evidence of pages having been torn out. That had to be what happened, but he couldn't prove it. No one could.

"Norma." *Please don't let her hate me.*

"Hi, sweetums. Come on in and sit a spell. What's on your mind, darlin?" Norma rocked in her favorite chair, a grin plastered on her face from ear to ear.

"You mean you're not mad at me for how I treated Noah?"

"Oh, child. I'm so glad I didn't know what was going on and who it was going on with." Norma fanned herself with a quilt catalog. "The Lord. . .He had plans. Delicious ones. And I would have meddled and messed them all up. This way, it's all Him. As it should rightly be." She sighed like her life was complete.

"Norma, please tell me about Brad Hopper." Hadley dropped to her knees beside the rocker.

The old woman's face darkened like a shadow cast from the moon descended upon it. She moved her lips, as though in prayer. Praying for permission? "I'll tell you, child. But only because of what's happened. Now, you know I don't believe in gossip."

Hadley nodded.

"That boy—he went to college with my grandbaby boy. That Brad gave Noah such a time of it for his faith. He made Noah stronger—that much I know. But Brad wasn't satisfied. Seemed like every time my boy had a girl he liked, Brad had to prove he could get her."

Hadley grimaced. She'd been used as a tool to hurt Noah. Maybe not at first, but as soon as Noah appeared interested. Or did Brad know from the beginning who she was to Noah? She might never know.

"But that boy didn't just date 'em. He chewed 'em up and then spit 'em out."

Hadley nodded. That could have been her.

"But the final blow. . .what shut off any hope Noah had of reaching Brad, came when that Hopper boy took Noah's sister from her husband and from Noah and from me. She left her husband for good a few months after they lost their baby boy. She chose Brad Hopper over all the good that God had brought into her life. She was hurting, sure. But we all were. That baby. . .oh, he was so beautiful. Chubby. Giggly. Happy. He drowned in the lake. Off Brad's dock."

Hadley gasped. Brad had used the same location where a baby had died to draw her into his web. The pain that family had endured because of a man she might have loved. How could she have been so blind? "I'm so sorry, Norma."

"Oh, sweet child. You didn't know. You didn't do this. Noah. . .he's an innocent. He loves big, but he hurts hard. He's been aching over you for years and years, I just know it." Norma grabbed Hadley's hands. "Don't hurt him. Please. I know you wouldn't on purpose. But please don't hurt him—even on accident. I can't lose my boy, too."

A car pulled into the driveway, and a door slammed almost immediately. Noah bounded into the kitchen, and both women stared at him in shock. "What's the matter, boy?" Norma croaked.

"We have a problem." Noah's skin was pale, and his hands were shaking.

He sat beside Hadley. "I know you worked so hard for this. We have to find a way to prove it's a lie."

"What's a lie? What are you talking about?"

Noah whipped open the logbooks, spread the print-outs

from the website on the table, and showed her the results, the grief lining his face. "I've only looked at the top few so far. I need to compare everyone's web records with the logbooks to find any other discrepancies that would be caused by missing pages."

Hadley waved a hand. "Oh, proof? Is that all you want?" She reached in her purse for her phone. "I have art."

"What do you mean?"

"Oh, I took pictures when I signed each and every logbook. Not because I thought something like this would happen, of course. But I just wanted a record for myself."

"Oh, bless you, sweet girl." Norma grabbed them both and pulled them to her bosom.

It was a little hard to breathe, but Noah caught Hadley's eye above the crumpled cotton and winked.

Tires scuffed the gravel driveway, and the three of them sighed.

"Oh, Lordy. What now?" Norma rose to see who had arrived. "Good gracious." She opened the screen door and stepped back to let a young woman move past her into the house.

Noah gasped. "What are *you* doing here?"

Hadley looked from Noah back to the girl. Was she an ex? Someone who'd hurt him?

"Crystal, what are you doing here?" Noah's eyes softened as the shock wore off.

Crystal? Like Brad's Crystal? Understanding flooded her senses. "Oh no. Is Crystal your. . .is she your. . . ?" Hadley grabbed Noah's hands and pulled him to look in her eyes. "Hear her out, Noah. Please?"

Pretty blue eyes, mirror images of Noah's, turned to Hadley. "Why would you help me?"

"Because when you've been forgiven for something, you want to share it with others. And we're both victims of something—or someone." Hadley reached her arms out and pulled the woman to her.

"Of course I'll hear her out, Had."

Crystal's lower lip began to quiver, and she looked at Norma, then Noah. "I am so sorry." She covered her face with her hands and dissolved onto the floor, sobs wracking her body. "I miss you so much. I miss. . .I miss my baby so much. I can't live another day without forgiveness. From you guys. . .from God. . . and from Joshie. If I can't have it, I'll leave from this place and never return. I promise you that. I can't live like this anymore. I broke my family. My baby died because I was selfish. . .stupid. Please. Please. . .oh God. . .please."

Reality swam in Hadley's consciousness. Too much. She finally understood what true pain felt like. It lay at her feet. Her own troubles paled in comparison to the agony she witnessed. She looked to Norma, to Noah. *Do something. Help her.*

A smile creased Noah's face. Not one of pleasure, but one of peace. He bent to where his crumpled and broken sister lay and scooped her in his arms, and pulled Hadley into the embrace.

"Welcome home, Chrys."

"And the winner is. . ." Noah's eyes sparkled as he opened the envelope Lyssa had handed him moments before.

Of course it would be her name he called. Hadley had been tracking the results through the entire hunt. No one was close enough to win, even if awarded all the extra points possible. And she had found the bonus coin. Hadley was a shoe-in for first place. Then why was she so nervous? If only she didn't have to be in front of all these people to accept her prize. Couldn't she phone in her acceptance speech from some far-off island in the Bahamas?

"Hadley Parker."

Here goes.

The crowd roared and whistled as Hadley climbed onto the wooden stage.

Noah gripped her hand while the crowd continued to clap. "One of these days you'll know who you are—how I see you and how God sees you. I'm going to make sure of it." Noah tweaked her nose. "But now. . .the prize."

Noah held a purple polka-dotted gift bag in his hands. "We've had so many donations and have added a long list of prizes to both second and third places, which you've seen already. But first prize. . .well, I've taken the liberty of donating first prize myself." He pulled one end of the green ribbon and untied the bag then reached inside and lifted out a tiny white box.

Several gasps came from the audience.

A few women moaned, "Awwww."

No way. Was he going to propose to her? It was so soon. What if it wasn't the right move? Hadley had hardly ever dated. How could she make such a choice with no warning. . .in front of all of those people?

Noah's shaky hand lifted the lid from the tiny box in his hands, and he looked Hadley in the eye.

In that momentary gaze, Hadley felt peace wash over her like a waterfall. Freedom. Joy. Love. Her choice was an easy one, after all.

Noah stooped to one knee as the crowd silenced.

He lifted the box toward Hadley and opened his mouth to speak.

Hadley gasped and leaned in to see, shifting her weight and placing her foot to her right.

In slow motion, she saw the crowd rear back in horror as one end of a loosened plank flew up and Hadley was flung to the ground as though abandoned on a teeter-totter.

Noah reached for her and set the law of gravity in motion again. He landed in a heap right on top of her.

Was he hurt? Was she? Hadley felt the heat rise up her neck and tinge her ears. How could she face these people? She lay motionless a few more moments, listening to the silence of the horrified crowd and the click of a camera shutter. Oh, great. This would be all over Facebook within an hour.

Did it matter, though? She'd ruined Noah's proposal. Humiliated them both.

Hadley felt movement on top of her, and then the board shielding her eyes from the sun and the stares of the crowd disappeared. She peeked through a slit in one eye to find Noah mere inches from her face, his eyes crinkled in laughter, the corners of his mouth fighting a losing battle with hilarity.

"Are you. . .okay?" He sputtered the words and waited for her nod before dissolving into gales of laughter.

Hadley waited. She didn't find it so funny, though Noah and the crowd sure did. She gazed around her. On the ground lay the open ring box, the sun glinting off the facets inside.

"Hadley Parker, will you marry me?"

Hadley's eyes traveled upward to lock with Noah's. "Really?"

Noah nodded.

Hadley nodded.

The crowd erupted.

Noah clambered to his feet then reached a hand down.

Hadley grabbed it and stood up.

Noah pulled her into a tight embrace. "Welcome home, love."

Nicole O'Dell has worked as a youth director, a Bible study leader for women and teens, and a counselor at a crisis pregnancy center. She lives in Illinois with her husband, Wil, and her six wonderful kids—including a set of toddler triplets.